More praise for *Besieged*

"There is a compelling precariousness to these stories: is something scary going to happen? Will there be a worm in the bud? . . . Versatile as well as subtle and dazzling."　—Ruth Pavey, [London] *Observer*

"Whether as satirical fabulist, or as purveyor of his own brand of suburban Gothic, James Lasdun is now an assured master of his form."
—Jonathan Keates, *The Independent*

"His writing reveals a fine apprehension and perspicacity. . . . He is a real find. Read him."
—[London] *Daily Telegraph*

"The best of these stories are brilliant enough to point a shadow—long as shadows are at sunrise— from this first book toward a valuable literary career. . . . [They] reveal a combination of talents—narrative, rhetorical, inventive, meditative—so rare that one forgives all else."
—Jonathan Penner, *New York Times Book Review*

"[Lasdun's] rich style and psychological fearlessness are . . . qualities to reckon with and savor."
—*Kirkus Reviews* (starred review)

"Mr. Lasdun surprises us again and again, by painting in the details of his characters' lives with such authority and imagination that we become thoroughly absorbed in their dramas."
—Michiko Kakutani, *New York Times*

BESIEGED

ALSO BY JAMES LASDUN

Fiction

Delirium Eclipse
Three Evenings and Other Stories

Poetry

A Jump Start
Woman Police Officer in Elevator
After Ovid: New Metamorphoses
(co-edited with Michael Hofmann)

James Lasdun

BESIEGED

W. W. Norton & Company
New York • London

Library of Congress Cataloging-in-Publication Data

Lasdun, James.
  [Siege and other stories]
  Besieged / James Lasdun.—1st American ed.
    p. cm.
  Originally published: The siege and other stories. London : Vintage, 1999.
  Contents: Property—The bugle—Dead labour—Snow—The siege—
  Delirium eclipse—Ate/menos, or, The miracle—The coat—Spiders and
  manatees—The volunteer—Three evenings.
  ISBN 0-393-32074-X (pbk.)
    I. Title

PR6062.A735 S49 2000
823'.914—dc21

W. W. Norton & Company, Inc.
500 Fifth Avenue, New York, NY 10110
www.wwnorton.com

W. W. Norton & Company Ltd.
10 Coptic Street, London WC1A 1PU

1 2 3 4 5 6 7 8 9 0

CONTENTS

BESIEGED

Property

A small parcel arrived on the first morning of my visit to my grandmother at her flat in Mayfair. I watched her opening it amid the debris of our breakfast. The process was very slow and laborious; her fingers were gnarled and weakened by arthritis, and could barely gain sufficient purchase to loosen the bow, let alone break the string. The sight of those hands, I remember, was like a dream of helplessness; it sapped all the strength from me. She tried, and failed, and tried again to slip the slackened cradle of string around the edge of the little box. A small cluster of rubies nestled beneath a knuckle, as startling there as the tiny brilliant cherries that sometimes appear on ancient trees in derelict orchards. The back of each hand was mottled with purple veins and mauve contusions.

Inside the parcel was a pair of ornate silver scissors with a little box protruding from the blades. It was for snuffing candles. My grandmother held the scissors at arm's length, peered at them, and then gave a soft cry of recognition. There was a note with them, which she read, also at arm's length.

'How very peculiar.' She passed the note to me.

'Dear Mrs Cranbourne,' it read, 'I am returning these candle-trimmers which I stole from you when I was in your service. I hope it is not too late to ask your forgiveness. We are both getting on now. Yours sincerely, May Prosser.' No address was given.

'Isn't that peculiar?' my grandmother asked me. She read the note again and examined the trimmers. 'May Prosser. I'd forgotten all about her. She left me years ago, before you were born.' She rubbed the scrolled silverwork with a finger. 'What a funny thing to do. I knew she'd stolen them, of course. Only one didn't like to say without proof. What can she be up to, giving them back now? Perhaps she's gone gaga.'

'Gaga,' I echoed, with a giggle.

My grandmother shrugged, and laid the trimmers aside, seemingly unperturbed. But as the hours went by, it became clear that the episode had unsettled her.

We passed the time, as was our routine on these visits, in her cluttered, over-heated drawing-room. She would lie on a *chaise-longue* sipping cassis and scrutinising the fashion pages in women's magazines. She had worked for such magazines in her day, and still counted herself an assiduous student of style. Her cheeks were always heavily rouged, and her lips were pearly pink. Pomanders, pot-pourri and lavender bags filled the warm room with sweet dry odours, and such dust as I ever encountered while I idled on the floor was always scented with that same sweetness.

She loved jewellery, as did I. She wore quantities of it even though she rarely saw anybody, and she had books on the subject, filled with glossy pictures which I pored over with undiminished fascination each time I came to the flat. Sometimes she would let me open her jewellery box and spill its contents on to the carpet. Coral and lapis lazuli; pearls, jade, a ring made of gold that swirled like a turban, stripes of sapphire, florets of emerald and diamond, charm bracelets dangling silver animals with watch-jewels for eyes, a great brooch of aquamarine ... I could lose myself in rapture for hours over the contents of that box – 'You ought to have been a girl,' my grandmother would laugh, then reach for her cassis, and sigh.

Sometimes, too, she would read to me. Our favourite tale was of the old Russian soldier who frightened death away by squeezing blood from a stone, only the stone was a beetroot. I liked the story for its cunning; she, I suppose, for its conclusion. I think she would have piled her kitchen high with beetroots had her sanity ever so much as wavered.

We passed much of the time in silence, absorbed in our own activities; comfortably aware of each other's presence, but feeling no obligation to speak.

However, on this day, the day of May Prosser's parcel, my grandmother became increasingly restless and talkative. From time to time she lowered her magazine, frowned, and observed how *very* peculiar, or strange, or odd it was of that woman to do what she had done. 'A horrid little woman she was too,' my grandmother said. 'What can she want with me I wonder?'

Then by degrees her attention turned from May Prosser to the candle-trimmers themselves.

'They belonged to *my* grandmother. When I was your age – ' A stream of reminiscence began then to pour from her. The parcel had prised open a fissure in her, and her early life welled through. She talked and talked, quite oblivious to me, and was still talking when the nurse arrived to administer her drugs and help her bathe.

The following morning a registered letter arrived with May Prosser's writing on it. My grandmother looked at it with distaste. 'You can open it,' she said.

There was a banker's draft inside, for two and a half thousand pounds.

'Dear Mrs Cranbourne,' read the accompanying note, 'please accept this money in payment for the vase I broke and denied breaking. You knew I broke it but were kind enough not to make trouble for me. I don't know how much it was worth, you said thousands. I hope this is enough, it is all I have. Please do not think too ill of me. Yours sincerely, May Prosser.'

'Oh,' said my grandmother, 'how dreadful.' She looked forlornly at the draft. 'How dreadful. She's sent me her life savings. She must be going senile. What shall we do?'

I looked up from my cereal uncertain what to say. For my part, I could see no problem. I had just begun to make the connection between money and happiness. I periodically made myself miserable wondering how someone so feeble as I felt myself to be could ever make enough money to be happy. Through sheer force of anxiety I had established a custom among my relatives, that they should tip me handsomely whenever I met them. I hoarded pennies, and felt it my sacred duty to appropriate any untended loose change I found in the households where my parents deposited me on their frequent travels abroad. I wanted to tell my grandmother that I would gladly take the money from May Prosser myself, if she felt unable to accept it. I had enough delicacy, however, to realise that now was not the moment to do so.

She looked so weary and troubled, there in her veils of gauze, her eyelashes not yet on, her sparse wisps of reddish hair spirited into a frail dome over her scalp.

'What could I possibly want with her money? She must be mad. The vase was insured anyway. We were hoping somebody would break it. Such a horrible thing. A relation of your grandfather's gave it to us as a wedding present. It was a piece of expensive antique tourist junk from Germany. A great big glass goblet with enamelled views of Bavarian castles all over it. Quite the ugliest thing I ever owned.'

We went slowly into the drawing-room, her arm on my shoulder, rose-scented talc swirling invisibly about the folds and tucks of her gauzy night-gown.

'I shall dress after lunch,' she said. She lay on her *chaise-longue* and reached for a magazine. I could see the wrinkled flesh sagging from her arm as she stretched it towards the pile. The blotches on her skin were big and far apart, like the first raindrops on a pavement. I poured out her glass of cassis. She gazed at the furred and jewelled models.

'I had a coat with a collar like that,' she might say, or 'Those hats were fashionable in my day.'

I took a pack of the stiff, brand-new playing-cards of which she had an endless supply, and spread them on the floor for a game of Pelmanism against myself. Net curtains made an area of milky light behind her. The deep red bloom of an amaryllis on the television testified to the tropical conditions of the room.

'She knows I don't need her money,' my grand-mother murmured. 'Why does she send me these things?' Then, as I matched two queens and proceeded to redeem pair after pair from the spawn of cards on the floor, she said, 'Your grandfather was just like you. He never forgot a thing. I, on the other hand, was always too muddled and light-headed to remember very much at all.'

But now, as she lay sipping her cassis and watching my little feats of memory, her own memory began to belie those words. At first she picked randomly at her married life, much as I had done at my jumble of cards, mismatching people and incidents, dates and events, until gradually the episodes fell into place, and started to resurface in her mind with something approaching clarity.

'We visited Europe's capitals for our honeymoon. It took us almost a year.'

She recalled the doorman's braided piping at a Viennese hotel, heat rash in Rome, how her husband was mistaken for the Grand Duke of Luxembourg in a lobby in Baden-Baden, an itinerant jeweller in Amsterdam tipping on to the embroidered cloth of their restaurant table a chamois pouch full of unset amethyst and tiger's eye, red champagne in Prague, triplets in maroon cloche caps tipsy in the enclosure at Chantilly ... She lay back sipping her cassis, remembering these things and the later years. She was not addressing me. The words streamed from her lips as if autonomous, and she, sallow beneath her rouge, seemed at once oblivious to and enrapt in them, like an exhausted medium transmitting a dead soul's testament. Elisions, not lacunae, fixed a quarter-century into the two or three hours before May Prosser's successor came to prepare our lunch.

My grandmother talked incessantly, the memories soon flowing too fast for her mind to separate them so that the past became populated with strange hybrid events comprising such occasions as my mother's birth, my aunt's fiancé dying of shrapnel wounds, and a series of picnic breakfasts one summer on the South Downs. I could not follow her, and she too seemed estranged from her own loquaciousness. By lunchtime her forehead was moist enough to reflect the milky light of the netted window.

'I am over-exciting myself,' she said. 'Here – ' I helped her to her feet, and we walked unsteadily to the dining-room. 'I haven't thought about these things for years,' she told me as she served the veal and asparagus. 'I don't think it is very healthy to dwell on one's past. Do you?'

And to distract herself from it, she switched on the

television after lunch. She liked to watch the races, and was giving me a taste for them too, by encouraging me to gamble. She would hand me a pound to bet with – I invariably chose the outsider with the longest odds, thinking thereby to make my fortune. I would take the pound down to the hall porter and ask him to place my bet for me at the bookmaker. The porter was inclined to pocket the money himself if he thought the horse had absolutely no chance. We could see from the window whether or not he went to place my bet, and long ago we had discovered the added amusement of gambling with each other on his capriciousness.

'I bet he doesn't go,' I said to my grandmother, handing her a half-crown which she was to return doubled if I were proved correct.

I was, and anyway the horse fell at the first fence, as it almost invariably did. It pleased my grandmother immensely to benefit both myself and the porter in this way. She was a gracious giver; it flustered her to receive.

We allowed the television to divert us for the rest of the day. My grandmother had personal feelings towards the presenters and compères. She was of a generation that experienced them as real people, not the corporative chimeras we now know them to be. She adored the new breed of camp comedians taking over the shows. '*Terribly* funny,' she would say with a guilty smile, as if apologising to someone who disapproved, or else, 'He *does* make me laugh.' To be made to laugh was, for her, the principal reason for having a television. She watched, figuratively speaking, with her ribs exposed, willing the performer to tickle them. The News bored her, quiz programmes she disliked, though her real contempt was reserved for the soap operas that left life as dreary as it was. 'Why on earth do people want to watch these programmes?' she would ask if we accidentally alighted on one in our quest for amusement.

By night-time, when the nurse arrived, it seemed the morning's disturbance had been quite forgotten. And when nothing arrived in the post with the following breakfast, it seemed also that the remainder of my visit was going to pass in its customary tranquillity.

'Perhaps we might have tea at Fortnum's this afternoon,' said my grandmother as she finished her last piece of toast.

But shortly after breakfast the doorbell rang, and there was the porter, a cigarette in one hand, and a vast bouquet of roses in the other.

My grandmother caught her breath as I brought them into the drawing-room.

'Dear Mrs Cranbourne,' the note with them read, 'I am sorry to disturb you yet again, but I have just remembered one last thing. Some roses once arrived for you from a man called Geoffrey Isaacs. You had gone out, having lost your temper with me for no good reason. I took the roses myself out of spite. Please forgive. I hope I did no damage by my wickedness. God bless you. Yours sincerely, May Prosser.'

My grandmother's face slackened into a look of haggard helplessness.

'Geoffrey Isaacs,' she said quietly. She started to tug at the Cellophane wrapper covering the roses, but soon gave up and laid them on the window-ledge beside her. The roses were a lush velvety crimson. The wrapper glazed them, and they were wet too, big dewy beads of condensation dripping on to the furled red petals and dark green leaves from the inside of the Cellophane.

We were quiet again that morning, but it was not a calm quiet. We lay as if we had eaten excessively and any activity beyond breathing was uncomfortable. We were super-enriched – I have had that sensation since; it is as if your blood has been exchanged for some sweet creamy substance that swells in your veins until you feel over-ripe, over-laden, and all you want to do is unburden yourself of everything that clots up your life. It can herald a severe depression, or a nosebleed, or a bout of insatiable sexual desire. It is pleasure taken to an unbearable extreme; a refined torment, only for those among whom superabundance is an occupational hazard. We lay still in that hot room; we were like Keats's bees in their over-brimmed, clammy cells.

Unanimated, my grandmother's face looked glum and old. Occasionally she sipped thoughtfully at her cassis and murmured to herself. 'She oughtn't to have taken them,' I heard her say, and 'She oughtn't to have returned them,' and once or twice 'Geoffrey Isaacs, well I never.'

She looked drowsy on her *chaise-longue*, and dishevelled. She sighed. Neglected by her, I too became anxious and disconsolate. I was yearning to be older; to be able to control things. I had brought out my bubble-blowing kit to entertain myself that morning. I can remember dipping the plastic hoop into the soapy liquid, and then feeling incapable of breathing life into the taut, translucent membrane. Instead I watched its oil-bright colours swirl and dilate as if they were about to resolve themselves into some dazzling, tremulous sesame, never doing so before it burst.

I brought my grandmother's lunch in on a tray, but she laid it aside after staring at it miserably for a few moments. 'I don't think I'll manage Fortnum's this afternoon,' she said. Then, remembering her duties as my hostess, she added, 'But shall we watch the races instead?'

I selected an outsider running at a hundred or so to

one. She gave me a pound. I took the lift down to the mirrored hall and gave the money to the porter.

'I bet he will go today,' I said, handing my grandmother one of the half-crowns she had paid me the day before.

'Very well, dear.'

I watched out of the window, and sure enough the porter presently ambled out of the building, cigarette in one hand, my pound note in the other. I was aching; full of indefinable needs. Too much was passing through me, but I craved for more. I had to help myself to my half-crowns from my grandmother's handbag, she feeling too listless to search for the coins herself. I opened the stiff, shiny bag, fingered through its freight of lipstick, tissues, powder-compacts, credit cards, mirrors and receipts, opened the soft leather purse and, thinking it would assuage my desire, took all the silver it contained, and the copper too.

We watched the race – I, with my habitual excitement, she with a fearfulness that turned, as did my excitement, to a kind of nausea as we realised my outsider was going to win.

'Well there you are,' my grandmother said when it was over, 'we've won a race.'

We waited for the porter to arrive, avoiding each other's eyes, as if we had been caught at something shameful.

The bell rang. The porter stood there in a cloud of smoke, chuckling and twinkling, thrilled to be a bringer of such good tidings. He strode past me into the flat, holding our winnings in a carrier bag.

'You've done it,' he bellowed. 'I never thought the day would come. My congratulations to you, Mrs Cranbourne, and to you, sir.'

We wanted him to leave the bag and go, but he was waiting for us to rejoice with him. 'Everyone's winning today,' he said. 'They ran out of notes. Here – ' He reached into the bag and tossed me a dozen polythene envelopes full of coins. Some of the envelopes burst open with a clink as they hit the floor. The rest of the money was in notes which he handed solicitously to my grandmother. We thanked him, but he wouldn't go. He stayed there grinning and puffing, as if he expected us to tip him, or at least count the money with him. Then he caught sight of my bubble-blowing kit.

'Look,' he said to me, 'I'll show you a trick.' He dipped the hoop into the liquid, and inhaled deeply on his cigarette. He thought he was so cheerful, but at that moment he was hateful to us. Slowly and carefully he blew smoke into the drumhead of soap. We looked on silently as three big smoke-filled bubbles billowed out and drifted heavily towards the window. Daylight showed the smoke swirling inside the bubbles. It was the colour of jaundiced porcelain. The heaviest bubble fell back towards my grandmother. She closed her eyes as it approached. It burst on her gemmed knuckle, releasing a gout of smoke that dispersed about the notes she was holding.

He blew a stream of smaller ones that fell like silent bombs on the floor about me. We could not bring ourselves to applaud him, and waited silently for him to make his exit.

'Well,' he said, 'that's it. That's my trick. I'll be off then, shall I?' We made no effort to delay him.

Left to ourselves we neither spoke nor barely stirred. My grandmother's eyelids drooped and she fell asleep. I tipped out the coins from all the polythene envelopes, and played with them. I counted them, I arranged them in big concentric rings, I stacked them into crooked columns that tottered precariously and crashed to the ground, I filled my mouth with them and spilt them out

like a human fruit machine; I built them into mounds
and swam my hands through them.

It was not until much later that it occurred to me
that the notes, too, were mine to play with. The sky
had darkened and the room was grey. I whispered
Granny can I have my money. She made no response. I
knew I should have let her be, but I could not help
myself. I crept up to her. She was holding the notes in
the air below the window-ledge. The dark little rubies
sparkled secretively from her knuckle. I reached my
hand towards the fanning wad of notes clasped in her
fingers. I pulled gently at the money but it refused to
slip from her grasp. I was perplexed; I thought perhaps
she was teasing me, or that she had decided not to let
me keep the winnings after all. A tiny sensation of
panic passed through me. I tugged sharply at the
notes. They came away immediately, and as my hand
shot upward it struck the bouquet of roses lying over
the window-ledge. Condensation had gathered in a
dipped corner of the Cellophane. As I struck it, the
water slithered out of the hole in the corner and
splashed down on to my grandmother's face. She did
not flinch. The water broke into little quicksilver
drops which trickled over her powdered skin.

By the time the nurse came it had collected at the
scoop of her throat. It glinted there like a colossal
jewel.

The Bugle

David didn't recognise the woman who opened the door to him when he arrived back at his parents' home.

She looked at him questioningly, awaiting an explanation.

'I'm David Pesketh, I think my parents are expecting me.'

'Ah yes. Come in.'

He could smell smoke on her clothing as he passed by her into the hall. Her face, under crimped grey hair, was downward-inclined, forbidding.

'They were expecting you yesterday.' There was a calm assurance about her that inhibited him from asking her directly who she was, and what she was doing here.

'I know they were – there was a strike in Tokyo. I'm very sorry.' He wondered immediately why he had apologised to her. 'Where are they now – are they in?'

'They're resting.'

'I see. Well I'll go up and say hello … ' He slid his two bulging suitcases into the shadowy alcove beneath the stairs. He was about halfway up when he heard her calm, flat voice again –

'They're asleep. I think you ought to wait … '

He turned on the stairway and looked down at her,

astonished. He had not seen his parents for three years.

'I don't think they'll mind, you know ... '

'No,' she looked directly up at him, 'but they do need to rest.'

He lingered a moment, registering the power of this stranger who was forcing him, after a minute's acquaintance, to appear churlish by proceeding, or submissive by descending. It seemed oddly familiar, that dilemma, and associated somehow with the smells, brightnesses and shadows of the house itself. And this familiarity in turn thrust him abruptly back into the long untasted atmosphere of the place. He was home, back home.

He came down the stairs with a conciliatory smile.

'All right – I'll wait if you think that's best.' He stood beside her, supposing that she would now volunteer some information about herself.

'I'll pour you a glass of milk' was all she said.

'Who are you ... I mean are you, are you staying here?'

'I live here.' She looked at him a moment, her eyes unblinking – 'You don't remember me do you? I didn't think you would.'

'*Remember* you?' He peered at her in the gloom of the large hall. The blue pigment of her eyes had all but crumbled into glazed dust, but what remained was of a tint again faintly familiar, again associated with the house itself.

'I'm Alice Cottle. I looked after you when you were small. Now I am looking after your parents.'

'Ah ... Goodness ... '

Alice Cottle ... So she was back too. Miss Cottle the Confiscator, back home again, back before him, a spirit unbottled from the distillation of his childhood ...

'It is strange, yes,' she said, 'but here I am you see ...

Now you go in and I'll bring you a glass of milk.' She walked briskly away.

'Actually I'll have a cup of tea,' he called after her, 'I'll make it myself.'

She stopped, and paused a second in the corridor before turning to face him.

'We'll have tea in half an hour, when your parents come down.'

David watched her turn and recede down the narrowing parallels of the corridor; tap tap tap ...

He opened the living-room door, then thought for a moment, and closed it without entering. He doubled back, and tiptoed up the stairs. Only when he reached the second landing, where his parents' bedroom was situated, did it strike him as laughable that he should feel he had to tiptoe up the stairs in his own home. He strode over to the bedroom door, knocked loudly once, and burst in with a cry of greeting.

There were dust sheets on everything. The great brass bed, the lacquered bamboo tables on either side of it, the plump little sofa by the window – all were shrouded in a pale grey drift of cloth.

The air was musty. Light billows of dust scudded away from his feet as he moved. He raised the sheet from an object beside him. It was the nutwood escritoire from which his mother had run her affairs. He tried the little drawers and hidden chambers that honeycombed its interior. They were all locked. A distinct feeling of weakness came over him. He crossed to the window. A large incinerator was smouldering on the back lawn, just where a japonica bush had been. The ground beneath it was scorched in a black circle.

A voice startled him –

'They don't sleep here any more.'

She stood in the doorway with a glass of milk in her hand. David stared in shock at her a moment, then relaxed, and eased his collar from his neck.

'Ah. I see. That explains it ... Where are they then?'

'On the first floor. They found the stairs too much. Your mother's in the blue guest room. Your father is in your room.'

David sat – almost sank – down on the bed. It was like being told of a bereavement.

'It's all rather ... odd.' He freed his collar again. 'Where do I sleep then?'

'We thought the nursery. Most of the other rooms are closed up now, like this. I'm working on the attic rooms at the moment. There's a lot of rubbish to burn. Here – '

She handed him the glass of milk. He gulped it down. He could see her watching him as the last of the liquid slid into his mouth, her wrinkled face held bunched and contorted in the thick glass at the base of the tumbler. She put out her hand for the empty vessel.

'I'll wait for them downstairs,' he said, wiping his lips.

The reunion at tea had an hallucinatory quality which David attributed to jetlag.

His father had seemed to move down the stairs with the leaden slowness of a shadow creeping round the calibrations of a sundial. His mother, who had been ill while he was away, had shrunk dramatically. She looked at him absently, her head half-sunk in the shadow of her sweater's voluminous polo neck.

'It's lovely to have you back,' she said. The words reached him as if from an enormous distance, bereft of power.

There was a tinkle of porcelain as his father raised cup and saucer to his lips with trembling hands.

'Tell us all about Japan,' his mother said, 'was it like Thailand – no you enjoyed Thailand. Where was the other place you were unhappy in? Peru was it? Algeria?'

He felt acutely the judgment her confusion passed on the haphazard nature of his adult life. He had passed the same judgment himself, and sentenced the culprit to begin again, begin afresh.

'Japan is a very nice country. I've had enough of that way of life, that's all. It's galling to pass thirty and realise the only claim to distinction you have is the ability to teach your native tongue to foreigners. I could have been replaced by a box of cassettes. I probably have been by now ... '

Begin again. He knew about the state of affairs in England. The appointment of an American to dismantle the steel and coal industries had greatly tickled the Japanese businessmen he taught. One of them had compared it to a dishonoured Samurai blundering even in his self-disembowelment, and begging a former vassal to finish the job.

Even so, even so ... In his dejection abroad, he had allowed himself to blur the idea of flying back across the world, with that of leaping as swiftly into a new existence. There would be a space for him somewhere, a little gap in the margins of the economy, the shape of David Pesketh, and *voilà*, out of the plane he would step, and into the gap ...

He was tired, and went to bed early, but he was unable to sleep. He sat up and opened his eyes. As the dark of the big nursery receded, he could make out the dappled rocking horse in the corner, the children's books and annuals ranged by series on the bookshelf, their different sizes giving the outline a battlement effect. He could see the silhouette of a kangaroo squatting on the toy-cupboard, a glint of moonlight in its glass eye. It was very strange to be among these things again. In their faint visibility, they formed the eerie picture a device that could summon particles of light from the past might produce. A grainy, dreamy image no human hand could ever alter. He rose from bed and crossed to the window, drawing back the curtain. Abutting from the wall below him was the sloping glass and steel roof of a greenhouse, where his father had once cultivated tomatoes. He could see in the moonlight that it was empty now, and derelict. A faint glow came from the ashes of the incinerator on the lawn.

The days were warm and quiet. If he rose before nine, there would be a tinkling breakfast of crustless toast and tea. If later, nothing; Alice locked the pantry between mealtimes.

His mother wandered about the garden, pruning and digging. His father sometimes played patience, or leafed through an ancient copy of the *Illustrated London News*. Time distended itself immeasurably in the old man's presence. Vast flights of imagination could be accomplished between two ticks of the clock in the room where he sat snoozing in his high-backed chair, his eyes half open like an old dog's, a pool of cards under his limp hand.

Neither of them drove any longer. The car was still in the garage, but only Alice was insured. She went into town once a week, to do the shopping and have her hair done. The rest of the time she moved about the house, tidying, preparing meals, taking box-loads of junk from the attic rooms to feed the incinerator on the back lawn, standing immobile as a flurry of sparks rushed up before her. The smell of burning came and went on the breeze. Sometimes a moth-sized flake of ash was blown inside the house.

David could see her through the nursery window as he sat filling in application forms. She had found a chest full of old clothes. Flames gave way to thick white billows of smoke as she stuffed the wool, tweed and cotton into the hot steel basket. She looked up at the nursery window, and David dropped his glance back down to the forms.

It wasn't long before letters began to arrive back for him. *We are sorry to have to inform you. We regret we are unable. I'm afraid we cannot. There were three four five thousand applications for the post. We were looking for a younger person. For someone with more relevant experience. We are sorry. We regret.*

The summer days grew long and slow.

He lay in bed watching smoke disperse from cumulus to cirrus to nothingness. Alice brought him a glass of milk. As he drank it, he remembered a childhood whim of leaving a half-inch of liquid behind, in case the last mouthful should unveil a spider. 'All of it up now' Alice would say. White milk sluicing away from the black tangle of the creature, limbs bedraggled and awry like the stem of a tomato; tumbling on to his lips ... *all of it up now, all of it* ... He drained the glass and handed it back to her.

By the time he had roused himself, she was back at the incinerator, cramming big objects from a tea-chest into it. The sky was a heavy ochre, patched with dark clouds; Alsatian colours. Tall flames with peacock greens and blues in them streamed upward in front of her. A table lamp disappeared into them, an enormous book ... There was an abandon in her movements. She took a black box from the tea-chest and shoved it into the fire. David watched it smoulder and ignite. Through the comb of flames devouring it, he could see the wooden sides disintegrate. Peeping through burning slats was something shiny and metallic. More charred material fell away. The object was gold and curved. It was the bell of a brass bugle. For a moment it

shone out brighter than the fire around it. Then gradually it tarnished, and blackened with soot.

There were forms to fill in, and letters of application
to compose. There was nothing else to do. He wrote
his name on a form. His hand was shaking violently,
and the letters came out malformed, like a child's. He
let the pen drop, and went to lie down on his bed. He
stayed quite still. Soon he was conscious of nothing but
the smell of burning.

'I hope we're not too quiet for you ... ' his mother said
at lunch.

'I'm all right. I'll soon, you know ... '

Minute nibbling sounds.

'Yes?' Alice said.

'Get something ... '

There was a silence.

'You need cheering up!' his father exclaimed, surprised at the discovery. A moment later he announced
he had an idea.

'I'll get the projector out. We'll put up the screen in
the drawing-room and make some popcorn like we
used to.' He looked cautiously at Alice. She folded her
napkin into its silver ring, and rose to her feet with the
air of someone conscious of exercising magnificent
self-control.

'I'll see to the dishes,' she said, leaving the room.

There was some ancient popcorn in a jar at the back
of the pantry. David attended to it, while his father
ambled off to set up the cine show. He heated the oil
with a few grains of corn in it. Alice was in the kitchen
with him, washing the dishes. She made no attempt to
speak to him as he stood by the saucepan waiting for
the grains to explode. Nothing happened for a long
time.

'Wouldn't you like to watch a film with us?' he

asked, purely to break the silence. She didn't answer.

Pop pop pop.

'Your oil's ready,' she said, without turning from the sink. 'Please don't leave a mess.'

'Don't worry. I'll clear it all up.' He poured a cupful of grain and some sugar into the pan.

'Please do.'

A hailstorm erupted under the heavy lid. The cartoon sound stirred residual memories ... gleeful anticipation ... excitement ... a whiff of brilliant dreamtime ...

He took the pan off the heat, and lifted the lid to view the miraculous increase in its contents. The smell was shatteringly sweet. Shiny amber husks the shape of ladybird wings were splayed around the burst corn. He poured the golden mass into a bowl and carried it through to the drawing-room.

The curtains were drawn. His mother turned to him in the gloom and patted the space on the sofa beside her. His father stood by the cumbersome projector, adjusting the angle of its beam until the square of light was flush with the four sides of the screen.

The two big spools revolved at a stately pace, whirring like a ratchet. Blurred white numbers on a grey background counted down to zero. A brief tumult of flickering words and shapes followed, and suddenly they were watching Charlie Chaplin eavesdrop on gold prospectors in a Western saloon.

David sat back into the sofa, feeding himself popcorn, surrendering to the grainy transmutations on the square of light. Dust showed up in the white areas, hair-fine coils and strands like broken watch-springs.

He was comfortable in the darkness of the warm drawing-room, listening to the whirring spools, the crunch of popcorn. He was aware, in a peripheral way, of Alice moving briskly about the house, opening and closing doors, carrying boxes down from the attic. The activity enhanced rather than disturbed the comfort of his enclosure, like rain on a car.

A villain fell over a precipice and plunged down into a turbulent river that swept him away like a piece of flotsam. David chuckled.

'Ah yes,' his father said, standing up to flick a switch on the projector. The river's flow reversed. The man swirled back upstream, slid out of the water, and rocketed back up to alight on the lip of the precipice.

David could see the illumined outline of his mother's face bulge into a smile. She turned and patted his leg. He leaned against her.

The film ended. His father switched on the light and took another reel from the box. They remained hushed while he threaded it on to the projector, anxious not to break the room's fragile spell. Footsteps thumped overhead.

It was a home movie. A card bearing the legend *Pesketh Films Inc.* wobbled on the screen, followed by another: *Tuscan Rhapsody*.

A stream of clouds seen from above through an airplane window. Mrs Pesketh in a bright red dress gazing up at a cathedral front, her streaked blonde hair half hidden in a silk scarf. Camera follows her gaze, giving a blurred, unsteady impression of stonework and statuary. Mr Pesketh, tanned and dapper in a light summer suit, standing by a high stone balustrade looking out over vineyards and yellow hills tiered with olive trees. A breeze ruffles his hair. The scallop-shaped piazza at Sienna milling with people. Scarlet and gold banners fluttering from balconies. Horses and riders in fantastical heraldic costume flash by …

They sat bewitched. There were thundering sounds from above; a trunk or another tea-chest being hauled down the attic stairs.

More clouds. David sat bolt upright. He remembered what was coming next.

A shot of the garden gate, and there he was in the porch, standing in front of Alice, her hands on his shoulders. He was in shorts and a T-shirt, and looked impossibly delicate. He was smiling into the camera.

Smiling directly at David, who drew in his breath and stared back at himself, electrified.

He shook off Alice's hands and ran forward over the bright green lawn. The camera followed him to his mother, who bent down to kiss him and handed him a little present which he opened, his eyes alight with curiosity. It was a walnut. He peered at it bemusedly. His mother showed him a concealed button to press. The nut sprang open at its rim, and out of it poured a cascade of white silk embroidered with the gold and scarlet emblems of the Siennese banners.

'Ah yes,' Mr Pesketh said, and stood up to flick the reverse motion switch.

'No,' David cried ...

The tumbled silk gathered itself up and disappeared inside the walnut, the hinged shell snapping shut behind it. The boy wrapped it up and handed it to his mother, embracing her. He ran backwards across the lawn, back to the woman waiting in the doorway. Her hands came down on to his shoulders.

A while later, some family friends came with their daughter Lucy, his own age. She had ginger hair and blue eyes, a pollen of golden freckles scattered all over her face and arms. It was the first crush of David's life. The feelings she aroused in him were like amazing, invisible toys. He almost believed he could conjure them into visibility by making her laugh just a little louder at his clowning, goggle even wider at the feats of daring he performed for her. What would they look like if he could see them? Shimmering things dusted in gold.

They sat up in a tree, watching the yellow roses and lilac blossom turn luminous in the summer dusk-light, the green of the lawn deepen. It was still light when Alice Cottle came to fetch them to bed. Lucy was put to sleep in the nursery, next door to his room. He crept in there when Alice had gone. They stood by the window. The noise of woodpigeons in the distance was like flute sounds bubbled through water. The chalky red flowers of a japonica bush took fire from the disappearing sun. They talked and giggled, louder and louder, breaking into snatches of songs they both knew, abandoning themselves ...

There was a sound of footsteps stomping into the corridor.

It gave the situation a new complexion: a thrill, but a peculiar, queazy sort of thrill. They heard Alice open the door of his room and call his name. He whispered to Lucy to get into bed and pretend she was asleep. He climbed out of the window, lowering himself on to a steel rib of the greenhouse roof, then dropped to the ground and slipped in through the door.

He stood trembling among the darkened foliage of the tomato plants. The thrill, the queazy thrill, was intensifying not receding. Warm air, moist and sweet with the musk of the plants, enclosed him. He felt weightless, afloat. What was happening to him? His whole body was tingling. Clusters of new tomatoes dangled from the plants like the smallest, most secretive of baubles on a Christmas tree. They were tight and gold, some beginning to redden, so that the gold sheen was no more than a powdering. There were masses of them, gleaming faintly in what remained of the light. Was it from them, or from the rich air, or the giggles of Lucy still ringing in his ears, or from inside himself, that this sweet tingling dizziness radiated? He played his hands through the plants, trailing his fingers around the hardsoft fruit, toying with them. A great pulse of sweetness travelled through him. He felt he was about to burst into some dazzling world of unimaginable power and pleasure.

He had to move. He stumbled out of the greenhouse. The air was cool, the zodiac freshly tattooed on the deep blue sky. He entered the house through the back door and ran up to his room. He stood there in a delirium of wonder, his heart racing. Euphoria was like a wild animal in him, struggling to break out. There was a black instrument case on the table. He opened it up and took from the blue plush of its interior his shiny brass bugle. He put it to his lips, filled his lungs, and blasted a reveille on to the silent night.

He turned, and she was there in the doorway as if summoned; her face taut and white, her hand outstretched –

'Give it to me.'

Dead Labour

Summer, and my mentor lay in hospital. I was apprehensive about visiting him. I had done things I ought not to have done, and left undone those things that I ... I was neglecting my duty, yes, joining the rats.

I realised the extent of my dereliction as I set off to visit him one moist, breezeless afternoon. I tried to summon an image of his face, but my summons was met with a blur; a blur topped with a great hank of absolutely black hair, but a blur all the same. I thought of my admiration for the man, my gratitude and affection. These, undeniably, were my feelings for Samuelson, but they lay quite comatose.

I tried to prod them into life.

I began to observe my surroundings as Samuelson would have had me observe them. There was plenty here for the Samuelson vision of life. The long road was flanked by a colossal and classically ravaged housing estate. Children were playing in pits full of smashed glass and excrement. This was Samuelson's melancholic England. It could have been an extension of one of his stage sets; mothers in floral housecoats sitting in the mean balconies contemplating suicide ...

I hurried past the place. It was having no effect on me, and I switched it off as you switch off a favourite piece of music heard once too often. I did not want it to be spoiled for ever.

The sky was pavement-grey with a shapeless lemony stain in it, just too bright to look at. Miniature irises with remnants of petals the same lemon colour grew against a wall, their triangles of dead flowers resembling burnt out catherine wheels. Laburnum corals too were turning from yellow to an ugly brown. These small corruptions drew my mind away from Samuelson. All along the side of the hospital were huge horse-chestnut trees in full flower, multitudes of deep crimson blossoms showing through the dark leaves, each one like … like … like a …

… Like a giant mulberry, a marzipan tree, like the excised innards of a glass paperweight … I was looking into metaphor and simile. My new friend Philippa was indirectly to thank, or blame, for this. My new friend Philippa had stirred me in a way that urchins and ravaged housing estates no longer seemed to. She was to thank, or blame, for much. She was Gardening, Antiques and Restaurants for a new magazine about to be launched at income groups A and AB. She was looking for people to write for her; I was looking for work, Samuelson's Open Theatre Project no longer funded and no longer functioning since the second month of his absence. She offered me Restaurants, and in a fit of gallantry I swore that she and she alone would be 'my guest', 'my friend', 'my companion' wherever I consumed in the name of her magazine.

After the party, I dropped her at her flat in Wandsworth. She repeated her offer; I, my oath. I drove away into the quiet night watching the great breweries and power stations reel in and out of my rear-view mirrors; feeling, as my car sped me across the Thames and through Chelsea, the peculiar vibrancy of an illicit joy to which guilt will attach itself but has not yet done so.

A formal commission arrived from Philippa on the day before I visited Samuelson. Three restaurants, 2,000 words, budget £200, fee £200, to be delivered in three weeks. Scribbled in biro beneath were the words, 'Ring me soonest. My mouth is watering already! Love Philippa XXX.'

Ring me soonest. The affection excited me, the affectation made me wince. The task too, suddenly a reality, attracted and repelled me in equal measures. To write that kind of thing, and for that kind of magazine ... but then the money, and the food, and then Philippa herself ...

I bought the glossies and spent the afternoon immersed in banquets, balls, and the sundry other pursuits of income groups A and AB. I read with detachment, holding in check my Samuelsonian distaste for this world, in an effort to learn how to write for its creatures. An appreciation of the nuances of class, an allusion pitched just within bounds of the knowledge guaranteed by a private education, an amusing coinage, all these were prized. But the stylistic commodity most highly valued of all was the surprising simile; the ingenious metaphor. These were delivered with superlative dash; the author knew that here, if nowhere else, he or she was giving readers a proper return on their investment – an echo of the satisfactions of a good business deal where two items were had for the price of one. *My bream came in a faintly yellow creamy sauce flecked all over with green herbs, as if it had been dressed by Laura Ashley.* Olé!

A fractional stirring of the air caused one of the crimson chestnut flowers to topple through the branches. I picked it up as I entered the hospital, and saw how here too the pristine colour was beginning to turn.

A nurse showed me to a small annexe off one of the men's wards. I stood in the doorway and looked for the thick black swatch of Samuelson's hair. I couldn't see it. I was about to go away and ask again for his ward, when I heard my name called. The voice was Samuelson's, but the head it came from bore no immediate resemblance to his. The face was sucked in around the contours of the skull. The skin was blood-less. An egg-sized patch of darkness surrounded each eye. His hair was white, and stood up in sparse sprouts, areas of scalp visible beneath them, the whole thing altogether like a half-blown dandelion clock.

His right arm protruded, naked and white, from the side of the bed. I'd seen this arm reach down and hoist to the safety of a platform a woman bloodied by a bottle at a rally. It looked now as if the weight of the bedside glass would snap it. Sticking into what remained of the bicep was a needle attached by a tube to a polythene drip-feed bag half full of a clear liquid.

'All it lacks is a goldfish ... ' he said, looking up at the bag. A timpani of rattling phlegm accompanied his words. I smiled for him and kept my mouth shut. There was so much I wanted to avoid telling him.

'I gather we've lost our grant.'

I nodded.

'You must have a – excuse me – ' He broke off to dribble into a wad of tissues, ' – a lot of time on your hands now ... '

'I suppose I do.' Would he question me, and if he did, would I be able to lie to him? He could be a formidable inquisitor. I wanted to go before I was forced to witness those cavernous eyes absorb and echo back whatever deceits and evasions I might address to them.

'I wonder if you would do me a favour?'

'Of course,' I said, relieved.

He raised himself up slowly, and took from his bedside table some pieces of paper covered with notes.

'I was asked a while ago to write something about my work for an anthology of essays on politics and theatre. I wasn't all that interested. But I said I'd give it some thought – you know – when I had time ... ' He paused to regain his breath, then went on to tell me that he had decided to produce a statement for posterity, that he was at the moment too weak to write anything but fragmentary notes, and that he considered me the one person capable of turning his notes into a presentable essay.

'They wrote a week ago, saying I had another month if I wanted to get in the book. That would give you about three weeks ... '

He passed me the papers. There was a heading: *Dead Labour*, followed by the quotation from Marx – 'Capital is dead labour which, vampire-like, lives only by sucking living labour, and lives the more, the more labour it sucks.'

I looked at Samuelson, feeling my sense of relief turn to unease. Two months ago, one month even, this task would have presented no difficulties. Now however, it appeared distinctly problematic. To do it at the same time as the magazine piece would require me to split myself into two irreconcilable frames of mind. Something told me I should try to duck out of it. But I had immense obligations to this man – for a long time almost everything I valued in myself could be attributed to his influence. I had yet to judge whether I had drifted clean away from this influence, or was merely on holiday from it. Either way, he was calling in a debt. No means of evading it came to mind, short of a flat refusal, and I was too much in awe of him for that. My tongue was enslaved to the forms of politeness.

'It looks very interesting,' I heard myself say.

We discussed the details. I promised to return in a fortnight with a preliminary draft, and left him crackling and wheezing on his bed, like an ill-tuned radio.

My companion's Steak Ambassadeur was delicious. No. My companion's Steak Ambassadeur was of a tenderness so exquisite you could have –

'What's that you're writing now?' asked Ringmesoonest with an impish grin.

I looked up from my jotting pad. 'Secret,' I whispered. She made a play of grabbing for the pad, but I snatched it away, tut-tutting her.

'Tell me or I'll scream.'

'Oh all right then: my companion's ... My companion tossed back a large brandy with her customary brio, extinguished her cigar, and staggered to her feet, saying, "My place honey, I'm gonna ride you ragged."'

Ringmesoonest laughed a tinkling laugh. She didn't; her laughter aspired half-heartedly to the condition of tinkling. She knew what she was doing. She had a passing attraction to me, and was happy to let her gestures refer to the flirtatious premise on which this attraction was based, in order to help it flourish. Everything about her could be read as a series of concessions – her precision-cut hair, her seamless charm, her big brown eyes with their perfectly white whites, the endless variety of smiles that played on her face, each one showing you something new to like in her lips or cheeks; her pale throat, the discretion of her scent ... These things mean nothing to me, her manner suggested, they're all yours, only let me have what I want of you in return.

A waiter came to remove our plates. Another joined him to replenish my glass with wine from the silver bucket beside me. A third hovered behind him with a menu in his hand. It excited us, all that attention, made us into a source of energy as if we were living under a new decree where it was the candle that fed off the moths and not vice versa.

A feeling of power crept into me as I read the menu; a little rush of magnanimity, as if I was up above the world and could order anything – *I'll have Chartres please, and the Guggenheim. My friend would like Mauritius* ... I recognised it as a corrupt sensation. I let it bloom in me, observing it like a scientist at a controlled explosion. A necklace of condensation on the ice bucket broke, and the beads streaked down the silver surface. It struck me that Samuelson was dying. I passed momentarily into crisis. I felt like someone awaking in a room altogether different from the one he went to sleep in. What was I doing here? Who was this girl? The myth of intimacy that had wrapped itself around us seemed suddenly to be disintegrating. I felt cold and exposed. I vowed to myself that I would start work on Samuelson's piece tomorrow morning; no, tonight.

How was our myth patched up? By glass after glass of wine and brandy? Partly, but also by the sensitivity with which she adapted herself to my shift of mood. She became quiet now, and engaged me in serious conversation. She asked me about my work with Samuelson. I had a faint feeling of unease, talking about him to her, but she listened with such absorption and concern that I soon found myself telling her all about his life and how I had come into it. I mentioned also the task he had given me.

'I must get it started tonight.'

It all made her feel so frivolous, she said in a soft, pensive voice. I took her at her word and told her that I, for one, thought she was very far from frivolous. I felt a tremendous affection for her, and great relief at having recovered so precious and pleasant a feeling.

I drove her across the river to her door. She asked me in. Her flat was leafy and cushiony, trinkets everywhere, perfume atomisers, scarves, records, bracelets, a printer's tray on the wall with a little ornament in every niche, masses of patterned fabrics, a bentwood hat-tree in full, exotic fruit. There was a coal fire too, facing the sofa. A pinkish glow peeped through cracks in the blanket of white ash.

'Summer fire,' I remarked.

'I know, but it's pretty. You could revive it if you like. There's more coal in the scuttle. I'll get some drinks ... '

She went into the kitchen. I heard the creak of ice being prised from its tray as I blew on the coals, and the clink of ice in glass as I tipped the smooth black ovoids from the scuttle into the fire. The old ash fell away. The fresh coal reflected the red light of the embers, and slowly the reflection became the thing itself, blazing out brighter than the weakening originals.

We drank gins rapidly on the sofa, talking a little nervously, but sure of our ground. The fire became an orange sea with diminishing black islands in it, thin bluish flames playing overhead. I took her hand. The hand squeezed mine, though its owner affected not to have noticed.

'Look,' she said, and with her free hand tossed the ice cubes and slice of lemon from her tumbler into the fire. A spectacular plume of steam hissed out. The sea shimmered. Patches of darkness were sucked in around each gleaming nugget of ice as it sapped the heat from the coals in its melting. The lemon slice writhed, shrivelled, and released a sweet citric scent in its candleflame apotheosis. She put down her glass and leant towards me with her eyes wide open looking into mine; conceding to me, as we kissed, all her softness and charm, her pale throat and discreet scent, the white whites and deep brown pupils of her eyes, her repertoire of smiles . . . a warm tumbling of herself into me, so it felt. We lay there kissing, growing blood-heavy and languid under each other's touch. The coals in the fire had recovered from their icy assault and were now a single golden mass, so that, as jackets, blouse, trousers, skirt, fell away from us, we felt the brazier heat directly on our skins and glowed like coals ourselves in its reflection. She lay naked in my arms, light and delicate, an exquisite instrument taken from the plush-lined mould of its case, a faint trace of amusement on her lips to remind me as I caressed her that all this was provisional, transactional. She was almost passive in her enjoyment; receptive, glazed in her own sensations, feeding delicately on me. A pink blush rose on her pale cheeks. She pressed my mouth gently to her nipple, and then brought me into her, closing her eyes. Her breathing stayed quiet as it grew faster and higher in pitch, and when she came she did so in one silent, extended, blissful, private shimmer.

Traffic sounded in the distance. A clock ticked in the bedroom.

After a while she disentangled herself from me and went to run a bath.

'What about Mr Samuelson?' she asked as she left the room. There was no mockery in her voice, but I felt mocked. It was three in the morning. The notes were all at my place and I could do nothing without them. I wondered if this was her way of telling me to go. But then she shouted from the bathroom, 'There's only enough hot for one, shall I leave you my water?'

Samuelson, I decided, would do much better by me in the morning.

I lay in the warm, soapy water, sponging myself with her sponge, feeling happy and satiated. She was much lovelier than I had imagined. I could feel her presence in my mind, a warm soft radiance.

As I climbed sleepily from the bath, I caught a whiff of her perfume on my skin. Her large, damp towel carried the same fragrance, and as I dried myself I could sense it impregnating me like the subtlest of varnishes; a sheen of Philippa's existence enclosing my own.

No accident that textures of fringe stage predom. matt while W. End stage aims glitter & shine. Impression given of massive industry, what sparkles is labour-intensive. Forests & millennia required to crystallise one seam of diamonds. (Adam Smith on rel. value of water & diamonds) ...

The notes were square on the desk before me, illuminated by a beam of bright midday sunlight. On one side of them was a green mug of steaming coffee. On the other side was my portable typewriter, a piece of crisp white paper wound about its roller. I sat there marshalling my thoughts, feeling absolutely confident in my power to execute this task. Whenever I moved, a hint of Philippa's scent rose from me, filling me with rich, pleasurable sensations that in turn seemed to fill everything inanimate around me with glimmerings of benevolent life – the green mug with its dancing genie of steam, the Olivetti's dial of levers waiting to transform thought into print; an occult conspiracy to make me feel loved and intimately connected with the world. I looked up, and tried to shape the first sentence in my mind. I was getting there, and had my fingers poised above the keys, when the telephone rang.

It was Philippa's boss; a cajoling male voice speaking with an expression I recognised at once as simulated deference. He was awfully sorry to disturb me only they'd had a crisis at the magazine and he won-

dered if I would do him a favour. The chap doing the
Nightlife and New Openings pages had dropped out,
and they needed someone urgently to give them copy.
Philippa'd said ...

I sensed danger in this voice, and kept quiet. It began
to flatter me now, its owner interpreting my silence as
reluctance. 'She says you're exactly the man for us.
I have this good feeling about you.' The words filled
me with panic. I made noises of uncertainty, but he
pressed on. 'It should be a lot of fun for you. Do it
myself if I had the time. Free tickets to everything –
discos, cocktail bars, new restaurants on top of the
ones you're doing for us anyway ... Actually I've had
my secretary post you a batch of invites. Go to them all.
We just need a few sentences on each one – glorified
listings really. Won't take you any time. Pay you over
the odds of course. Money for old rope between you
and me ... '

I felt cornered. There was a vague threat floating on
his words; a shadow of something cast just too faintly
to be identifiable. 'We're gambling on Philippa's
say-so of course, but I have a hunch about you ... ' An
intimation of knowledge that somehow gave him
power ... 'We'd like you to get yourself known a
bit – be a sort of man about town. We'll print a card
for you ... ' I could feel myself submitting to him, like a
creature entering metamorphosis, powerlessly witnes-
sing its familiar shape mutating into something new
and strange ...

'What d'you say to it then?'

'Hm. Okay. Yes. Thank you. I'd love to. It's very
kind of you to ask me.'

'Good. Now here's a surprise; your first assignment's in an hour. Philippa's waiting for you at a new
lunch revue place in Fulham. She can do it herself if you
absolutely can't make it. I think you should though ... '

The chestnut blossoms had succumbed to summer. Crimson petals had shrivelled away to reveal antlers of stem that made me think of Philippa's bentwood hat-tree. I saw emblems of her wherever I went. Over the past two weeks she had become installed inside me. She was no longer so much a source of pleasure as a prerequisite for it. I was abandoning myself to her. A thimble's worth of me was watching it happen, unable to do anything about it.

Three days after the lunch date in Fulham, I had slunk reluctantly back into my room. A bruise of turquoise mould had risen on the scum of milk fat riding the unconsumed coffee. No miracle had occurred, translating the notes into formal prose on the piece of typing paper now warped around the shape of the roller. The task awaited me still. I forced myself to sit down and concentrate. My ears – all my senses – were still ringing with the weekend's excess of free drinking and dancing with Philippa, of making love on the sofa with an escalating urgency and passion ... We had become a *perpetuum mobile* of arousal and appeasement. We would abandon, mid-flight, the simplest of domestic tasks as desire seized us, and fall back together tugging at buttons, zips, laces, clasps, fasteners ... Continually radiant in my mind's eye was an after-glow of tumbling body-forms – cloven spheres, softened cylinders – a cubist kaleidoscope of Philippa that sometimes occluded everything else around me.

Dead Labour ... How difficult it all looked; how impossibly complex the world it postulated. Would I ever be able to think my way back into Samuelson's theories of drama, his vision of theatre as an economic microcosm where new forms of living could be experimented with like shapes and spaces in an architect's model? That thimble's worth of me tried valiantly to lead the way. It was as unappealing a prospect as drinking the cold, rancid coffee beside it would have been. By a stupendous effort of will I managed to become Samuelson for one, two, three sentences. I then sat back, exhausted. That was the worst over, I told myself. But my conscience was still nagging me. To appease it, I set to work on my restaurant notes. I had the same obligations here, after all.

What a contrast this work was! Far from distracting me, my tape loop of breasts and thighs and moss-mounds of dark brown pubic hair seemed to be *generating* the stream of words that now slipped out of me — *My companion's Steak Ambassadeur was of a tenderness so exquisite you could happily have fed it to a toothless infant* ...

So it continued; a week and more of sipping A to Z through cocktail menus, of dressing up to dance under searchlights or strobe lights, undressing to make love and sleep stickily in the musky sheets of Philippa's bed, of cramming our bellies with *pâté en croute*, hot fruit soups, ocean creatures in aspic, surprises, *bombes*, *sukiyaki*, chicken in chocolate, sea-slugs, fish-lips, duck-webs, calf-heels ... of lying all day in a kimono, half-stupefied, while Philippa went out to work.

Three or four times, my former self reared its head above this sweet miasma of sensations, and I raced home full of guilt and good intention. But as soon as I was sitting before Samuelson's notes, the impulse would always ebb away. A tortured sentence or two might trickle out, and I would end up once more appeasing my conscience with a review or a listing — *The only creatures likely to feel at home in Lulu's Kitchen are dysentery bacilli* ... Slick, glib little gobbets that spurted out of me like — ah no ...

A doctor in a white coat was adjusting Samuelson's polythene drip-feed bag as I entered the annexe.

Patients and visitors were murmuring quietly together. I felt numb and distant, sealed off from the place as if I or it were enclosed in thick aquarium glass. Samuelson was flat on his back. His hair was even whiter and thinner. One more puff and it would all be gone. The shadows around his eyes seemed to have entered deep into the pigment of his skin. The protruding arm was skeletal.

'Good of you to come.' His voice was scarcely more than a whisper.

I smiled and said as little as possible. As long as my bubble remained intact, I was safe. I'd brought the piece of paper with my few sentences on it. I had no plan.

'Did you ... did you get anywhere with those notes then?'

The timidity was out of character. It was the tone of a man relinquishing his claim on others. I could see that Samuelson had moved, in two weeks, from a central, to a peripheral relation with the living world.

I began to formulate an excuse, but couldn't summon the conviction to see it through. I showed him my piece of paper.

'I did a little. Not very much. I'm sorry.'

His eyes flickered from me to the paper, and back again.

'Too busy on your own work I suppose.'

'Yes,' I said, 'that sort of thing.'

'Well ... good. You look healthy on it.'

There was a silence while he read my sentences, and a silence after he'd finished them. I was trembling.

'I will get it done,' I said.

'There's only a week – '

'I know. I'll do it though. I'll bring it here and we can go over it, then I'll take it straight to the publisher's myself.'

'Will you? That's kind.' He closed his eyes. I stayed a moment, looking for signs of activity in the drip-feed bag, imagining it as the sac of a giant tick with a grotesquely long proboscis, not feeding Samuelson, but sucking out the glass-clear essence of him. I rose, and left him sleeping peacefully.

There is a passage in Freud's essay, 'On the Universal Tendency to Debasement in the Sphere of Love', describing psychical impotence. The victim 'reports that he has a feeling of an obstacle inside him, the sensation of a counter-will which successfully interferes with his conscious intention.'

My conscious intention was to write the piece for Samuelson. Morning after morning I would see Philippa off to work, and sit down before the notes, which I had now transferred to her flat. Time after time I read them through, and each time the meanings they dealt with seemed more remote from me than ever. Even so, I should have been able to perform. I was not required to understand or create arguments, merely to articulate them in clear English. But I could not do it. A paralysing lassitude came over me every time I tried; an inertia that was not indolence but a powerful negating force – an anti-magnetism that made myself and the notes mutually repellent.

'Where they love', continues Freud, 'they do not desire, and where they desire they cannot love.'

We awoke late and bleary-eyed on the morning of the sixth day. Philippa was staring at me listlessly as I opened my eyes. I detected minute signals of hostility. I rolled over to embrace her; unreproved, if undesired … At breakfast she hardly spoke. Her silence made me unnaturally talkative. I could sense my words grating on her, but I kept on chattering.

'I *must* get Samuelson done by this evening,' I said.

She turned away.

I sat down at her writing table with the notes. Tomorrow was the deadline for both pieces. The reviews and listings were all but done. This evening an old friend of Philippa's was opening a night-club – a small once-a-week place with dancing, seafood, and some sort of cabaret. The idea was for me to write it up as the final listing on my Nightlife page, immediately it was over, and send the completed copy with Philippa to the magazine the following morning.

I heard her cleaning up the kitchen as I read through Samuelson's notes. Shortly afterwards, she moved into the drawing-room with a spherical Hoover in tow. It began to hum resonantly. I pretended to be undisturbed, but the drone of the machine was mesmerising me, emptying me of thought. I turned round and stared at it gliding smoothly behind Philippa as she moved, stopping when she stopped, filling itself with the dust three weeks had milled from our bodies and possessions.

'Am I disturbing you?' She said it sharply, and before I could stop myself, I replied in kind, 'Don't you have to go to work?'

'I'm taking the day off. Is that all right or would you prefer me to leave?'

'I'm sorry.' I turned back to the piece.

She abandoned the Hoover and marched into the bedroom. The silence she bequeathed was as disturbing as the noise had been. I went into the room. She was lying on the bed, staring at the ceiling and chewing her lip ruminatively. I knelt by her and put my hand on her shoulder. She smiled wanly without looking at me. I slid my hand from her shoulder to her breast. She lay immobile for a moment while I squeezed it. Then she exploded – '*Get* off!' – and recoiled to the other side of the bed. I left the room stunned, as much by my own gesture as by her reaction. I looked at the notes, but I might as well have been looking at a tablet engraved with hieroglyphs.

I went back into the bedroom, to propitiate. My reception was warmer than I might have expected. She was not a callous person; she would not abandon an affair without first examining it for signs of life. We embraced, and kissed fondly, struggling out of our clothes. She twisted herself tightly around me, kissing me methodically all over, as if searching for ingress back into our former intimacy. There was a frenzied-ness in our movement, and a hopelessness too. Some-thing was wrong; each time one of us rose to a pitch of desire, the other would go dead, cold, flaccid. Thus we stopped and started, and broke off again for cigarettes, gin, air ... until at last we rolled apart, sweaty and frustrated, miserably defeated by a fact which neither of us had willed into existence, but which was un-assailable.

We spent the afternoon in considerate silence, avoiding each other, as far as this was possible in her small flat. We had had our fill of each other; that was the fact. We were like two swollen drops of rain on a window pane – if we so much as touched, we would fall and disintegrate.

I sat staring at the white wall above the notes, wait-ing for the night, a prey to one sensation after another. I would feel weak, then angry, then a current of sexual desire would travel through me, the sweet blood col-lecting at my groin dispersed in turn by a sudden irradiation of guilt about Samuelson. Where did these feelings come from? I appeared to have no control over them at all; to be no more than a receptacle, a vacuum into which they strayed at random. I wondered how far into my psyche this principle extended; were my rational faculties – my opinions, beliefs, interests, after all as haphazard and involutional as my emotions, and did they share the same mysterious provenance? What was the essence of this creature leaning on a table in a darkening room, what was its irreducible quality? I sat still, probing its archaeology, passing layer after layer of superimposed ideas, acquired mannerisms, mimicry repeated until it felt like personal conviction ... I was merciless, inquisitorial; I saw the mildew of corruption everywhere, nothing was untainted, or if anything was, it was no more than that minute, lost particle of life you wake up to in the small hours, panicking at its insubstantiality ...

The place was hot and crowded, dimly lit. We settled into a table with half a dozen of Philippa's friends. I had the impression she knew everybody there, had known them all her life. It was quite a network – A and AB at leisure. Groups of them in gorgeous colours milling between tables, bar, dance-floor; dispersing, regrouping ...

The young proprietor came over to us, a bottle of champagne in each hand. He crossed the bottles around Philippa's neck and bent over her, searching for her lips. Afterwards he took my hand in both of his, greeting me like a long lost friend.

Glasses were brought, and we held them up in a bright cluster to collect the overspill of foam, the cuckoo-spit. At the back of the room a waiter in a white coat was shucking oysters and stacking them on beds of crushed ice. Deep-pink sides of smoked salmon were laid out along a table, between sunflowers with king prawns for petals and caviare for seeds. There was a tank with long sea-trout speeding to and fro in it. Another with lobsters and giant crayfish, snouted, plated, bristling with spines and wiry antennae; pre-historic. Coloured lights shone from within the tanks,

submarine blues and greens on coral trees and arches
of rock. Silver bubbles streamed from a plastic tube
immersed in the water.

I gulped my champagne, feeling the sting of its fizz
on the roof of my mouth. Aqueous light and a boom of
music pulsed from the dance-floor. Philippa went off
to dance with Baz, a gaunt-faced man wearing purple
shoes. Her friends tried to include me in the talk.
They'd heard I was reviewing the place, and traded
comic send-ups of the kind of thing I might write. They
saw I wasn't listening though, and left me alone in my
corner.

I had the notes with me. I took them surreptitiously
from my pocket, and unfolded them under the edge of
the table. I was drinking steadily; every time I picked
up my glass it had been refilled. People came and went
with plates of seafood. A pile of oyster shells grew in
the centre of our table – stiffened frills, a tang of brine
… Noise came in waves, swelling and receding. Time
was streaming out. I wrote, 'There seems also a more
than symbolic significance in our society's preferred
method of neutralising its most toxic waste – by con-
verting it into a form of glass.' Then I scribbled as a
memo for the morning, 'Cross a mermaid with a
rhinoceros and you'll have an idea what I mean when I
say the crayfish here are *giant* … '

Philippa was still dancing with Baz. I heard waves
crashing on a pebble shore – a background tape just
audible in the occasional lull. The sound filled me with
sadness. I was losing touch with the party. A curtain by
our table was opened to reveal a stage. Philippa came
back sparkling with secret exuberance. Someone sang
a song on the stage. Jugglers and fire-swallowers followed. The men at my table hooted their appreciation
and stamped their feet. They were drunk, and I too was
drinking myself to the verge of something.

A man with a skull mask and an undertaker's outfit appeared on the stage. He was part magician, part mime. He mimed stalking a rabbit, then produced from thin air a real rabbit which he held upside down. It was freshly dead; a drop of dark blood splashed to the floor. I had a feeling of déjà vu, and a sense, too, of foreboding. He was going to ask for an assistant. I tried to make myself invisible. He called out the names of a dozen guests and asked them to check their pockets. He'd picked them all earlier on. The victims filed up sheepishly to collect wallets, cheque books and so forth. One or two of them looked faintly nettled, but he had the power of the audience on his side.

He produced a tabloid newspaper. There was no print on the pages. He mimed bafflement, exasperation, fury – tearing the paper in half again and again, ripping it to shreds while the audience roared with laughter. He folded all the pieces into a little wad, tapped it with his white-gloved hand, then unfolded it. It had become a creased, but perfectly intact copy of the *Daily Mail*. Quelling the applause, he announced that he was going to teach the trick to a member of the audience. He scanned us with his skull face, sprang down from the stage, and made straight for me.

'You sir, I wonder if you would do me a favour ... '

He had a firm grip on my arm, and was pulling me to my feet.

'And bring these pieces of paper with you, yes yes, bring them along.'

There was no disobeying him. I rose and climbed the stage. I was in a glassy champagne trance, far away from the clusters of green-lit faces angled upward at me. Waves broke on shingle in the quietness.

'Do exactly as I do.' He had another blank newspaper which he tore in two. I tore the notes in two. He tore again and I did likewise, again, again ... My body was trembling. The wall at the end of the room was like the sail of a giant windmill, slowly revolving. I could see the white-coated waiter clearing up the buffet tables. He flicked a switch by the shellfish tank, cutting the air-feed from the plastic tube. He drew the last crustacean from the tank and dropped it, flailing, into a saucepan behind him. A bald head in the audience caught the green light and sank back into shadow. I could hear a groundswell of laughter.

'Tap your hand like so. Now open it up ... '

A chill tingle, a *frisson* of terror, came and went as the shreds of Samuelson's notes fluttered from my hand to the ground. I felt his presence in the room; a ghostly analogue ... The laughter rose as the magician jeered at me, waving his own intact paper at the audience. I noticed, as I left the stage, that his shoes were purple.

Snow

My great-uncle Dominic, the inventor, took me into the small workshop that stood between the back of his house and the large kitchen garden behind it. 'This will amuse you,' he said, pointing to a box-shaped contraption with what looked like a headlamp encased in it. 'It's called a stroboscope. They are going to become very popular.' He switched on an electric drill, and brought it into the flashing, acetylene-blue light of the contraption. With his free hand he adjusted the frequency of the flashing, and I watched, enchanted, as the drill-bit appeared to slow gradually down to a complete halt. 'There, you see,' he said, 'it renders the most violent things harmless. Touch the drill, go on ... '

Such was his solicitude, however, that before I had raised my small hand a fraction, he clutched it with his own. 'Now let this serve as a lesson to you. Watch ... ' He brought a piece of wood from the work-bench to the motionless drill-bit. A harsh rasping came as the one contacted the other, a flashlit spray of sawdust plumed out in a staggered curve, and in a trice the innocent piece of metal had bitten clean through the inch-thick piece of wood. 'There you are. If something looks peaceful then leave it alone or else you get

crucified. The stroboscope makes machines look still
because it only illuminates one point in their cycle.
Terrible accidents happen in factories where they have
flickering neon lights ... Now I must go and have a nap
before Inge and I go out.'

Uncle Dominic was a man of extraordinary mild-
ness. Family legend has it that his only retort to the
irresponsible nurse in whose charge his son drowned
forty-five years ago was, 'If this sort of thing happens
again you'll have to go.' He made his fortune when the
patent for a guidance device he had invented was
purchased by an aeronautical company, which then
adapted it for use in naval missiles. After the war he
calculated that he had been instrumental in the deaths
of some twenty thousand people. The fact haunted
him. He wrote countless letters to the press warning
scientists to guard their discoveries from the Military,
and was much ridiculed for them. In an oddly inverted
piece of *folie de grandeur*, he papered his workshop
with the dead and wounded of Hiroshima, as if he had
been personally responsible for the carnage. The projects he worked on became increasingly trifling, as his
concern over their possible abuse grew more obsessive.
That winter he had perfected a machine for feeding
minced chicken, at twelve-hourly intervals, to Salome,
his beloved Persian Blue, so that he and his second wife
Inge could take short holidays without troubling the
neighbours to look after the animal.

He had also built the prototype of a hair-plaiting
device for Inge, and as we returned from the cold
workshop to the warm house, we heard Inge shouting
from the bedroom upstairs – 'Come and get this
wretched machine out of my hair. It's stuck – ' Uncle
Dominic quickened his pace, then checked himself. 'I
mustn't run,' he said to me, 'you go and help her.'

Inge, twenty-six years my great-uncle's junior, sat at

her dressing-table in a blue silk *peignoir* embroidered with tiny bright humming birds, the plaiting device sticking incongruously from her long golden hair. 'Ah. Little Thomas,' she said, 'how sweet you are ... ' I stood behind her disentangling the golden strands from the silver tines of the device as gently as I could. 'None of his machines work these days,' she whispered, as Uncle Dominic's footsteps approached the door.

He fell instantly asleep on the bed, while Inge had me brush her hair with her soft, ivory-handled hairbrush, and plait it with my own hands. I can remember wanting to tell her how lovely I thought she was, but having the courage only to let my all-licensed hands linger in that gleaming floss some moments longer than were necessary. She coiled the braid into a bun, and fixed it with two tourmaline pins. 'Now go', she said, 'while I dress,' and kissed me on my forehead.

I saw them off from the front entrance; my great-uncle immaculate in evening dress, black of his tall gaunt frame and the silver hair repeated in his tipped ebony stick; Inge's sable stole collecting the first white crystals of the frozen evening. 'We won't be long,' she called to me from the bottom of the marble steps, 'Anne-Marie will look after you. If Mr Morpurgo arrives before we do, then ... offer him a drink.' She climbed into the car giggling at the thought, and they drove off to their cocktail party.

I sat on the living-room sofa drawing Christmas cards for them, while Anne-Marie – or Claire or Gabrielle – buffed silver knives and piled them on a salver where they gleamed like fish spilt from a net.

Mr Morpurgo, their dinner guest, did arrive before Dominic and Inge. He wore, as I remember, a yellow suit with pieces of brown suede clasping the shoulders and elbows. His face was a porous, piecemeal assemblage of unrelated features that could never agree on one expression. Smiles dissolved into scowls then into parodies of misery, swiftly, and with no apparent reason. He was the kind of man who awakens in children their first sensations of snobbery. I offered him a drink, and when he asked jovially if I was joining him, I declined with a delicious sense of disdain. He addressed me as 'little man', but I knew he had only been invited out of pity, because his wife had left him, and it was Christmas Eve, and he happened to live across the garden. He tried to flirt with the au pair, but she feigned ignorance of English. He put on a French accent, as if that would help, and she quickly found an excuse to leave the room. He wandered about picking up and examining ornaments from shelves, and when I intimated that the silver- and glass-framed wedding portrait of Dominic and Inge he'd pulled from its hook, was fragile and perhaps rather special to them, he made a great show of replacing it exactly as he'd found it, smirking at me while he did so. 'Whatever the little man says,' he added, and in an attempt to amuse, clicked his heels together and saluted me.

The slam of the front door brought in Dominic and Inge, rosy-cheeked and vibrant from their cocktail party. As they greeted Mr Morpurgo, apologising for their lateness, I watched the powdery snow on Inge's stole melting into tiny seed-pearls that clung, sparkling, to the wet tips of fur. The arrow-heads of her pale blue high-heels were rimmed with moisture, and I remember this pleasing me, because it meant the snow was settling.

At dinner, Mr Morpurgo tried to draw out my Uncle Dominic on the subject of his pacifism. 'Go on, admit it,' he kept saying, with what was presumably intended to be a roguish grin, 'you're deluding yourself. No real progress has ever been made in the name of peace or love. Greed, aggression and lust – that's what motivates people. We're beasts really – I'm one, I don't deny it. I organise my life and work accordingly. Stab your neighbour before he stabs you, that's the only way. Admit it, go on … ' Out of courtesy, Uncle Dominic made a token defence of his position; the lazy, tail-swishing defence a horse makes against a mildly irritating fly, and it seemed entirely proper to me that he should not waste energy doing battle with so unworthy an adversary.

After dinner he dozed on the living-room sofa, Salome dozing on his lap, while Inge and Mr Morpurgo played backgammon, quietly accusing one another of cheating, and giggling quietly so as not to wake Uncle Dominic. Mr Morpurgo risked a stab at his sleeping host – 'That's how he preserves his illusions is it – by sleeping most of his life, and only waking up for the good bits?' Inge smiled sadly at her husband, and said nothing.

As ever, no effort was made to send me to bed, although Mr Morpurgo twice expressed his amazement at 'the little man's stamina'. I went, eventually, in the wake of Uncle Dominic who, roused by the bite of Salome's claws, declared himself a little sleepy, and retired, wishing us all a happy Christmas. When Inge came up to say goodnight, she let me unpin her hair, unfurl it, and separate the three golden locks which she rustled back into one dishevelled tress before returning to Mr Morpurgo.

I found myself very suddenly wide awake long before the dawn of Christmas Day. I left opening my stocking until my great-uncle and aunt would have woken, and I could open it on their bed, the quilt wrapped about my shoulders, while they received my tribute of delight in return for their generosity.

Through my bedroom window the dark blue sky with its sprinkling of stars coaxed pale shades of silver from the snow-covered garden and surrounding houses. The snow on the garden was pristine, except for a dotted line that ran across the centre from our house to the one opposite, like the perforations between two stamps seen from their white, shiny backs.

I put on my slippers, went downstairs to investigate, and yes, parallel with two sets of snowed-over footprints leading out from the back door, past my great-uncle's workshop, was a set cut freshly into the crisp snow, the arrow-heads pointing back into our house.

The significance of these footprints remained in chrysalis within me until the recent death of my great-uncle reminded me of the occasion; though by then I, like everyone else except perhaps Uncle Dominic, knew all about Inge's affair. The sight thus provided me with no sorrowful descent into knowledge. It did, however, give rise to a tableau which now seems a peculiarly expressive coda to my Uncle Dominic's life.

The busy Christmas morning rituals on the day itself demanded I put the image of the footprints temporarily out of mind. At lunch, though, it rose once more from its suppression. The ten or twelve assembled relatives had finished eating, and we were leaning back in our chairs telling stories and sipping *eiswein*. Whether it was an excess of that extraordinary distillation of frost-corrupted grapes, or the air's intoxicating fragrance of tangerine peel, burnt brandy, and cigar smoke, or the way the candle flames were splintered and multiplied in the table's debris of silver cutlery and dishes, I don't know; but something released in me the image of those tracks again, catalysing a thought that seemed to me astoundingly clever, and well worth the immediate attention of the company.

'Uncle Dominic,' I called out in my shrill voice. The

table hushed, and my great-uncle's eyelids opened a crack. 'Your stroboscope is like snow. There were footprints leading to the back door this morning when I got up, and I've just thought ... ' but to my chagrin the relatives at once resumed their conversations in unnecessarily loud voices. I piped louder, but my ingenious explanation – that all the action happens *between* the footprints, so that only the moments of stillness are made visible by the snow – was drowned by my relatives' voices that rose with mine, fell briefly at intervals when they thought I'd given up, then rose in chorus again as I persisted, so that all my Uncle Dominic was allowed to hear were the disjointed words that rang out during the brief pauses.

He looked perplexed for a moment, but made no attempt to hear more than the babble permitted, and soon let his eyelids drop again. I was finally silenced by Inge's mother who asked me, with a fatuous (though unreturned) grin at her daughter, whether I thought those footprints might have been Father Christmas's. Mortified by this snub, I fell into a sulk from which I did not recover until I had flown back to my parents, who worked in a place where Christmas is not celebrated, and where snow has never been seen.

The Siege

Marietta was woken one night by a rumbling sound in the wall beside her bed. She switched on her lamp and opened the door to the dumb-waiter, which she used as a clothes cupboard. Her clothes lay neatly folded on the two shelves, as she had left them. But resting on a pile of shirts on the lower shelf was a piece of white cartridge paper. The address of the house was embossed in smart black print at the top, and below this was a large question mark painstakingly executed in turquoise ink: **?**

She had no word, in English or her own language, for a dumb-waiter, and she had never considered what the original function of her clothes cupboard might have been. But it was a matter of seconds before she realised that it was in fact a small lift connecting her basement flat with the house upstairs. There was only one person living up there: Mr Kinsky.

Marietta cleaned and ironed for Mr Kinsky, in exchange for accommodation in his basement. It was a convenient arrangement, enabling her to study, while supporting herself frugally, but adequately, with a weekend job supervising a launderette.

She turned over the piece of paper. There was

nothing there. A faintly disturbing thought occurred to her; she examined her shirts and blouses, bras and knickers, for signs of interference. Nothing seemed to be amiss. This did not greatly surprise her: she had judged Mr Kinsky to be an eccentric, overbred product of European capitalism, but not a dangerous pervert. He had treated her with impeccable courtesy since her move here over a year ago. If anything, he was a little shy of her.

She resolved not to jeopardise her position by making a fuss. Whatever hopes and desires were encoded in that scroll of turquoise ink – and it was not difficult to guess – it seemed a harmless enough way of expressing them. She would say nothing; Mr Kinsky would understand, and that would be that.

She threw the piece of paper away, closed the cupboard door, and went back to sleep.

She had lectures and classes the next day, and did not see Mr Kinsky. But that night she was woken again by the rumbling of the dumb-waiter. This time it served her an orchid. Orange freckled with mauve, blue flames running along the centre of each fluted petal. Lying there naked and unadorned, curved and contorted into itself, it looked like the embodiment of an indecent suggestion. Somewhat reluctantly, she picked it up. It was cool to the touch, sprung firmly upon its involutions. She couldn't quite bring herself to throw away something so fresh and brilliant, so she stuck it unceremoniously in the chipped mug of water by her bed.

She thought uneasily of Mr Kinsky. Was he listening at his end of the shaft, trying to decipher a response from the sound of her movements? Foreseeing that this idea would only worry her into a sleepless night, she shrugged it off and climbed back into bed resolved, as before, to say nothing.

She was doing Mr Kinsky's ironing in the small utility room at the top of the house the following afternoon, when she heard his tread on the staircase.

The door was open, and she could see him from above as he climbed the stairs. He was a very large man with a slow, soft way of moving. His black hair was silvering but still curly, and always unkempt. He wore a baggy black suit, a white shirt buttoned at the collar, but no tie. His broad face was almost entirely unmarked by care or suffering, which gave it a serene handsomeness.

He did, however, look worried when he caught sight of Marietta at the top of the stairs. She smiled at him and said hello, in a perfectly nonchalant way.

'Ah ... ' he said, coming to a standstill in the doorway. He paused there, while she aligned the legs of a pair of pyjama bottoms and folded them up. He cleared his throat, and waggled his fingers as if trying to conjure more words from the air. None came, but still he lingered, making tortured expressions on his face, with an unselfconsciousness that suggested he had little idea how very imposing his presence was.

Marietta spread out a shirt on the ironing board and pulled a trigger on the iron. Steam rose in a puff that clouded out her hand. Mr Kinsky stopped fidgeting and stared at the phenomenon as if he had never seen anything so odd in his life. Presently he sighed, and padded off next door, to his music room.

Marietta smiled to herself as she heard the scales peal out from the grand piano. She had seldom managed to discourage a suitor with such ease. The key of the scales shifted up semitone by semitone, a steady spiralling ascent through the octave. The upward movement was exhilarating, and Marietta listened to it happily, confident that Mr Kinsky's affections were back where they belonged: with his Steinway.

That night the rumbling came again. Marietta opened her eyes, more startled on this occasion than she had been before, and for the first time fractionally afraid. She lay quite still in the darkness, listening, but the house was absolutely silent. She could see the cupboard handle gleaming in the faint light that seeped through the curtain from a street lamp. She sat up slowly and stretched her hand towards it. She opened the door as quietly as she could.

A ring lay cushioned in the pile of shirts. She held it up to the window, twisting it in the light. Dark jewels glittered; a sodium burnish slid about the gold. It was heavy, and blood-warm from a hand's prolonged grasp. She felt suddenly vulnerable in her nakedness, as if there were a hundred eyes glinting in the shadows of her room. She placed the ring beside the orchid and pulled the blankets tightly about her body.

The ring was slippery in her hands, as she climbed the stairs to return it the following day. Big chords and rippling arpeggios rained down through the house from the music room. Mr Kinsky had a taste for the rhapsodical to which Marietta, recognising it as the luxurious rhetoric of the *haute bourgeoisie* spirit, was more or less indifferent. She only liked it when he toiled through his scales: something in the drudgery made her uncloak her sensibility, and listen.

She was nervous about the confrontation that awaited her. Life at Mr Kinsky's had been simple and carefree. Now she suspected her luck was about to run out. It was an object lesson in the treacherous magnanimity of the powerful.

He continued playing, quite unaware of her as she hovered in the doorway of the music room, clutching the ring in her hand.

The grand piano was positioned against a huge,

gilt-framed mirror. Mr Kinsky and his reflection conferred closely over an operation in the bass regions,
then parted company for the upper extremities of their
respective keyboards. The instrument itself, its lid
propped open for maximum resonance, was doubled
into a gigantic butterfly.

When finally Mr Kinsky registered her presence,
he stopped mid-cadenza and blushed, quite unashamedly. Can a blush be executed unashamedly?
Yes, in that Mr Kinsky appeared entirely unconscious
of it: the blood came flooding into his cheeks, but he
looked Marietta in the eye as if nothing were out of the
ordinary, nothing at all.

'Ah ... hello,' he said.

Marietta walked briskly across the cork-tiled floor
and placed the ring on a stack of yellow Schirmer's
Library scores piled at the front of the piano.

'This is *yours* I think?'

He looked impassively at the ring – a big oval
emerald garnished with diamonds and gold filigree.
His look was so inscrutable that for a moment Marietta wondered whether he was going to disclaim it.

'My aunt's,' he said at last. He looked down at the
keyboard and pressed a white note with a long,
powerful-looking forefinger, so gently that although
the leverage was visibly transmitted to the felt-covered
hammer beneath the exposed strings, no sound was
produced.

Marietta stood in the opulent curve of the instrument, waiting.

She knew that Mr Kinsky had been brought up in
this house by his aunt, a sparky-looking woman whose
resplendent portrait hung in the dining-room. She had
wanted him to be a concert pianist. She drowned in a
yachting accident when Mr Kinsky was nineteen. *I
found I couldn't perform after that*, Mr Kinsky had

said, *but then again she left me the house and enough money* ...

'I was rather hoping you'd hang on to it, you know ... ' he said finally.

'Why?'

He stood up and lumbered over to the room's balcony window. Facing out of it, he began a long, meandering confession of love.

His shadow trailed out from his heels across the cork tiles. The floor surfaces in this house! Black and white chequered doorsteps, herring-bone wood in the hall, cold granite flagstones in the kitchen, rush matting, goat skins, Friesian cowhides clouded symmetrically like Rorschach blots, deep pile, junkers, Persian rugs so lustrous still that filaments of precious metal must have been twisted into the weave ... It was dizzying to think that the man who trod them carried in his mind an image of her which, if she caught his drift correctly, he had been worshipping in secret and with mounting fervour from the first week of her instalment in his basement.

He turned to her – 'I do love you though, Marietta. I absolutely ... ' he waggled his fingers in desperation ' ... love you. I'm in love.' He faced her with a trance-like stare, relishing the word as if it were some exquisite delicacy he had never tasted before – 'I love you.'

She felt mildly intrigued by the emotions of this peculiar man, but could not in any way connect them with herself.

He looked so innocent, and clownish, buttoned up like a schoolboy waiting for mother to tie his tie and comb his straggling curls ...

But then she happened to glance down at the piano-top, and notice a piece of manuscript paper with a bass and treble clef immaculately scrolled in turquoise ink at each stave, and back with a jolt came the question

mark, the orchid, the ring, the dumb-waiter's rumbling underscore to Mr Kinsky's quaint declaration ...
She decided it was time to retreat.

'I think I should go.' She made for the door.

Mr Kinsky strode across the room to intercept her.
He caught her wrists.

'Would you like to marry me?'

She could feel the beat of his heart pulsing through
his big hands, and she could smell him too, a sweet rich
tang.

'I couldn't possibly marry you!' She said it with a
laugh that came out as a shrill, nervous giggle.

He was serious, he said; he had never had such
feelings before. Marietta was determined not to let
indignation, or embarrassment, or fear get the better
of her, but she could feel herself shaking in his grasp.

He pulled her close to him and asked if she believed
he was serious. Yes. Did she love him? No, please let
me go ... Was there anything he could do to make her
love him? No, please ... Anything at all, was she sure?
Let go of me!

'*Anything*, Marietta ... '

She wrenched herself free. A furious glare burst
behind her eyes, and before she could stop herself she
shouted at him. In doing so, she revealed a secret she
had been guarding since her arrival in London: 'Get
my husband out of jail!'

A pause.

'Your husband.' Mr Kinsky sat down on the piano
stool. 'I didn't realise you had a husband.'

Marietta stepped back, and watched him with the
nervously satisfied eye of someone who has dislodged
a small, critically placed stone, and set off an
avalanche.

'May I ask what he is doing in jail?'

She emptied the bucket of water down the front steps. Steaming suds cascaded over the black and white chequered stone and slithered out on to the pavement, darkening it. She picked up the mop and began to clean, leaving the front door open. Pale sunlight glistened on the bubbles of soap. Scales poured down from the music room, a torrent of sound streaming out of the door and down into the street.

There had been a shift in the atmosphere of the house. It was like the modulation from major to minor in Mr Kinsky's scales, which always gave Marietta a feeling of foreboding, a premonitory tingle, when she heard it. The incident in the music room had pitched them into a sombre, melancholic key. To be sure, the dumb-waiter no longer rumbled in the night, and she had not been asked to leave. Nevertheless, she and Mr Kinsky were no longer comfortable with each other. For weeks now, Mr Kinsky had been conspicuously avoiding her when she came upstairs to his part of the house. She didn't mind this, but it coincided with a growing anxiousness on her part. She had begun to wake up in the mornings feeling worried and unrested. Certain questions about her life, which she had succeeded in shelving since her arrival in England, were now stirring again, clamouring for an answer. These questions concerned her husband, from whom she had not heard since his incarceration in the military barracks of her country's capital city four years ago. She had no idea whether she would see him again, or whether he was even alive.

She was a conscientious worker. The steps were dazzling by the time she had finished them. She went indoors and set to work on the shelves and niches in Mr Kinsky's drawing-room.

She was deep in thought as she moved about the room. Four years and an ocean away from a husband who might or might not be alive, she had remained wedded to the idea of him. It was surprisingly easy to consecrate oneself to such a mystery, like falling asleep in snow. It formed a backdrop to her life in London that made this life less purposeless than it might have been otherwise, though it did so only because she took pains not to examine it too closely. But since she had revealed its existence to Mr Kinsky, the mystery had begun to appear once more in the foreground of her thoughts, and when it did it was like one of those vast unanswerable metaphysical questions that creep up and stun you into panic at the sheer unlikeliness of your being alive, here, now.

There was one shelf which Mr Kinsky had asked her to take particular care over. It contained a number of objects that were without exception, he said, quite priceless. Her hands were long accustomed to the shape and weight of them all, so that she could give each one its due care without needing to break out of her reverie. Scarcely seeing what she was doing, she steadied and dusted a winged grey bust of Mercury, an art nouveau vase fashioned from the attenuated bodies of a man and woman entwined, a frail and worn fragment of an ancient ivory horse ... absently she put out her hand to grasp the little statuette of shepherds and nymphs that had always stood next in line. She found herself grasping at air. The statuette was gone.

The absence stalled her for a moment, but she gave it no further thought.

Until a week later, when she noticed that a framed original manuscript, signed by its composer, was missing from the upstairs landing. She wasn't inquisitive by nature, but her curiosity was aroused, and she kept her eyes open for other disappearances.

She came upon four square patches of paler paint on the wall in one of the spare rooms; memorials to a row

of watercolours depicting scenes from Kiev, one for
each season. A circular imprint on top of a corner
cupboard was all that remained of a large oriental
vase. And hadn't there been a little clutch of enamelled
lockets in that wicker basket?

She had never been greatly interested in Mr Kinsky's
affairs. She assumed he lacked for nothing. He lived off
a private income, from which she deduced he had
money invested in countries such as her own, where
governments could be relied upon to keep wages neg-
ligible, and profits correspondingly enormous. This
made him reprehensible, though in too passive a way
for her to be able to maintain an individual grudge
against him. She merely hoped, and believed, that his
breed would one day vanish from the face of the earth.

But the disappearance of these objects conferred an
air of mystery upon him. Was he simply bored with
them or did he need money? If the latter, then ... It was
good to be able to think about someone not connected
with her own affairs. Mr Kinsky was out at the
moment. The only sound was of the spring wind rattling windows in the big, airy rooms. She began to
search the house. An ornamental silver bowl was missing from the dining-room table. Was he in some sort
of trouble? She went into his study. Where was the
chair with lion paws at its feet, a gilt lion head carved
at the front of each armrest? What was going on?

She began to feel uncomfortable lingering in Mr
Kinsky's private study, so she turned to go, but as she
left she glimpsed something in the wastepaper basket
that made her stop in her tracks. It was an envelope,
crumpled but with part of the stamp still showing. She
picked it up and smoothed it out. It was addressed to
Mr Kinsky. The stamp, as she had suspected, was
familiar to her, more than familiar. It bore the face of a
man with a general's hat and a thick-jowled look of

military displeasure. He was the president of her own country. She looked at him in wonder, and as she stood there thinking, her wonder turned to amazement, and finally to a kind of helpless awe as a suspicion of what Mr Kinsky might be doing, or trying to do, assembled itself from the evidence in her hand and all around the house, and rose up within her, creeping under her skin, like a blush ...

Mr Kinsky was learning a new piece. He started practising it in the morning before Marietta went to her classes, and would still be at it when she returned in the afternoon. Day after day he played nothing but this piece.

It began with a childish melody, a simple nursery tune of no particular distinction. The tune was played again and again, but at each repetition a new element was added to the accompanying harmonies, deepening and darkening its resonance, so that it was gradually transformed from its bland cheerfulness into something haunting and disturbing, in the way that a child's toy might be if you were to see it in a series of successively gloomier backgrounds, beginning with a nursery and ending with a graveyard. Then when it had reached its graveyard phase, the tune was abandoned, and the piece burst into the most voluptuous, ecstatic progression of pounding bass notes and dazzling runs cascading down from higher and higher.

She heard the piece now as she sat at her desk by the window, trying to gain a foothold in the huge textbook that lay before her. Through sheer force of repetition, the music had begun to get the better of her customary immunity, and steal its way into her system. Here was the tune again – la da da *da*-de-da ... Here was that first hint of shadow in its harmony, then another, deeper, deeper ... She stared out of the window and watched the breeze winnowing white blossom from an almond tree. Flurries of fallen petals were swirled up into ghostly tops and sent spinning across the street ... Here was the tune in its twilight stage; she felt her body tensing up in expectation ... There! The first pounding volley as the piece exploded into rhapsody – bombs and shrapnel, starbursts of sound.

It was impossible to work. Like Mr Kinsky's confession of love, the discovery of her president in the wastepaper basket had transformed the atmosphere around Marietta. She had begun to feel peculiarly sensitive, alert to every movement and disturbance. And there was a profusion of disturbances, of stirrings and awakenings ...

The house was steadily being denuded. Every time she went upstairs something else was missing, and each time she noticed it her heart gave a jump. She was in a state of mild, but continuous trepidation. One by one the prize possessions had disappeared from their special shelf. Now only the grey bust of Mercury remained. Seeing him standing there alone, she had been struck for the first time by his beauty. He had clusters of curls under his winged helmet. His face had been sculpted with great delicacy – a trace of Olympian amusement on his lips, his cheeks cool and smooth to the touch ...

And yesterday an unsigned letter had arrived for her. *My dear Marietta, news of your husband: he is alive. He has been transferred from the barracks to an ordinary prison. I shall write again as soon as I know what is happening.*

Mr Kinsky stumbled over a note, paused a moment, and returned to the beginning of the piece – la da da *da*-de-da ... How unnerving it was to be at the centre of all this activity, but not its source. The powerlessness of her position made her feel by turns blissful and resentful. Several times she had been on the point of confronting Mr Kinsky with her discovery, but to confess that she had guessed what he was doing would oblige her either to tell him he shouldn't, or else to acknowledge herself massively indebted to him. It was easier to pretend she knew nothing. Besides, Mr Kinsky had become less communicative than ever. When he wasn't at his Steinway, he would be sitting in his unlit study, gazing into space with an air of broody preoccupation. She did not like to disturb him: she had begun to find his presence daunting, almost forbidding, as if with the disappearance of each possession, a commensurate space had been hollowed out in him and filled with shadow. He loomed large in her imagination.

She could not concentrate. She took her finger from the left-hand corner of the enormous book. The thin, silky pages bulged towards the centre. Four or five of them slid in succession from the sprung sheaf and swung through the air in a lazy arc, settling gently on the other side.

It was raining. Thin drops crackled against the window. Water trickled in plaited sluices from the gutters. She shuddered. Her room felt sparse and constricting. She had an urge to move.

She went upstairs. Today was not one of her working days, but she could always find some task. For a while she wandered aimlessly over the rugs and mats, the wood floors and stone floors ... She opened the drawing-room door to look at Mercury. When she saw the gap where he had stood she had to steady herself against the door-frame. Wind made rumbling sounds in the windows, playing them like kettle drums.

She climbed upstairs to the utility room. La da da *da*-de-da ... Here it was again, at full volume now, percussive chimes so bright and loud the space about

Marietta seemed to be occupied not by air but by sound. She set up the ironing board and switched on the iron. Above her, suspended from the ceiling, was a cradle of bars over which the two large white sheets of Mr Kinsky's double bed were draped. She reached up and pulled one towards her, furling it in as it slid free of its bar. It smelt sweet and clean. Bunched against her breast it was like a colossal almond flower. She laid it over the ironing board. It was satisfying to cleave the iron through the linen waves and see the smooth white wake stretch out behind. She moved her arm in time with the music. She was thinking of her husband, or trying to: it was difficult to focus her thoughts while the music was swirling about her. A long swelling crescendo brought it to a pitch where it no longer sounded like a single piano, but a whole orchestra. She glanced through the open door of the music room. There he sat, lost deep inside his broad bulk, pouring out music like some mythical hoof-struck spring. And as she returned to her thoughts, the sound became a stream flooding down through the house, bearing a flotilla of enamelled lockets, silver bowls, water-colours, Persian carpets, statuettes, engravings, jewels, furniture ...

It was like a forcible initiation. Day by day the music inducted her further into its secret language of nostalgia and desire. She had always considered it the height of decadence to have one's emotions tickled and stroked and cosseted in this way, for the sake of nothing more than a series of fleeting sensations. But as she became increasingly attuned to the nuances of the piece, so it grew more difficult for her to recall with any conviction the context within which the pleasure it gave was corrupt. She observed herself succumb to it with a certain mortified fascination.

She sat in the Blue Ocean Launderette. Her duties here were minimal – dispensing change, tending the occasional service wash, sweeping the floor, closing up.

The machines were like a row of submarine portholes, looking on to a sea swirling with bright clothing. The melody was playing in her head – la da da *da*-de-da. She looked absently through the portholes ... Another letter had arrived that morning – *My dear Marietta, your husband has been granted a trial* ...

As she stared at the machines she tried to imagine what it would be like to start living again with a man she had not seen for four years. But she found herself instead remembering Mr Kinsky's confession of love – the turquoise question mark, the orchid, the ring ... turning from the balcony – *I do love you though, Marietta, I absolutely* ... waggling his fingers, grimacing, lumbering across the room – *would you like to marry me?* Grasping her wrists – *anything at all ... anything, Marietta* ... Clothes tumbled round and round. Lacy white suds splashed against the glass and slid away. Glissando runs echoed in her memory ... She had a sudden desire to be back in the doorway of the music room, watching Mr Kinsky play. She closed her eyes. She realised that she could hardly wait to lock up and go home. A strange feeling ran through her: it had in it both exultation and dread.

It was still light when she locked up. It had been raining, but now a chink of blue had opened up in the clouds, and the sun was shining through, reflecting in gutters and puddles. She walked briskly along the street. Everything looked very clean and shiny. The buses seemed a brighter red, the taxis a glossier black. There was a bracing, astringent smell, like the smell of a new leaf crushed between two fingers. She felt almost light-headed among the jostling pedestrians who were afflicted by a rare and visible exuberance of spirits. A chef stood in the doorway of his restaurant, sharpening a knife and looking critically at the sun. He was dressed in spotless white, a white scarf knotted at the side of his neck, and a lop-sided hat. Every time he brought the blade down against the honing bar, it came out of the shadow of the doorway and flashed brilliantly in the sun, as if repeatedly puncturing a vein flowing with light. He smiled at Marietta as she passed, and without thinking she smiled back. Pigeons were strutting about, surveying the pavement cracks for the rainfall's harvest of worms. They cocked their heads and swelled their necks in jerky spasms; and when a puffed-up throat twisted in the light, the modest gloss of green and violet made Marietta think of a black and white photograph puffing and straining to be colour, and she giggled to herself at the thought. She had an urge to run. How peculiar this feeling was—a strange, aching elation. She turned into her road. The almond trees were sparkling with waterdrops. They had been stripped by the wind of all but a few tight white bunches of blossom that clung like crowns of fleece to the shiny black twigs. The trees gleamed in their mantles of water like moss in agate.

Something seemed to be happening at the house. She could see people standing on the pavement outside. She quickened her pace. There was a small crane that had been hidden by the angle of the building. She began to run. She could hear the deep rumble of the crane's motor, and the squeak of revolving pulleys. She arrived in time to see the grand piano, trussed in thick ropes, rise up from the music room's balcony window, swing slowly away from the house, and descend majestically to the pavement, where a removal lorry awaited it.

The silence in the house was terrible. It resonated in the big, empty rooms.

Marietta sat at her desk in a daze. She could no longer even pretend to work. From time to time she heard the music in her head – la da da *da*-de-da ... twitching like a phantom limb, and when she heard it, she was filled once more with that strange, dreadful exultation, only now the discomfort of the feeling far outweighed the pleasure.

She had been once into the music room: where the mirror had formerly doubled the piano, it now doubled its absence, and the bareness of the place made her ache. She found herself waggling her fingers as Mr Kinsky had done when searching for words to express his feelings for her.

The next letter to arrive was from her husband himself; a short note telling her that he was free, and that he would be arriving in England in a fortnight, five days of which had elapsed since the letter was posted. No need to meet him at the airport.

It wasn't unexpected; all the same, Marietta was surprised at her lack of reaction. It might have been a gas bill for all the effect it had on her. She wondered if this was the numbness people are supposed to experience when they first go into shock. If so, what would she feel when it wore off?

It occurred to her that she ought to inform Mr Kinsky. She went upstairs feeling as apprehensive as she had done months earlier, when she had climbed up to return his ring. She was struck by the peculiar symmetry of the two occasions – every aspect was inverted: anger had turned into a kind of furtive gratitude, fear into wonder, unheard music into this tumultuous silence.

He was lying on a sofa in the drawing-room. It was a long sofa, but he was even longer; his legs stuck out over the armrest. She could see a section of very white shin between the end of his puckered trousers and the beginning of his socks. He wasn't doing anything. He looked calm and self-possessed.

'Hello, my dear.' He used the endearment with the authority of someone who has acquired a right to it precisely by virtue of his grace in defeat as a prospective lover.

'I just wanted to ask you if ... ' She could hear her voice wobbling like a timid child's; 'I just wanted to ask you if it was all right for my husband to move into the flat. He's been released.' She looked down at the bare floor. She could sense him staring at her. She peeped up; he was. It was a complex, eloquent stare. It invited her to divulge more about this turn of events; it forgave her if she chose not to.

'What marvellous news. You must be very happy.' He didn't sound in the least bit surprised.

'Yes,' she said, 'I just heard. He'll be here in a week, just over a week.'

'That's frightfully exciting.'

'Yes.' The space in the room seemed taut, contracted: a bubble that the slightest slip would burst. She realised that this would probably be her last opportunity to acknowledge Mr Kinsky's magnanimity. The charade of ignorance she was going through would otherwise soon harden into an established version of the truth that would be difficult ever to breach without awkwardness and embarrassment. An act of monumental generosity would simply evaporate from history if she did not speak now.

They looked at each other for a moment, both watching the opportunity go by. Then Mr Kinsky said of course her husband could move in, and that he looked forward to meeting him. She gave him the faintest of smiles, and went back downstairs, her legs trembling, ever so slightly.

What had she been afraid of? That he would attempt to hold her to an ironic, rhetorical promise? She tried to make herself believe that this was the case. With that in mind, she reread her husband's letter, attempting to induce the rush of joy that had failed to materialise first time round. If she succeeded, then she would be able to attribute the feelings of elation that arose in her whenever she thought of Mr Kinsky, to his services in bringing back her husband; the feelings of dread to what he might ask in return.

She did not succeed. In fact, she felt her spirits beginning to sink. How appalling ... She struggled; *he's free* she told herself, *he's coming back to me* ... She pictured him walking through the door. The first kiss... would it be passionate? Sexual? Would he want to make love before they spoke? Would she want to? Would the circumstances oblige her to? She hadn't slept with a man for four years. She imagined herself naked in his arms, his mouth at her breast, his hands sliding between her legs. Her heart burst into life, but it was not desire that beat there. It was panic; dread.

Thus it was that Marietta drifted into the realm of pure emotion. Her flat and the streets beyond were less real to her now than the shimmering landscape of feelings she found herself stranded in. She had never been anywhere so strange and treacherous. She had a clear objective: to persuade herself that she loved her husband, and that she did not love anybody else. She was perfectly sincere in her desire to do this. Her husband was a good and brave man for whom she had the utmost admiration and respect. Their marriage – an alliance of idealists against a common oppressor – had been exciting and happy. A certain anxiety was to be expected after an interval of four years. But this was much more than anxiety: this was cold sweats in the small hours when she thought of him in bed beside her; nausea at mealtimes when she considered the unending wifely devotion he was entitled to, and would certainly need after his ordeal; a sudden flushing out of all the strength from her limbs as she imagined the sheer saturation to which his presence would subject the little flat.

The closer the day came, the worse these symptoms grew. The harder she tried to overcome them, the more exhausted she became. She had never before experienced the full waywardness of feelings. It exasperated her that an invisible, intangible phenomenon like love, which could barely be said to exist at all, could not be brought to heel.

Love, desire, fear, revulsion ... Feelings are like a physicist's massless particles; the hypothetical agencies by which the universe coheres and makes itself visible. These miraculous phenomena combine all-pervasiveness with absolute elusiveness, ceasing to exist when not in motion. Devoid of any intrinsic qualities, their secondary effects are none the less momentous and ineluctable. A particle of desire is as improbable as a photon or a graviton; its effects are as undeniable as light, or gravity.

In the middle of the night before her husband was due to arrive, Marietta awoke with a jolt. Her hand was at her groin, and her groin was moist. She could hear, as an internal echo rather than an actual sound, a deep rumbling, as though she had just been woken by such a noise. She opened the door of the dumb-waiter. There was nothing there. In her groggy state this seemed wrong. She rummaged frantically through her clothes: nothing at all. She felt cheated out of something. Her dream had lurched her into wakefulness just as she had reached the pitch of arousal, and it was like being lurched into a void. She remembered lying on an odd-shaped bed. There was a radial of taut silky strands running through her body from her breast. A hand touched her nipple; squeezed it gently between finger and thumb. The strands tautened, transmitting a vibrant current of desire throughout her body. The owner of the finger and thumb was in shadow. The slightest movement of his hand sent a sweet shudder of pleasure through her. She peered into the shadow. A face loomed forward. That was when she imagined the rumbling sound, and woke up. Recalling this, she could not avoid also recalling whose face it was that had loomed towards her. She closed her eyes and buried her head in her pillow, trying to stifle both the recollection and the renewed pang of desire it brought with it.

Her capacity for self-deception, never great, was now all but exhausted. None the less, as she got out of bed she told herself it was only to make herself a hot drink. And as she went, not to her kitchen, but to the stairway leading up to Mr Kinsky's house, she told herself she merely wanted to sit for a while in his music room, alone. Even when she opened the door to Mr Kinsky's bedroom and crept in, she half-believed that all she wanted to do was look at him as he slept.

He was fast sleep, breathing quietly and deeply. His massive body swelled and subsided beneath the pale blankets. The strands of silver in his black hair were just visible in the darkness. She felt tranquil looking at him; not in the least like an intruder. She slipped into the double bed beside him. The bed was warm from the heat of his body. She caught the soapy smell of his pyjamas, which she had ironed only that morning. She put her hand on his waist, and leaned over to kiss him on the lips. His eyes opened.

'Marietta,' he whispered.

'Sssh.'

He lay still as she caressed him, as if afraid that the slightest stir would make her vanish. She slid over his body, and she was astride him, sighing to herself. She grasped his wrists. The tighter she held them, the further away she was, tilting back her head, her shoulders, arcing her back like a bow, shuddering. Somewhere in her protracted orgasm he felt his own – a minor detail it seemed – drowned out by the high, inhuman cry that burst from her lips and echoed through the empty house long after she had fallen asleep at his side.

Shortly after daybreak they heard the squeal of a taxi's brakes outside the front steps. They held each other tightly in the short pause before Marietta's doorbell rang.

Delirium Eclipse

Lewis Jackson had about ten million dollars of multi-national aid at his disposal. It was a large sum for a man as young as himself to be tending, but he was properly aware of his responsibilities, and perfectly confident in his ability to shoulder them.

His ascent through the hierarchies of his chosen career had been rapid and smooth. His still-boyish face was glazed with the angelic patina acquired by people who work in the medium of success. He now found himself representing quite a substantial node in the planet's economic grid, and he could feel the hum of power in his veins.

His assignment – the first serious one he had been given – was in the south of India, where he was to budget the finances for a series of projects ranging from the sinking of village wells, to the planting and irrigation of thousands of hectares of new orchards.

There were six weeks to go before he was due to begin, and he decided to fill the interval by visiting the great Mogul sites in the north of the country.

Shortly before he left, he met a girl called Clare at a party in a Kilburn squat. They could see the bronze glitter of the canal from the window where they stood.

The brick houses facing it were sepia in the lamplight, and the sky was violet.

'Imagine if that canal was the River Ganges, and those houses were temples,' was Jackson's opening line, after which he was able to steer the conversation quite naturally round to his ten million dollars and his projects. He spoke of peaches, plums, mangoes and limes, of fungicides and fertilisers, of crop yields waiting to be multiplied tenfold or more ... His eloquence was lit up with the immediacy of personal involvement, so that even if Clare wasn't interested in the subject matter, she couldn't help noticing the energy with which it was communicated, and this energy drew her towards him.

She was carefree, relaxed, and quite without guile. She lived on the dole, and spent her time at the dance, language and craft classes her local council provided for its unemployed, at a nominal fee.

Her hair was a very shiny gold on the top, but increasingly dark towards its roots – burnt stubble colours. It was thick and unkempt, and hung in a tea-towel girdle like a sheaf of wheat. Her eyes were a pale slate colour when looked at; a perfect blue when remembered. Her face was broad and strong, but also faintly childish in a Nordic way. It looked well accustomed to expressing pleasure, and little else. A Kirlian photograph of her would have revealed a brilliant aura burning about her body like St Elmo's fire, indicative of unusual spiritual and physical vigour.

Within minutes of meeting her, Jackson had set his heart on taking her with him to India. There was some urgency, as he intended leaving in a few days, but as he unfurled before her his visions of plenty, he felt certain that whatever it would take of charm, cunning, and will-power to persuade her to come, he possessed it in abundance. He felt invincible. In the event, the only

serious obstacle he had to overcome was her reluctance to let him pay her way, she having no money of
her own. She allowed herself to be swayed when he
told her how much he was being paid, and hinted at the
latitude of his expense allowance. It was as much the
spontaneity of the idea that appealed to her, as its
promise of adventure, and having agreed to it, she
couldn't wait to go. Jackson congratulated himself on
his good fortune in finding a travelling companion as
pleasant and equable as Clare, though he didn't doubt
he deserved it.

Pearl mosques, incense, cane juice, desert forts, the
deft hands of itinerant foot masseurs, the unearthly
sound of vultures at carrion ... They travelled in a
leisurely way, stopping for everything.
   They enjoyed each other's company. Clare, a
natural hedonist and libertine, was content to focus
the entire range of her sensuality on to Jackson alone,
which made him feel like a prince. His health was so
good that he soon gave up dissolving chlorine tablets
in his water, and joined Clare, who disdained such
precautions, in drinking from the tap. He was in fine,
magnanimous humour. He scattered coins before beg-
gars, gave liberal tips to rickshaw drivers, and patron-
ised street vendors avidly, accumulating garlands of
colourful bead necklaces, shiny silk scarves, and
innumerable little trinkets, decking Clare out in
increasingly sumptuous combinations of his pur-
chases.
   The closest they came to a quarrel was outside the
Red Fort at Agra, where Jackson wrote a warm, witty
postcard to someone whom he had only that morning
described to Clare in terms of the most crushing contempt. Clare coloured as she read it.
   'You shouldn't send that,' she said.

'Why on earth not?'

'It's hypocritical.'

Jackson told her not to be so silly, but she persisted in a slow, painfully obstinate way. 'I wish you'd tear it up,' she said, and, 'I would never send a postcard like that to someone I despised.'

Finally, Jackson snapped at her: 'If you attach your integrity to something as trivial as a postcard, then it can't be worth much. I reserve mine for more important things.'

She recoiled into a puzzled, hurt silence, while Jackson went off to buy a stamp.

He was pleased with his retort; at first because it seemed so clever, and then because it began to seem true. It crystallised the Jesuitical sense he had, that the gravity of his work licensed him to trade in the sort of deceptions Clare objected to, with impunity. A mission to irrigate orchards guaranteed your soul against damage from these minor acts of dissembling. If anything, the more you exposed yourself to them, the stronger your conviction was proved to be. Reaching that conclusion, Jackson felt a twinge of pity for Clare, who had nothing weightier in her life than the sincerity of her postcards, against which to measure herself. He bought a sapphire from a gem hawker outside the post office, and gave it to Clare when he got back to the tea stall where she was waiting for him.

'There you are,' he said, 'that's what I call an important thing.'

She looked at him warily, uncertain whether to believe him. He faced her with his most unflinchingly honest gaze. As he watched her gradually giving him the benefit of the doubt, he felt a curious, complex sensation of joy: he had made her believe the sapphire was a token of love, which it wasn't, by sheer force of will, and it gratified him to see that he possessed this power. But simultaneously, the sight of Clare *accepting* it as a token of love, gave him a rush of the kind of elated yearning he had only previously felt for complete strangers – beautiful women at airports or concerts, whom he would never talk to and never see again ... To feel like that about a girl who was looking at him as lovingly as Clare was now, whom if he wanted he could take back to their room this minute and ravish, was blissful.

Mr Birla, the manager of their hotel in the holy city of Varanasi, was a friendly young man dressed in jeans and a tight floral shirt. He spoke English well, and informed them he was an Anglophile. He said he had a stocklist of English delicacies which he was working through alphabetically. Last month his kitchen had been filled with boxes of lime cordial, lemon curd, and luncheon meat. This month it was marmalade, muffins, macaroons, malt loaf, and Marmite. He sincerely hoped they would not feel homesick.

He showed them to a room with a small balcony from which they could just see the far shore of a massive brown tract of water, calm beneath an oily haze: the River Ganges.

He said they had arrived on a very important day. There was to be a partial eclipse of the sun that afternoon, an event of great significance in the Hindu calendar. There would be processions along the river, chanting, 'All these kind of things.' He offered to accompany them.

The streets were already beginning to swarm as they set off. Sadhus were striding about singing and praying. A Mercedes van with smoked glass windows pulled up on one street and disgorged a dozen pink-skinned devotees of Krishna who danced off like fully wound-up clockwork toys, banging cymbals and drums, and singing their song. Here and there they or the sadhus sent a charge of fervour rippling through the crowds gathering around them, though it was still a tentative, experimental fervour, and a man seized by it one minute might easily break off to buy a popadum or a cup of hot spiced milk the next.

Everyone was making for the great stone steps that led down to the Ganges. These were carpeted with people, milling, jostling, weaving about in processions ...

Jackson could see that Clare was already entering into the spirit of the occasion. A look of delight was fixed on her broad, healthy face. She beamed at everyone who passed. An old crone, muttering an incantation, was reeling from person to person, annointing foreheads with greasepaint. Mr Birla saw her off with a little gesture of disdain. Jackson followed suit. But Clare solemnly parted her hair and lowered her head towards the woman, rising again with a smudge of red above her eyebrows. 'Who was she?' she whispered to Mr Birla. 'Holy woman,' he answered, in a matter-of-fact voice. Clare looked exultant. A moment later she was caught in a crush of human traffic. She rose a few inches into the air, and glided along, borne by the pressure of the crowd. She turned round to look at Jackson, shaking the dark golden mass of her hair out of her eyes. She was smiling rapturously at him. As he smiled back, Jackson's heart swelled with pride, as if he had conjured this radiant creature into being from the excess of his own vitality, and her smile was nothing less than an acknowledgment of her creator.

They were down at the river now. Rowing boats tethered to jetties jostled each other in the brown water. People were swimming and washing themselves. Jackson could see trickles of effluvia, glistening like snail-tracks, dribbling into the water. Right beside him, a boy was washing a herd of water buffalo in the shallows, scraping the matted dung off their rears, scrubbing their dusty black hides until they looked Brylcreem-slick, and the sunlight made a blue gleam on the cusp of each muscle corrugation in their necks.

... A surge of noise, cymbals crashing, drums ... Something happened to the daylight. It didn't darken so much as distort. The whole dome of sky was like an eye being squeezed askew. Jackson could hear a roaring, but far away; he was fixed in the space immediately about him, as if in bending it had become vitreous – a great glass orb. He squinted up at the sun: quartz-cold brilliance. 'Do not look at the sun,' he heard Mr Birla say. It cut a glittering trail of light across his vision as he turned away; coruscating, like diamond dust. For an instant he was snow-blind, his insides curling from some obscure discomfort. The sun had been misshapen. He had the impression of having seen a scimitar edge of absolute blackness probing into it – a tiny penetration of darkness into the source of light itself.

On the way back to their hotel, they passed the general post office, which Jackson had given as a *poste restante* to his employers and family, should they wish to contact him. Leaving Clare with Mr Birla, he went in to see if there was anything waiting for him. A telegram was eventually handed over the counter. He tore it open. 'Agency closing down. Funds transferred. All projects cancelled. All staff kaput. Please no more expenses. Will explain on your return.'

He sat down on a bench at the back of the stuffy, paper-strewn room, breathing deeply, to regain his composure. He was acutely conscious of the fatigue of his body, which flushed all over like a fanned ember when he looked at the telegram again. When he could, he stood up and walked slowly towards the exit. On his way out, he crumpled up the telegram and threw it into a bin.

'Anything?' Clare asked.

'No. Nothing at all.'

The following morning Jackson's eyes were ablaze with conjunctivitis. Scarlet threads of vein straggled out from each canthus towards the pupil. His eyeballs felt like they'd been doused in acid. He smeared them with Chloromycetin ointment from a tube in his washbag. As he looked at himself in the mirror, he flinched, as if he had seen not himself, but some unsavoury acquaintance from long ago in the past, who was swimming up to him, grinning like a black-mailer.

'Don't even think about it,' Clare whispered, kissing his eyelids. 'It'll soon disappear.' He said as little as possible to her; he was still trying to calculate how much of his news he could conceal from her, and how she would react to what he chose to reveal.

They walked down to the river, Jackson's eyes streaming behind a pair of sunglasses. There was a bitterness at the back of his throat, where some of the ointment, diluted by tears, had trickled down his sinuses.

They had planned to swim, but when they actually reached the river, Jackson began to have doubts. He could see one of the snail-trails of sewage he had observed the day before, trickling into the water. There was a smell of barbecued meat on the air from the Burning Ghats, where corpses were cremated on wooden pyres, their ashes sent floating out on to the river on little rafts. He had read the passage in the guidebook, describing the miraculous medicinal properties attributed to the Ganges; tests – 'scientific tests' – had shown that water from cholera-ridden tributaries was purified within seconds of its penetrating the holy river. The time when these myths would have sufficed, and he would have plunged in without hesitation, already seemed remote from him.

'You go in. I'll wait here with the things.'

Dressed in a blue swimsuit, Clare stepped down through the sandy mud to the river. Her skin looked very dusky in the gloom afforded by Jackson's sunglasses. She waded into the water, splashing it on to her waist and shoulders before kicking herself free of the ground and plunging in. She swam out from the shore, covering yards with each thrust of her strong arms and legs. Her body churned the water into bronze scoops and billows that fanned out behind her, tiger-striping the surface with big ripples. Jackson watched her, his mind a jumble of desire and misgiving: the free abandon with which she plunged and twisted in the water had in it something distantly threatening as well as graceful. A dangerous self-sufficiency. Perhaps after all he ought to join her in the water; it might make her less likely to suspect there was anything seriously the matter with him.

He stripped to his trunks and stepped gingerly down to the river. He felt peculiarly naked and vulnerable, as if he had taken off not only his clothes, but also a layer of skin and there was now nothing between his internal organs and the water. Clare waved, and called to him. She was a good thirty yards out. He could hardly retreat now. Goose bumps swarmed over his back and shoulders. The water was warm and thick with detritus. His toes sank deep into the soft riverbed. He kicked free and started to swim towards Clare. Something solid bobbed against his thigh. A fish, he tried to think, but could only imagine human excrement, or charred human remains; a burnt hand touching his thigh, a blackened tongue ... An involuntary spasm quivered through him, and he panicked, jack-knifing round, thrashing wildly at the water in his haste to get out. Quite soon he was shivering.

He lay alone on the sagging double bed. That morning he had taken his temperature, and sent the silver thread straight up to a hundred and two.

Clare was with Mr Birla, who had invited them to visit his family's carpet factory that day. She had offered to stay behind with Jackson, but he could see she wanted to go, and although he would have preferred not to lose sight of her, he decided there was less to be lost by a show of carefree acquiescence than one of possessiveness.

He was in quite a poor way. There was a fever ache in his bones, and dysentery in his bowels. His eyes were still so inflamed that direct sunlight caused him unbearable pain. The curtains were shut, the dark room stifling. Now and then he had to drag himself upstairs to squat at the cracked and stinking porcelain throat that connected the hotel with the river. He voided himself there with a ferocity that left him shattered. He was in a groggy, twilit stupor of aspirin, streptomycin, and Chloromycetin. Thoughts drifted through him, but he hadn't the energy to seize hold of one for more than a few seconds. They slipped by, inconclusively. The telegram had blown him wide open. He didn't know what to do. He wondered what the matter with him was; he seemed to have lost all his powers of resistance. Clare wasn't getting ill. Had her life provided her with some crucial immunity that his own had not? He remembered himself as a schoolboy: shy, insecure, unaccustomed to attention, deeply affected by it when it came his way. A washroom surrounded with mirrors ... Someone teasing him for his baby face ... He'd blushed with pleasure as the insults flew at him. Nothing like this had happened to him before; he was being celebrated, never mind why. He started laughing wildly, braying. He could see himself in the mirrors. His face was incapable of expressing so much ecstasy, and it began to twist and curl in all the wrong ways, absolutely out of control. Finally tears started pouring down his cheeks – 'It's all right,' he sobbed, 'I'm still laughing, I'm still laughing,' and the place had frozen up in an embarrassed silence ... It was that schoolboy's face he had seen in the mirror yesterday morning. What is wrong with me? The question hung in abeyance. He was sleepy by the time Clare returned.

She was in a jubilant mood: 'What a place!'

She whisked open the curtains, letting in a bright sunbeam that hit Jackson's eyes like a punch.

'Don't.'

Instead of closing the curtains, she picked up Jackson's sunglasses and stuck them on his face. 'There we are. No need for Clare to sit in darkness all afternoon is there?' She kissed him on the forehead. She had never babied him before, and the unprecedented tone had a faintly depressing effect on him.

'There were huge copper vats full of dye, and bales of thread the most gorgeous colours stacked all over the place. And then these little children, tiny little things, just everywhere, little mice ... ' She giggled. 'They get four rupees a day which Shiva says is a fortune for them – '

'Shiva?'

'Mr Birla. He's a lovely man ... I told him all about your projects. He'd love to talk to you ... I said you'd like that too and he could come up any time. He took me into a room completely covered with the carpets they make. I wish I could describe them to you ... ' She attempted, and even though she stumbled clumsily from one superlative to another, her words worked on Jackson's drowsy imagination to produce an impression of bright patterns, stylised animals, birds, flowers, all glimmering through a medium of peacock plumage alloyed with silver and mother-of-pearl. She was more than usually voluble; the place had evidently had an effect on her.

'The best thing was how they were made – you'd've adored it, Lewis – half a dozen of these toddlers sit in a pile of thread weavering away like mad, with an old man beside them just singing, and the thing was that what he sang was the pattern of the carpet, which was how the children knew what to do. What they wove depended on what he sang. Do you see? Isn't that good? The carpet is a song turned into a silk tapestry. Lewis? Lewis?' She lowered her voice to a whisper. 'Are you awake?'

'Hm.'

How tired he felt. He yawned. He could hardly hear what Clare was saying. Was she saying anything now? A hand touched his forehead. His various discomforts floated away just far enough to let his mind relax its vigil over his body ...

He woke up at dusk, his head reverberating with an absurd dream-phrase spoken in Clare's voice: 'Shivaring away like mad.' She wasn't in the room. His sunglasses had been placed on the bedside table, on top of a note, 'Back soon.'

He wondered what she could be doing. An idea came to him: she was downstairs having sex with Mr Birla. He sent it packing. He wished he could read a book, or get up and go for a walk. He turned over the bolster and straightened the sheet on top of him. He could feel the idea hovering in the wings. Shivaring away like mad. Resist it, he told himself. He tried to think of something else. Nothing. A pulse of alarm struck up beneath his ribs. An image of Clare and Mr Birla locked together in a naked embrace blossomed in his mind like a big pink and brown flower. He winced, shook his head. But there was nothing between him and the idea. He seemed to have as little immunity to it as he had against the microbes swarming in his body. Here was Clare again. It was like a film, a conscientiously scrupulous pornographic film. He sat up and tried to block it out by reciting the only thing he knew by heart, which was the Lord's Prayer. Our Father which art in heaven, Hallowed be Thy name … but there was Clare sighing while Mr Birla's fingers slid under her loose silk shirt to fondle her breasts … Thy kingdom come, Thy will be done, on earth as it is in heaven; Give us this day … and Mr Birla was underneath her while she slid the cushioned chassis of her hips to and fro astride him, a flush of pink washing her body … Jackson sat up appalled. A cold veil of sweat surfaced on his brow – Give us this day our daily bread and forgive us our trespasses; As we … and there were two Mr Birlas now, one of them calmly fucking Clare from behind, the other stroking the golden hair buried in his groin. Why is this happening to me, Jackson thought. He did not want to see these things.

He looked around the shadowy room for something to distract himself with. The room service buzzer … If he pressed it and Mr Birla came up within … within a minute, that would bring an end to these anxieties. He pressed it.

Mr Birla arrived with such alacrity that Jackson hadn't even begun to think what he would actually say to him. But he was spared the trouble by Mr Birla himself.

'Hello,' the summoned manager said. 'I was just thinking of popping up and looking in. How are your spirits?'

He hardly looked like a cuckold-maker – tight polka-dot shirt shadowed at the hollows of his bony shoulders and collar-bone, a crumbling battlement of dentistry silhouetted in his grin.

'I'm all right, thanks,' Jackson said, feeling a little relieved.

'Oh good.' Mr Birla stepped right inside the room 'I understand you are engaged on important business. Distributing welfare, is it?' He half V'd the W of welfare, and concluded with a charming smile, eager for conversation.

'Oh yes. That's right,' Jackson said. Now of course it was necessary to get rid of the man; 'I wondered actually, could I ... ' Inspiration struck him: 'Could you bring me some muffins, please, with marmalade, and Marmite?'

Mr Birla looked momentarily startled. His smile went glassy as he reverted from would-be conversationalist to hotel manager.

'Of course,' he said. 'Thank you.'

Clare had been swimming. She came back with wet hair, and hung her costume up to dry.

Like his dysentery, Jackson's feelings of jealousy were tidal. They could ebb so far away that they would seem no more than a vague, dispersed nightmare. But when they rose, they engulfed him, and this they tended to do whenever Clare went out. Within minutes of her departure, her blithe, relaxed manner began to curdle in Jackson's memory. He realised her poise was a sham, performed in order to quell precisely the suspicions he was harbouring. The realisation coexisted with a full awareness that it was groundless, but this didn't in the least diminish its effects. His imagination began to seethe, his fever to rise; he would start trembling and sweating. Finally he would hit the room service

buzzer, summoning Mr Birla, whom he would scrutinise with increasingly blatant hostility before ordering a
plate of macaroons, or a muffin, or a slice of malt loaf.
An incidental benefit of this procedure was that it
supplied Jackson with nourishment bland enough for
him to consume: he had come to regard eating Indian
food as a form of Russian roulette, where every
mouthful might be loaded. He had lost his taste for it.

The frequency with which he summoned Mr Birla
increased rapidly. Soon he had him running up and
down stairs five or six times a morning. By then he
hardly knew why he did it, but it satisfied him in an
obscure way to exercise the power. 'Thank you,' Mr
Birla always said when Jackson finally snapped his
order at him. He didn't try to engage Jackson in conversation again.

Meanwhile Jackson was growing steadily more ill.
His eyes were swollen and rheumy. He developed a
streaming cold. A small colony of itchy red spots between his toes ran riot, covering both feet with a livid,
burning rash. He lay all day in shadow. Sometimes he
would be aware of Clare lying beside him, talking
about her day, cooling his forehead with a flannel.
Then somehow she would have vanished, and in
no time Jackson would have to hit the room service
buzzer again ...

One day she produced from her bag a bottle of Dr
Collis Brown – an opium-based panacea which she
had discovered in the bathroom cupboard of her
squat. It was the only medicine she had brought.

'Why don't we try this for a change?' She poured out
a spoonful for Jackson. It was sweet and fiery.

'Maybe I'll have some too.' She took a swig straight
from the bottle, and passed the bottle back to Jackson,
smiling mischievously. 'Go on ... ' By the time they
had finished it, Jackson was feeling a pleasant, slightly

drunken sensation. Clare snuggled up next to him on the bed. Her bushy hair brushed against his skin, and set him tingling. He was floating, immensely happy. A lot of time went by very quickly, or else a little, slowly. His body wasn't hurting at all. He plied his fingers through Clare's hair. A rustle like a breeze through copper-coloured leaves ... Tiny golden sparks began to tumble out of it with each stroke. The more he brushed the brighter they grew, and when he stopped they faded.

'Are you seeing things too?' Clare asked in a far-away voice.

'Oh yes ... so I am ... '

They lay still. He was in a room like this but different. Clare was kneeling by the bed.

'Look,' she said, placing a hand on each side of her head. 'Look ... ' She lifted away the top of her head. Jackson peered over: a crystalline, miniature landscape ... mountains with snow and dark green pines. Still blue lakes, and on a far shore an icy blue sea with motionless white crests ...

'Now you ... ' she said. But he was looking at the wall. There was a hole in it he hadn't seen before, with a bird's nest inside. A spider the size of a hand was sitting on the twigs, its black head probing down into the broken shell of a pale blue egg. A bead of golden yolk was sliding down the side of the shell. 'Make me come,' he heard Clare whisper. She was naked, aroused. Her breasts had turned a rosy colour at their tips. She pressed them to his face and wrapped her legs around him. 'Come on ... '

'Look at the spider,' Jackson said. It took him hours to form the syllables. She knelt up slowly on the bed and leant towards it. As she did so, the bird's nest disappeared, and the hole shrank to a shallow cavity of flaked-away plaster. There was no trace of the egg or

its liquid treasure. 'Sweet little spider.' She reached her
hand towards it and picked it up very gently by one leg.
It wriggled, grappling with the air close to Clare's
naked skin. Jackson had to close his eyes for a
moment. When he opened them again she was at the
window talking to the spider, wishing it a pleasant
journey to the ground. It was much smaller than he
had imagined. 'Bye bye, little spider,' Clare said. She
drifted back to bed, and covered Jackson's face with
kisses. He rolled away. 'Don't feel like it,' he said.
'Sleep.'

It was evening. Beyond the window the dark pink
sunset was drawn, like a conjuror's silk handkerchief,
through a band of clouds, from which it emerged a
watery blue. Jackson stretched and sat up. He could
feel the imprint of the sweaty, crumpled linen on his
cheeks. Clare wasn't there. He had no idea when he
had last seen her.

There was something on the floor by the bed. Jackson peered down, touched it.

It was a rolled-up carpet about six feet in width. He
stared at it a moment, wondering where it had come
from. Clare couldn't possibly have afforded to buy a
carpet with the pocket money he gave her, and he was
certain she had no secret stash of her own. He checked
his own wallet; nothing was missing. How had she got
hold of it? It must have been a gift. Jackson felt the
familiar signals of alarm go off in his body. He pressed
the buzzer. A minute went by, two minutes. He pressed
it again. An old woman he hadn't seen before finally
appeared, wheezing and dragging her feet. She tilted
her chin at Jackson, questioningly.

'Mr Birla?' he asked. She shook her finger and ges-
tured with it towards the window: gone out. Jackson
thanked her, and she shuffled off.

He lay back on the bed with a feeling of acute
consternation. He told himself over and over that there
was absolutely no basis for his anxieties; and meanwhile he grew quite frantic. Images of Clare and Mr
Birla played in his mind with the intensity of an hal-
lucination. He had nothing to fight them with, and
they took on a life of their own, commandeering his
imagination, like the amoebas in his bowels. He
started shaking. Fever flushes rushed through his
body. The intensity and luridness of his imaginings
proliferated until he began to feel he was losing his
grip. He had to move.

He climbed out of bed and put on a pair of light
cotton pyjamas. His legs were wobbly from lack of
use, though this had the effect of making him feel
oddly light rather than heavy. He took his wallet and
documents so that he could leave the door unlocked in
case Clare came back before him. The evening light
being just tolerable, he left his sunglasses behind. The
old woman was sitting at Mr Birla's desk in the lobby.
She looked at him impassively as he stumbled by her,
out on to the street.

After a few yards he was panting; he was in no
condition to be out. He waved down a bicycle rickshaw and climbed into the chariot-like seat. They
rumbled over the cobbles, into the maze of alleys that
led down to the steps.

The city was coming to life as the day cooled. People
were out strolling. The street markets, some of them
already lit with kerosene lamps, were trading busily.
There was food everywhere. There seemed to be a
surplus of it. Unwanted mangoes and limes lay in
broken crates outside shops, fermenting into chutney;
Jackson could smell the sweet syrup odour of fruit rot
as he went by. Apple scab, he remembered from his
training, potato canker, honey fungus, white rot, black

rust ... Pomegranates and papayas tumbled from overladen stalls on to the cobbles, where their heedless owners watched them disappear into the mitts of furtive monkeys. A skew-horned cow patrolling one of the alleys dragged, like a prisoner's ball, a giant watermelon she had stamped on, and which no one had troubled to prise from her hoof. There was meat in abundance too – garrotted guinea fowl, skinned lambs dressed in living fleeces of big black flies, goats' heads, foamy swathes of what looked like, but surely could not have been, tripe still green with cud ... Jackson watched a beggar tip ruefully from his brass bowl a mound of sticky rice that even his elastic appetite had been unable to accommodate. There were smells in the air of cooking – garlic and coriander, spice smells of cardamom and cinnamon, acrid odours from the dung-burning stoves over which soot-blackened vats simmered and steamed, and floating over these, the soapy smells of incense, frangipani, sandalwood ...

Too much was going on. Radios and klaxons were blaring out, flutes, drums, voices ... There were too many people and the rickshaw driver kept stopping to let them pass in front of him. Dogs and monkeys were rooting in the gutters. Cows choked up the alleys until they felt like ambling on. Jackson had an urgent desire to get down to the river. It made him feel uncomfortable to dawdle among all this plenty. He felt lost and insignificant. 'I'm in rather a hurry,' he said to the rickshaw driver, who smiled and said nothing. They were hardly moving. Come on, come on, Jackson thought. 'Come on,' he shouted. He could see knotted veins bulging like worm-casts on the driver's skinny calves. Looking at them he had a brief intimation that if he'd had a whip, he would have used it. His fever was running high.

It was almost dark by the time they reached the steps

that led down to the river. Fires were burning here and there, and the level sun made the sullage in the water look like gold-dust. The steps were staggered, uneven, muddied by a mulch of crushed marigolds and rose petals. The whole higgledy-piggledy embankment with its crooked paths and terraced buildings stacked precariously on top of each other, saris flapping on the vast web of lines stretched between them, was more like vegetation than carefully assembled stone. The budding tip of a new shrine pushing its way through a crack in the ground would not have been an altogether surprising sight. Jackson climbed down, scanning the water for Clare. He was in a particular state of mind that internalises everything perceived, giving it the viscosity of a dream landscape – temples flowed past him, people in prayer or meditation dissolved into the glare of torchlight, shadowy figures swam into focus and then ceased to exist. His head was throbbing. The steps seemed endless and unreal.

He was still some way from the water when a head of fair hair rose up from it, followed by a body in a dark blue swimsuit. Before it had reached full height, the head of hair had already bushed out from its water-sleeked anonymity and taken on a burnish of firelight. Water streamed from the body, draping it for a second like a glassy dress; leaving behind a few beads in which the last of the light took refuge ... She walked slowly out of the water, smiling faintly to herself. Jackson stayed very still. He felt invisible. He watched her stoop for her towel and hold it round herself with one hand, while with the other she slid the swimsuit from her body. She knelt down to dry herself. There was nothing but twilight between her nakedness and the eyes of people wandering by the river. She was oblivious. She dried herself slowly and carefully, lux- uriating, it seemed, in the sensations of her body. She put on a dress and strolled towards the steps, several yards along from where Jackson stood.

He hung back, following her from a short distance, half-thinking Mr Birla was suddenly going to appear at her side, half-knowing he would not.

A figure approached her from the shadows … not Mr Birla, but a leper hobbling on a pair of makeshift crutches tied under his shoulders. His feet were bandaged in rags and his skin was mottled like a wall with bad damp. There was a box hanging from his neck. Clare fumbled in her purse for coins, which she held out to him at arm's length. The leper stood still with his head bowed as she dropped the coins in his box. From where Jackson stood, along the steps, he could see it dawning on Clare that the man had interpreted her outstretched arm as a sign that he was to come no closer. A look of anxiety at her unintended coldness crossed her face as the leper thanked her and turned to go. 'Oh … wait.' She put her hand on his shoulder to detain him, and as he heaved himself back round on his crutches, she ran her fingers lightly down his arm, resting her hand a moment on his scabbed stump. The leper stood obediently still while Clare stared at him, her mouth open as if she were on the point of uttering some phrase that would magic away his disease. Then, remembering herself, she dug into her purse again, taking out not coins, but something that sparkled as she dropped it into the box: the sapphire Jackson had given her.

Jackson watched it all with a feeling of vertiginous wonder. What was he to make of this? There was too much new, bewildering information crammed into Clare's gestures and actions for him to comprehend it all at once. It was like being dazzled by a glare. As he watched her disappear into the dark city, he realised he had seriously underestimated her. There was a side to

her he had failed to appreciate. Her uncomplicated-
ness wasn't the same as simplicity: he had glimpsed
behind it, into a world where his own labyrinthine
relations with people and possessions had no place,
where you gave and took as you felt like or needed, and
that was that. He walked back slowly, feeling faintly
ashamed of his furtive behaviour, and trying to assess
how much damage it had done. He resolved never to
indulge his suspicions again, and as he did so, it occurred to him that the only probable explanation for
the presence of the carpet in their room was that Clare
had borrowed it, just so that she could show him one.
How extraordinarily thoughtful she was. He felt like
someone coming out of a delirium: feeling his way
back along a frail vein of reality. And it was the way
back to health too; all he had to do was concentrate on
holding on.

There was no one at the desk when he re-entered the
hotel. He climbed up the stairs, feeling rather stronger
on his legs than he had when he'd set out. I'm recovering, he told himself, and felt an anticipatory buzz of
well-being. The dimly lit staircase smelt of stale
incense and drains: not a place he would be sorry to
leave. There was enough money left for another week
or so. They could go somewhere they hadn't planned
to visit – Assam perhaps, or Kashmir, hire a wooden
houseboat on Lake Srinagar – mountains and snow,
lush valleys ... There was time to make a fresh start.
He would tell her about the agency closing down; she
wouldn't give a damn. He'd pretend he'd just been
down to the post office, and found the telegram.

The light was on, peeping under the door, but the
door was locked. He rattled the handle. 'It's me.'
Scuffling sounds, a delay: 'Open up, it's me.' Clare
opened the door: 'Oh, there you are. Where on earth
have you been? We thought you'd been kidnapped.'

Mr Birla was in the room. Jackson stepped inside, screwing up his eyes against the electric light. He looked at Clare and at Mr Birla. Clare was talking breathlessly. 'Did you see this carpet Shiva gave us?' he heard her say. 'Isn't it beautiful? Look – ' She knelt down and began to unroll it. Flowers and grasses appeared, tree-trunks, boughs, foliage ... Jackson stared at it intently while Clare went on talking, 'Have you ever seen anything so lovely ... ' A dizzy feeling went through him as he tried to resist wondering why the door had been locked, why Mr Birla was there, and why Clare was talking so wildly. Bright lemons and limes hung between the leaves on the carpet, and on one tree there were big lustrous peaches, shaded at the cleft and toned miraculously through from yellow to scarlet. 'A small gift,' Mr Birla said. Jackson peered even closer as Mr Birla edged behind him towards the door. He noticed how the leaves were individually veined, how some were curled to show a paler reverse, how there was even a silvery down of furze visible on the peaches if you looked carefully. 'I have received my new shipment,' Mr Birla was saying as he backed into the corridor. 'Nesquik, Nutella, a box of nougat – I'll bring you some nougat.' Then Clare stepped forward with his sunglasses: 'There's too much light in here,' she said, 'it's too bright for you. You'll damage yourself.' She stuck them on his face and went out, saying she'd be back in a while, that she wouldn't be long.

> I don't buy the ending ; would have preferred it ended with Birla leaving

Ate/Menos
or
The Miracle

1

Sunday morning. I awoke to a murmur of faint anxieties. The day held nothing and nobody in store for me.
I rose and prepared my breakfast. The radio was tuned
to a religious programme, but I hadn't the resolve to
switch channels.

How was I to fill the big blank freedom of the day?

I thought perhaps a walk, and set off along the High
Street, intending to continue in a straight line until I
had had enough, when I would board a bus and return
home.

Little traffic, few pedestrians, mute sounds and colours. A lamp in the distance had failed to extinguish
itself with the dawn. The silver light hung blurred in
the white sky like a dissolving pearl, and by its mild
incongruousness drew my attention to the ordinariness,
the celestial ordinariness, that Sunday morning confers
on London streets.

How immutable the bricks and paving stones and
plate-glass windows looked. Tarmac and hoardings,
railings, pillar boxes, drain-lids . . . Sometimes I would

give anything to glimpse a chink in the monumental
armour of stasis with which the material world cloaks
its fabled Heraclitean flux. I looked hard at the sturdy
frontage of a bank, as if staring would make its weighty
masonry shimmer and melt. How weak I felt, how
powerless.

I mention these details in the hope that they might
shed some light on the series of events that followed;
a series that began with my entering a church, where
a service was in progress, and committing a sacrilege.

2

As I reached the ugly portals of St Simeon's Church,
I found myself slowing to a halt. I could hear strains
of a hymn, the voices of what must have been a pitiful
congregation swamped by the swell of the organ. I am
not a believer, let alone a Christian, and had seldom
been near a church since leaving school. Nevertheless,
as I stood there listening, I experienced a strong, com-
manding urge to go inside.

Ate and *Menos* are the words Homer uses for states
of mental intoxication induced in humans by gods or
other supernatural agencies. *Ate* drives a man to
commit demonic acts of rashness for which he is duly
punished. *Menos*, which comes frequently in response
to a battlefield prayer, is moral spunk; a sudden access
of energy, confidence, strength.

What it was that possessed me is best described in
these archaic terms, there being no adequate modern
equivalent; though whether my actions were performed

under the aegis of *Ate* or of *Menos*, I am to this day unsure.

I pushed open the heavy wooden door. An usher – blue-rinsed and clad in thick tweed – stepped smiling from a pew, and handed me a small blue pamphlet with the words 'Holy Communion' printed on it.

There were twenty or so worshippers. Vicar, organist, and the three-person choir were all dressed in clean white surplices. The place smelt of cold stone and candlewax. A few faces craned round to look at me as I entered an empty pew; old, placid faces that paused a second to register this unlikely addition to their numbers. The priest was reading from the pamphlet. I flicked through it, and found my place.

It can hardly be termed an act of rash folly to enter an Anglican church on a Sunday morning, but nevertheless I knelt down on my threadbare hassock with the same sensation of wild recklessness I might have felt had I been installing myself in a brothel or an opium den.

I was struck immediately by the familiarity of the words the priest was saying. For a moment I thought I was experiencing a memory rush from boarding-school days of compulsory chapel. But the familiarity carried no poignant reverberations of that anguished period, and I realised the echo was of a note played much more recently. Played only this morning in fact, when I had been too listless to switch channels on the radio. At the time, I had not been conscious of hearing a syllable of the service it had been broadcasting. But now, as I listened to the priest's measured, impersonal voice, the words set their identical precursors, implanted that morning in my unconscious, chiming resonantly in sympathetic harmony, like so many ringing glasses, and the whole utterance hummed inside me with a vibrant power.

'Take, eat, this is my body . . .'

Slowly, on limbs for the most part decidedly unsteady, the members of the congregation filed from their pews, to form a queue in the aisle. The organist played long, reedy, wavering notes as one by one these shaky old souls dropped to their knees to receive their bread and wine. And when my blue-rinsed usher stepped forward to take up the rear, pausing at my pew to look at me questioningly, I began to understand why I had come here.

A feeling of abandon took possession of me as I moved towards the priest. I had never done this before, and was not entitled to do it. The priest moved and muttered in a sphere of candlelight and such daylight as the stained glass admitted from the sunless sky. He had the composed air of a man entirely taken over by his role. The operation of his limbs as he carried gleaming chalice and paten from head to head, was conducted with deft, balletic economy. There were now three people ahead of me. I kept my eyes on the fluted drapery of the priest's brilliant white robe. Two people. Tremulous organ notes filled the air. One person . . . and there I was, kneeling before the linen-draped altar, unchallenged, accepted by the priest without a second's hesitation or glance of appraisal. *The body of Christ* . . . I took the wafer, thin and translucent like an honesty pod, and held it melting on my tongue. *The blood of Christ* . . . metallic tang, iron-rich, finally sweet . . . I rose; I had known exactly what to do. The stray waverings of the organ collected themselves into a soft melodic tune that sounded like the music of forgiveness. Somewhere among the tumult of sensations welling up inside me I heard the peace of God which passeth all understanding being commended to me. Daylight flooded in through the opening door. As I left the church, the priest took my hand warmly in both of his.

'I do hope we shall see you here again.'

I smiled, and stumbled past him on to the High Street.

3

The same high street; an altogether different pair of eyes observing it. What had I done? Nothing at all, I told myself. Nothing of any consequence. Why then did I feel this preternatural energy tingling in my body? I was fuelled, burning.

I had stolen fire from Olympus, by which I mean that I, a non-believer, had tapped the energies of ritual without submitting myself to the acts of faith it asked in return. I wasn't sure whether I felt demonically mischievous, or consummately benevolent: that woman approaching me twenty yards off – I had it in me to run forward and throw her under a bus; but equally, had she in that moment chosen to throw herself under the same hypothetical bus, I could, in the split second available, have flown forward to pluck her from the wheels before they crushed her.

I must have been staring hard at this particular woman while I entertained these thoughts, because as she came nearer I realised she was looking at me in an

inquisitive way — an expression on her face of guarded
interest that burgeoned gradually into a nervous smile
of recognition:

'You're Matthew Delacorta,' she said, coming to a
halt two or three paces in front of me. 'We met in
Edinburgh.'

I stopped and looked at her closely. She was carrying
a bag full of groceries, fingers in black net gloves peeping up from beneath it. Her blouse, skirt and hat were
all black too, but trimmed with velvet and astrakhan,
so that they seemed fashionable rather than funereal.
A spray of crimson flowers was pinned to her lapel.
She looked ten years older than me, a face in the
process of exchanging hue and bloom for form and
character; more than enough allure in it to make me
feel glad to have been stopped in the street by its
owner. But it was her voice more than anything that
I noticed in that first moment: high and pure, modu-
lated like the voice of an exquisitely brought-up girl
of seventeen – full of fervent wonderment and respect,
at once timid and confident, startling in the way that
early recordings of legendary sopranos or film stars can
be, through the hints they give of a distant, dreamier
age. Hearing this voice weave its way through the syllables of Matthew Delacorta, I wished instantly that
this *was* my name, and that this woman and myself
had indeed met in Edinburgh, a city I have never visited
in my life. I was about to tell her she was mistaken,
when she spoke again:

'You mayn't remember who I am . . . I'm a friend
of Felix, you know, who did the lighting for you. He
introduced   us   after   the   show.   My   name's
Madeleine . . . '

Lucky Matthew Delacorta, that his imperfect acquaintance with this woman should have left her so eager to claim acknowledgement from him. There was an urgency in her voice, behind its diffidence – a determination to be recognised. She gazed at me, at Matthew Delacorta, with her eyes wide open, a look almost of pleading on her face. I paused before answering – I wanted to linger in this flattering delusion of hers for as long as possible.

And in that pause it dawned on me, as the reader will have guessed, that I had it in my power to extend this delusion artificially.

It was with a sense of breaking through into an opulent and altogether unfamiliar realm of living, that I smiled slowly at this stranger and said, in as relaxed and charming a voice as I could muster,

'Madeleine. Of course. I thought I recognised you.'

She rewarded me with a look of pure elation, and made no effort to move on. Clearly more was expected of Matthew Delacorta, and I had no intention of letting him down.

'How are things?' I ventured.

'Oh . . . ' She shrugged her shoulders, nearly causing a bottle of Cointreau to tumble out of her plastic bag, then with a rather graceful clumsiness, patting it back down with her chin. ' . . . Things are alright . . . not perfect . . . I was supposed to be doing Iphigenia in May, but the money . . . ' She finished the sentence with an eloquent tilt of her head.

'Oh dear,' I said, 'what a shame,' then added boldly, 'you'd make a terrific Iphigenia.' *Terrific* is not a word I use, but it came to my lips of its own volition, and sounded startlingly appropriate. She quickened visibly with pleasure at the compliment.

'Oh do you really think I would?'

'I do,' I said, then rashly, for the sake of colour, added that Aeschylus must have had her in mind when he wrote the part.

'Euripides.' A brief look of doubt shadowed her face, but I think it had less to do with my mistake than with my hazarded guess at Delacorta's style of charm. The camp hyperbole hadn't quite rung true with her, although there was evidently no serious damage done because, as she dismissed the doubt (she had probably been scarcely conscious of it anyway), she tried immediately to assuage any embarrassment the error might have caused me, with a bluster of platitudes about how impossible it must be for someone as busy as me to remember anything at all.

'I suppose,' she went on, 'things still are frightfully busy?'

'Well, you know . . . ' Although I had begun to form a plausible picture of our respective circumstances, I was far from ready to risk anything detailed. 'There are various projects on the go' was all I was prepared to offer.

'Gosh . . . I'd love to hear about them . . . ' She looked down at her groceries. 'The thing is Kiku's at home and I ought to get back . . . ' She bit her lip and studied me a moment. Bumping into Matthew Delacorta was obviously quite an event for her, and I could feel she was loath to let him go. I wasn't greatly surprised, therefore, when she invited me – nervously, her eyes alight with timid hope – to come home with her for a cup of coffee.

'I'm only round the corner.'

I made a show of consulting my watch. I was conscious of the double power of my position – my own power over the spirit of Delacorta, and Delacorta's evident power over Madeleine. The knowledge burned in me like a draught of something hot and invigorating. Involved in it was a complicated sense of danger, which I felt largely on Madeleine's account. How alarmed she would be if my mask slipped and she realised she had brought home an impostor. Should this occur, it would be like finding ourselves on a high wire, and while I would feel safe in the knowledge that I intended her no harm, she herself could know nothing of the kind.

'That sounds very agreeable,' I said, 'if you're quite sure.'

'Oh yes . . . I mean, if you have the time . . . '

We set off, back in the direction of St Simeon's Church. I was wondering who or what Kiku was, and trying to compose an innocently probing question, when Madeleine said, 'What you told me about Kiku was so true. I don't suppose you remember a word of it, but I've never forgotten . . . '

I smiled, and gave a non-committal shrug.

'You said there were infinite solutions to the problems of happiness, and Kiku's was almost certainly among the more successful.'

Well, there was nothing to be gleaned from that, other than a mildly ominous whiff of Matthew Delacorta's personality.

'Oh yes,' I said, 'I remember,' and tried to laugh it off as a piece of nonsense.

'No.' She sounded serious now. 'You meant it, and it's been a great source of strength to me.'

I was going to have to play Kiku by ear. Meanwhile there was Felix, my lighting man –

'So how's Felix these days?'

'He went off to Sydney . . . didn't he tell you?'

'No, he never did actually . . . '

'Probably too shy . . . they were all shy of you. It must be very strange for someone so young to have that effect . . . ' She tried to give me the indulgent smile of a seasoned woman, figuratively patting a brilliant young man on the head, but the smile was strafed with such visible anxiety, such genuine awe, that it quickly retreated, leaving behind the faintest of blushes.

'Terrific guy, Felix.' I sensed that, as Delacorta, I could heed or ignore her remarks as I chose; that she would willingly follow in whatever direction I took the conversation.

'Hm . . . ' She looked into the opaque sky, and out of her gaze flowed silence as eloquent as speech. I saw dimly – as if blurred in the silvery clouds she was staring at – the tangled line of a life coordinated by love and sorrow.

'Here we are,' she said finally. A shimmer of excitement passed through me as we stepped into the spacious, gloomy hall.

4

The dark, musty atmosphere of a house furnished with heirlooms; treasured possessions, inherited without the cash to maintain them; dust-covered trunks in the hall . . . We climbed to a living-room crowded with oils in chipped and tarnished gilt frames. A battered grand

stood in a corner, baring a row of carious, yellowing
keys. Its top was laden with silverware – candelabra,
vessels, a miniature silver phaeton – all badly in need
of a polish. Great curtains of dark green velvet, pep-
pered with moth-holes and mildew spots, were drawn
across the windows. Madeleine switched on a lamp,
the shade of which was patinated with dust, so that
only a hint of illumination was able to escape. She sat
down on an ancient sofa with intricately carved
wooden pillars supporting its back-rest, dust-coloured
stuffing hanging from the wounds in its upholstery.
Beside it was a coffee table bearing a wooden bowl
filled with limes and tangerines. These shone with a
jewel-like gleam, improbably mineral, as if it were they
that had drained all the splendour from the room, and
were thus alone responsible for its faded, threadbare
appearance.

'I'll make some coffee,' Madeleine said.

I sat quite still without thinking, while she was gone.
I was riding high on my *Ate*, my *Menos* – whichever
it was – and although I was aware of the extraordinary
precariousness of my position, the awareness was far
too remote to cause me any anxiety. My being here
was meaningless, in that it was founded on a deception.
And yet it felt, in a mysterious way, purposeful; as if
deception were only what the first, most superficial
analysis laid bare, whereas in the last, something altogether different was waiting to be uncovered.

The silence in the room was broken by a muffled
thumping sound. I sat up and looked around, trying
to locate its source. It seemed to be coming from the
room next door, a slow beat pounding through

the wall. I was about to investigate, when Madeleine reappeared.

'That's Kiku,' she said, putting two glasses down on the coffee table. 'I thought we'd have cocktails instead of coffee. But come and meet Kiku first.' The thumping grew louder and faster.

Kiku's room was locked, the key still in the door. Damp, human-smelling heat reared up at us as Madeleine opened the door. I stepped inside, onto an amazingly soft orange carpet strewn with toys. A girl of seven or so, in pigtails and a flowery frock, was standing on one side of the room, hitting the wall with her head. The wall was padded; covered in quilted gold corduroy to a height of about eight feet. The few pieces of furniture in the room were similarly padded.

'Kiku sweety, stop it. Kiku. *Suky*.'

The girl turned to us with a smile. 'Kiku,' she piped.

She was Madeleine in immaculate miniature: her mother's big dark eyes and delicate bones, her mother's high, dulcet voice, the same atmosphere of faint misalignment about her, but the sweetest, the most engagingly attentive of smiles.

'Kiku then. Say hello to Matthew Delacorta. She won't though.'

The girl ran halfway across the room, stopping suddenly to kneel on the carpet and pick up a toy aeroplane. The wings of the plane seemed to wilt in her hand. They drooped down like petals on a dead flower. I realised then that it was made of felt, and that all the other toys in the room – the dolls, the building blocks, the menagerie of furry animals jumbled around the bed in the corner – were made of similar materials. The room was entirely devoid of hard surfaces.

Kiku waved the plane around, jerkily following its movements with her head, still smiling. Then with a sudden, vicious twist of her arm, she hurled it tail-first at the wall, which it struck soundlessly.

'Suky's her real name then?'

'Yes, remember I – '

'– Yes of course . . . Hello Kiku . . . '

I walked towards the girl kneeling on the floor. I had an impulse to hold my hand out in front of me as if I were approaching a timid animal that might want to sniff a bit of me first. She was still smiling, bunching up the freckles on her cheeks and nose. She looked as though she was on the point of coming out with one of those comically candid remarks that children make – *Will you give some sweets*, or *I don't like you* – but she said nothing at all. I knelt down before her, conscious of the close attention of her mother standing in the doorway. Delacorta was being assessed for his rapport with the child.

'Hello there, how are you then?' I patted her head. Her smile was beginning to look like a fixture, a sort of benign facial disfigurement.

'I'm Matthew,' I said.

She was looking straight into my eyes, her own still dew-bright with infancy. 'Matthew,' I repeated. I took her little hand and gave it a squeeze. It lay unresponsive in my grasp.

'She's very lovely,' I said to Madeleine, still holding the limp hand.

'She's everything to me.'

'I can see why.' I turned back to the girl. 'Aren't you a sweetie, Kiku?' Silence. 'She's a shy one, isn't she?' At this Madeleine gave me a peculiar look, as if

I'd said something wildly inappropriate. 'I mean, ah ... ' I stopped myself from blustering, 'shy's the wrong word I suppose ... ' Madeleine looked a fraction more hopeful. And then quite suddenly the whole situation – the thumping, the padded walls, the soft toys, the rigid smile – snapped into place, and I recognised the child's condition. I assumed an expression of pious concern: 'She *is* happy though, isn't she, one can tell ... ' Madeleine's eyes were glistening. As I rose to my feet I noticed a dark patch spreading on Kiku's flowery frock. She was still smiling, no longer at me, but at the space my head had just vacated. Madeleine led her out of the room after me. 'Naughty Suky,' she said. 'Kiku,' the girl replied. 'Join you in a moment,' Madeleine said, steering me back into the drawing-room with a touch of her still-gloved hand. Somewhere in the depths of the house I heard a lavatory flush.

5

'I call this one Pina Madeleina. Tell me what you think.' Madeleine handed me my fourth cocktail. Like all the others it was foul, and in a distant way that foulness was reflected in the intimacy that the alcohol had established between us: a bogus intimacy in which I attempted to be wittily rude, while she pretended to be delightedly shocked.

I took a sip, and held up the glass before me.

'Too sweet, too thick, toothache,' I declared.

'Oh Matthew! You monster!'

Kiku was in the room with us, lolling on the floor, flitting from chair to chair, banging her head against

things until her mother got up from beside me on the
sofa, to stop her . . . She provided a point of choral
return for the conversational lulls, as a cat or a baby
does. But it made me uncomfortable having her there
– being faced with the disconcerting problem of having
to square her perfect physical presence with her complete mental absence. I found it difficult to believe that
she was not pretending; that she would not suddenly
shimmer and melt into laughter and tell us how silly
we were, how stupid it was of us not to realise.

'Tell me a story Mr Delacorta,' Madeleine said. 'Felix
said you were a great story-teller. He said you could
hold the Company spellbound.' She took off her net
gloves at last and, with the over-emphatic precision of
someone pretending to be sober, laid them hand to
hand on the coffee-table. Her naked fingers were
streaked red. I stared at them, startled, for some
moments, until I realised she must have put on the
gloves before her nail varnish had dried.

'Go on,' she said, ignoring the sight, 'spellbind me.'
She snuggled back into the sofa.

I stared up into the shadowland between the curtain
pelmet and the ceiling. Not being an imaginative man,
I could no more create a fictional human being *ex
nihilo* than I could a real one. But I sensed trailing
behind Madeleine's request – far behind it and nebulous
as the fleeciest end of a vapour trail – the unmistakable
scent of sexual promise. At that distance it did not
greatly excite me, but the possibility that it might if I
were to get closer, was enough to make me rack my
brains for a scrap of an anecdote to reconstruct for
her.

I might have been silent for ten seconds, or ten

minutes; drink had brought us into harmony with the secret elasticity of time. The darkness at the ceiling seemed to swell out and engulf me. I was adrift when the idea came, let loose in space. I spoke, and the sound of my voice was like a faraway disturbance. The story I told required no imagination; it was the truth, no more, no less. But as I told it, I felt the kind of nacreous, distempered thrill that accompanies the telling of an ingenious lie upon which momentous decisions will hang.

'Sunday morning,' I heard myself say, 'I awoke to a murmur of faint anxieties. The day held nothing and nobody in store for me. I rose and prepared my breakfast . . . '

I told her of my indecisiveness in the face of the big blank freedom of the day, of my walk, and the odd compulsion under which I had entered the church of St Simeon. *Ate* and *Menos* had not yet occurred to me as the alternative analogies for my behaviour. I kept to the facts; the sacrilegious communion, the preternatural energy tingling in my body as I left the church –

'I was fuelled, burning. I had stolen fire from Olympus . . . '

'What do you mean?' Madeleine asked, reaching with her streaked hand towards Kiku, who was revolving the fruitbowl with a finger, and had started to spin it out of control.

'I mean that I, a non-believer, had tapped the energies of ritual without submitting myself to the acts of faith it asked in return . . . '

I told her of the woman walking towards me, the purely hypothetical way in which she had first entered my consciousness, her looming into actuality as she accosted me with the name of Matthew Delacorta.

At this point Madeleine's face lit up with the realisation that she was the woman, and I myself the man. She was hooked. The words that left my lips as fact, reached her as fiction. I had no hesitation in revealing to her that I was not Matthew Delacorta. She listened with a drugged smile that seemed to struggle towards some more specific expression when I disclosed (or, as she would have received it, *invented*) the subterfuge by which I had inveigled my way into her home.

'A shimmer of excitement passed through me as we stepped into the spacious, gloomy hall . . . '

She looked around the living-room as I described it, relieved to be able to fall into her familiar attitude of delighted outrage as I itemised the mildew spots, the dust, the sofa's wounded upholstery. I spared her nothing of my reaction to Kiku. She heard it with a glazed look of entrancement such as I have sometimes imagined is found on the faces of the dead when their guardian angel shows them the life they have lived, with all the parts that were once obscure to them, rendered luminously visible.

It occurs to me that between reality and my account of it, there was precisely the difference that lies between the two mutually exclusive boxes contained in a drawing of a transparent cube. The lines were identical, but her cube was the inversion of my own. What happened in the process of this inversion was not so much a sacrifice of truth, as a diminishing of it to an entirely valueless quality. And under this devaluation, the currency of everything else became arbitrary. I was neither Matthew Delacorta nor myself, but a trick card on which either would show, depending on how it was held to the light. The ramifications of my connection with Madeleine – was she succumbing to my charm, to Delacorta's, to my version of his charm – went on like an infinite mathematical series. We had entered a realm where we were subject more to the laws of physics than those of human nature. And just as, under random stimulus, a quark is said to leave its own equivalent of a spoor along all the paths that it might have taken, but did not, as well as along the one it did, so I felt myself refracted into a mirror-hall of multiplicit possible selves, each one of them pressing a ghostly claim to being the sole channel through which these events were flowing. It was a vertiginous feeling.

'Tell me a story Mr Delacorta . . . ' I concluded, with a smile.

'What a *peculiar* story,' Madeleine said wonderingly, and gave a long, melodic sigh. The clear sound was like the sight of the gleaming limes and tangerines whirling beneath Kiku's fingers – a seam of pure tone lacing the shabby, crepuscular atmosphere of the room. Something in the contrast made the blood tingle in my capillaries. I downed the last drops of my cocktail, and asked for another.

'Make it bloody this time. A Delacorta Haemorrhage.'

Madeleine giggled, and walked unsteadily out of the room. Alone with Kiku, I performed some magic. I produced coins from thin air and exhibited them in the palm of my hand. I slid a cigarette into my ear and extracted it from my mouth. I balanced a chair on my foot and set it spinning. My life's accomplishments;

and Kiku gazed through them with her attentive smile, taking in nothing.

'Suky,' I said.

'Kiku,' she corrected me.

'Suky,' I repeated.

'Kiku.' There was, I thought, a note of anxiety in her voice.

'Suky.'

'Kiku.' Her eyes widened with alarm at this challenge to the single piece of herself she had chosen to share with the world. She looked agitated, and began to whimper. I felt I was on the brink of establishing contact with her, that all it required was the correct incantation in order to focus her mental processes on to me.

'Oliver,' I said, pointing at myself.

'Liar,' she replied without moving her lips, only of course it was not her, but Madeleine, returning with the drinks, her voice barely distinguishable from the little girl's.

'Why are you lying to my daughter?' She tried to look proprietorial, drawing herself up and placing a hand on the girl's head, but found she had sufficient self-command only to initiate the attitude, not to sustain it. She sank down on to the sofa beside me, looking momentarily lost. I took the drink from her hand while she gathered herself. Then I took the hand too, and answered her question with a question of my own.

'Why are you covered in nail varnish?'

'Oh,' she looked forlornly at her hands, 'I keep doing that . . .'

I drew her close to me and murmured something intimate, sentimental, and untrue. Sweet odour of

boudoir; roses and strawberries ... I kissed the prof-
fered lips. There was more pink powder on her skin
than I had thought, and an almost invisible pale down
glimmering over it. She looked at me warily, assessing
the balance of pain and pleasure to be had from a man
ten years younger than herself. She tilted back her chin,
showing me three cross-hatched furrows circling her
neck: this is how I am, the half-conscious gesture said;
stop now if you think you might hurt me later on. I
drained the cocktail in one, and followed her out of
the room as the last of the sweet emulsion crawled
down my throat.

6

The inner sanctum ... Kiku thumped in her padded
cell, while Madeleine and Matthew Delacorta made love
in the pot-pourri of crumpled sheets, lipstick-stained
tissues, and jumbled clothing strewn about Madeleine's
bedroom.

I was there as an intimate observer, having loaned
Matthew Delacorta the use of my body for the
occasion.

'Oh Matthew,' Madeleine said, 'Matthew Delacorta.'
I smiled for him. The sugar-fizz of pleasure swarmed
at my groin. But just as it is neither the glass nor the
mercury that registers heat in a thermometer, but the
eye that looks at the two in relation to one another,
so my body, temporarily removed from my ownership,
remained in an entirely mineral relation to this pleasure,
even to the moment of climax.

In the dozy period that followed, I became aware of

two things. First that Kiku was no longer thumping in her cell, and second, that my *Ate*, my *Menos*, had abandoned me.

It lay on the floor, a gloppy pearl tied up in the rubber sheath that Madeleine had produced from a little snakeskin treasure chest.

As I grew conscious of myself there in the bedroom of a stranger, I had a glimpse of the scale of my deception. It was so colossal I could hardly credit it.

'I can feel your heart thumping,' Madeleine said drowsily. 'What's bitten you?'

'Nothing.' I swallowed the short word before it was finished. My voice – I could feel more than hear this – had lost all trace of its preposterously confident timbre, and vibrated now to the higher, breathier pitch of fear. The room looked dismal; debris that had suggested dry, scented rose petals, took on the bleak look of mere refuse. Madeleine's eyes were closed. I tried to still my beating heart. I was afraid she would open her eyes and see not Matthew Delacorta, but me. My fear was vicarious as well as on my own account: I myself was as much the object of it as was the more practical danger I felt, of being found out. And this in turn, ironically but with a perfectly consistent logic, began to make me feel close to Madeleine in a more innocent way than I had previously. I wanted to communicate a tender, protective concern for her well-being. I wanted to reassure her that she was safe from her intruder while *I* was around. I pulled her close. She responded sleepily to my kisses. The alcohol on our breath had not yet gone rank, and there was a muzzy, intoxicating atmosphere around us.

'So you like me,' she murmured contentedly.

For the first time, a feeling of raw, carnal desire for her took hold of me.

'Very much,' I said.

We went at each other with deep, probing kisses. Out of shyness, or caution, or plain modesty, she had put on a short night garment when we had first gone into the bedroom. I had tried to slide it off her, imagining that I was expected to, but she had signalled resistance, and I had left it alone. Now, however, as my hand slipped between it and her skin, she raised her pelvis and let me pull the silky fabric off her, so that for a moment her naked body was thrust fully towards me, a scarlet flush spreading from her neck to her nipples, breasts dilated wide and shallow under their own gravity, looser flesh bunched spongily at her stomach . . . Outside, the first rumblings of the returning weekend traffic had begun, and the light was paling. The room, filtered once more through desire, resumed its aura of rosy *déshabillage*. Overcome again by modesty, or whatever it was, Madeleine pulled me tightly against her, wearing me. She drew up her legs and took me inside her.

'Shouldn't I put a thing on?' I whispered.

'No . . . it's safe.'

As Delacorta, I had been granted a limited intimacy – held back from ultimate communion by the thin veil of a prophylactic. As myself, however, I was given the full, ravishing candour of her nakedness enclosing my own. O rose, thou art sick! The invisible worm . . . did I destroy her in that moment? Was I with Satan or with the angels?

7

When at last we descended, it was not to the drawing-room, but to the kitchen in the basement below.

A bearded man in an old corduroy jacket was sitting at the table, with Kiku on his knee. Madeleine did not seem in the least surprised to see him, although a visibly charged look passed between them. Before him was a plate of biscuits and a jug of over-diluted orange squash. On the wall behind was a gleaming xylophone of Sabatier knives.

'This is my husband,' Madeleine said, gesturing brusquely towards him, 'and this,' she held my arm gently, 'is Matthew Delacorta.'

My first thought was that, far from having deceived Madeleine, it was she who had all along been deceiving me, drawing me into a domestic plot which, if obscure in its details, was instantly familiar in its atmosphere of banal squalor.

However, the husband betrayed no sign of anger or jealousy. He merely looked me briefly up and down and said, 'He isn't Matthew Delacorta.'

I remember gaping at him, speechless. His words had the impersonal, dispassionate ring of a judicial verdict. I turned to Madeleine, assuming my hour had come. But it seemed I had underestimated her powers of self-delusion. She closed her eyes wearily. 'Oh don't be like that, Dominic,' she said, adding for my benefit, 'husbands can be awfully trying.'

'He isn't Matthew Delacorta,' the husband repeated. His puffy, watery eyes (somewhere in them the melancholic stoicism of a drinker resigned to his condition) scanned me again. Kiku's rag-doll legs dangled from his lap. She stared at me.

Madeleine turned her back on them and lit the gas beneath a tarnished kettle.

'Take no notice of him Matthew. He'll be off soon, won't you Dominic? It's his turn for Kiku.' I sensed a quarrel between them of an antiquity that had turned it into habit. There was no pride left, even in appearances. I forced myself to recite the words the occasion demanded:

'Perhaps you know another Matthew Delacorta . . . ?'

For a while he didn't answer, but merely spread a hand out and looked at it gloomily, as if scrutinising the state of his nicotine-yellowed fingernails. The kettle began to make knocking sounds. I was at the depressed heart of a family, and wished I was elsewhere. I had a strong desire to cleanse myself.

Finally, without looking up, the husband said, 'I know Matthew Delacorta, and you're not him.'

Madeleine shook her head at me from behind him. A white rim had appeared around her tightly shut lips. Her eyes strayed over the Sabatiers, faltered, then returned to me with a wistful smile.

Her misplaced faith no longer amused or flattered me; I felt wretched. But for her sake I tried to make a stand. As politely as I could, I told the husband he had made a mistake, that I was indeed Delacorta, that I directed plays, had met Madeleine at the Edinburgh Festival through Felix, and was now as it happened looking for a Cleopatra.

'I'm hoping Madeleine will agree to audition.'

Madeleine stepped round and gave her husband a

triumphant smile. He ignored her, and said to me, 'What are you?'

Kiku twisted back her head and began to wriggle. A rushing sound came from the kettle.

'Oh go away Dominic. You wreck everything,' Madeleine said quietly.

'I can prove he isn't Delacorta. There's a picture of Matthew in Rosemary's book on the Fringe. It'll be in one of my trunks in the hall.'

He deposited Kiku on the floor, and stepped past me without a glance. He smelt of rain and tobacco, a distillation of autumn. Madeleine breathed in slowly, to calm herself it seemed. 'I'm sorry about this,' she said. She began to spoon tea into an enamel pot. Dried leaves scattered across a formica surface.

'Perhaps I should go,' I said. 'I'll contact you about this Cleopatra audition.'

She looked at me, glimmering with hope, and with despair. She dropped the spoon and ran out of the room. 'Dominic,' she cried, 'Dominic, please . . . '

Alone with Kiku, I realised I had to disappear. Wisps of steam rose from the spout of the roaring kettle. I picked up a biscuit and held it out to Kiku. 'Here you are, Suky.'

'Kiku,' she said, snatching it from my hand. I poured her a glass of orange juice. 'Drink it, Suky.' Her eyes widened. 'Kiku,' she said shrilly. Steam poured from the kettle, billowing into the room, blanching the blades of the Sabatiers. As I held the glass to her lips, I felt a last convulsion of my *Ate*, my *Menos*. From upstairs came the sound of remonstration. 'Suky,' I said, 'that's who you are, *Suky*.' She opened her mouth to whimper, dribbling out the orange juice. 'Suky,' I

repeated, 'Suky.' The whimper grew louder. 'Kiku,' she
cried.

'Suky.'

Her voice rose to a scream. Her face turned scarlet.
Footsteps tumbled down the stairs. Her mouth began
to shape the cry into strange, nonsensical syllables, as
if she were groping for words – *gaa, bey, cooo* . . . I
stepped, adulterer fashion, behind the door as mother
and father burst back into the steam-filled kitchen. I
vanished deftly behind their backs, taking the stairs
three at a time, bounding across the hall without pausing to look at the book lying open on one of the
trunks, while a high, grief-stricken female voice I could
not identify cried, 'No,' drawing out the word into an
anguished wail that pierced the air as I ran from the
house, repeating itself over and over, 'No, no, no . . .
o . . . o . . . o . . .'

The Coat

It was a light summer coat of yellow velvet with a silk lining. The velvet was soft and smooth. It might have been cut from the petals of an enormous primrose.

It had been given to Muriel by a dear friend (this was the term she had settled on), a veterinary surgeon, who had treated Muffy, Muriel's dog, for the numerous ailments she was suffering from when Muriel had first taken her in.

The pockets with their deep silk interiors were very cool to the touch. There were three buttons: ivory coloured, with sunflowers moulded in relief on each. The shoulders were styled a little outward, a little upward, not padded, but giving just a hint of regal breadth. The skirting tapered inward – a note of playful severity – stopping just high enough to disclose its owner's ankles, which, as the dear friend constantly averred, and as Muriel did not mind admitting herself, were something a seventeen-year-old girl could have been proud of.

In fact the whole garment flattered her. The colour revived a lustre in the remaining honey colour of her hair; the cut did credit to her figure which if nothing else was still erect. Wearing it Muriel felt a little more radiant, a little lighter-hearted than usual. It was, she sometimes felt, like being sheathed in an emanation from her own youth.

For this reason she wore it sparingly. She was in good health, not yet sixty, still worked in the college where she had been registrar since her husband's death. But after all, one's youth was not something to be called up indefinitely; its residue was volatile, like an ancient chrism that too much exposure might vaporise.

Then too, by an instinct for the higher subtleties of sympathetic magic, she made a point of never putting on the coat with a view to *inducing* livelier spirits; never wearing it to 'cheer herself up', as some of her more simple-minded acquaintances imagined they could by dressing up in some gaudy retrieval from the depths of their closets. No. She wore it only when the rare mood, the distant intimation of gaiety, was already stirring inside her. Then and only then would she wear it: not to coax but to facilitate, to enhance.

After checking the sky and the hall barometer (the dear friend had cautioned that water might spot the material), she would lift the coat from its padded hanger, swim her hands into the stream-cool sleeves, button up the three sunflower buttons, and step out from her small brick house (she preferred not to think of it as a bungalow), onto the lane that led to the village, pausing to smell a neighbour's honeysuckle, or buy stamps, or pick up groceries at the village store. Invariably someone would admire the coat, remark how well it suited her, how elegant she looked in it, how young, and she would answer graciously, feeling

a sensation of calm delight arising in her, as if a cool
flame were waving through her body.

The dear friend was a gentle, quiet soul called
Donald Costane. Their attachment was more consolat-
ory than passionate – they had come late into one
another's lives – though once or twice a remote craving
had passed through Muriel as she watched Donald's
long, white, well-manicured hands pick their way
through the mangy tufts of Muffy's ochre hair in search
of sores and parasites, then lave themselves in disinfect-
ant soap, and rub each other dry with a crisply starched
hand-towel. However, his regard for her appeared to
be restricted to the scope of formal veneration. He
admired her spirit, which he considered both proud
and refined. He cherished a notion that the two of
them were each other's reward for maintaining dignity
in the face of unspecified suffering. It was understood
that if they were not 'above' other people, they were
at least 'apart' from them, in possessing virtues too
subtle and discreet for the world to recognise; that they
must bear their obscurity with fortitude, but that now
at least they had each other to help them. Such, at any
rate, was how she interpreted his attentions.

And in a very little time she came to see that the
limits he tacitly set were not only sensible, but were
also conducive to unexpectedly rich and gratifying feelings; feelings that had more to do with possibility than
actuality, suggestion than statement, with consum-
mations subtly deferred that at another time might have
been eagerly sought. So that their friendship had
acquired the air of an eternal courtship: two parallel
lines moving together over horizon after horizon

toward some infinitely distant but perpetually beckoning point of convergence.

'I must admit I always believed I would come into my own at sixty,' Donald said once during a mild postprandial haze; 'even would you believe it when I was quite a young child.'

Muriel had laughed. 'It is a shame we didn't meet when we were younger,' she had ventured, then realising from his abstracted look that she had missed the point, added, 'but perhaps we would not have recognised each other.'

He was handsome in his own way: shiny grey hair always neatly brushed and set; dignified profile; grave, pouchy eyes that seemed to indicate a bottomless fund of sympathy. He collected Victorian pewter, dressed in well-cut suits or sports jackets, drove a plushly upholstered car, and was dependably punctilious in the matter of flowers and notes and little gifts at appropriate moments – all of them well-chosen, though none as bold, as presumptuous, as the coat, with which he had presented Muriel after their first outing to London, when she had complained of looking and feeling like all the other dowdy provincial ladies at the theatre.

It had astonished her, arriving by delivery van one afternoon, in a shallow box the length of a body, wrapped in several layers of tissue; lying there buttoned up, primrose yellow, with a fresh rose in its lapel, and a little mauve envelope with a note saying simply 'For the Metropolis.'

He spoke little about his past, and seldom asked Muriel about hers. The agreement seemed to be to banish all ghosts for the duration of their meetings; to create passages of perfect happiness while they were in each other's company.

Their outings were elaborate, and no doubt costly, though Muriel herself never saw a bill. They occurred perhaps once every six weeks, more in summer, a little less in winter. They had quickly established themselves as the high point in Muriel's routine, becoming downright necessary after her son Billy joined the navy and was out of the country for most of the year; so that, aside from the trivial solace of gossiping with the neighbours, there was effectively nothing but Donald between herself and whatever it was that pressed upon one during the quiet afternoons when there were no letters to write, no cardigan about to go at the sleeves, nothing to weed or prune in the garden, and one could see as if through glass straight into the empty ocean of the day.

But the coat.

There had been the occasion of the Losing of the Button.

It had happened during one of the outings to London. Donald had picked Muriel up as usual at eleven o'clock in the morning. They had driven to the city, eaten lunch at an Italian restaurant in Charlotte Street, strolled to the embankment and taken a boat ride along the river. Gulls, bridges, boat crews flat in the water like pond-skimmers, the Parliament buildings rising from the thumbed bronze Thames like needles of caramel combed up out of molten sugar . . . Donald had enquired in his solicitous way after Billy; Muriel began a lament about her son's deficiencies as a correspondent, then, hearing the unpermitted note of complaint in her voice, stopped herself and changed the subject, which Donald graciously pretended not to notice. After a drink at a newly restored Victorian pub in Shoreditch that Donald had wanted to investigate, they had gone to a musical in the West End, finishing off their evening with a light supper at a crowded brasserie in St Martin's Lane.

It had been an entirely satisfactory outing. Donald had told amusing stories about some of his animal patients, for whom he bore a tender and unashamedly personal affection. The musical had been cheerful and tasteful. The weather had been sunny but cool, and she had worn the coat all day except when they were indoors.

On the drive home, as she was drawing it a little tighter against the evening chill, her fingers had registered a bobble of thread where the middle of the three sunflower buttons should have been.

She waited until Donald stopped for petrol on the motorway, when she took the opportunity to make a search of the car; to no avail. Suspecting Donald would feel obliged to turn back in search of the button if he thought she was upset, and equally that he would be offended if she affected not to care, she refrained from saying anything when he returned to the car.

But all the small contentments of the day, stored up in her mind to be fondly relived later, had seemed to pour out of her in a single rush of annoyance.

The following morning she phoned the coat's makers and found that neither the coat nor the buttons were being manufactured any more. Without pausing – she did not want to give herself time to question what she was doing – she drove herself to the station (driving in the city made her nervous) and took a train to

London. Thinking she had probably lost the button towards the end of the outing – else she would surely have noticed it – she began retracing her itinerary of the previous day in reverse.

Nothing had been found at the car park or the brasserie. The cloakroom attendant at the theatre in Piccadilly had a box with odds and ends in it that people had left behind in the theatre: keys, gloves, fountain pens, a pocket-sized television, but no buttons of any description. Staving off her disappointment, Muriel took a bus to Shoreditch and walked to the Victorian pub. With its gilded cherubs and mirrors, its scrimshawed narwhal horns and enormous buttoned-leather sofas, the pub might have been expressly designed as a haystack for the concealment of her particular needle. A group of young men, catching on to her predicament, made a raucous display of searching every nook and cranny of the lounge and saloon and public bar, much to the irritation of the other patrons. The exercise was as fruitless as it was embarrassing. And what with the commotion, the heat, and the smell of beer and spirits, it left her feeling distinctly weak on her knees.

She took a taxi to the little shack on the embankment that served as the offices of the pleasure-boat company. The lady who sold tickets remembered her; remembered the coat at any rate, as soon as Muriel described it, and seemed as concerned as Muriel herself at the loss of the button, entering Muriel's by now unconcealable anxiety with a fullness of sympathy that made her feel at least that she was not being wholly ridiculous. It did not, however, produce the button.

At the Italian restaurant in Charlotte Street, the bow-tied manager who had attended to her with studied gallantry the day before, helping her both into and out of the coat, today not only failed to remember her, but treated her with thinly veiled suspicion, only grudgingly allowing her to inspect the cloakroom at the back of the restaurant, eyeing her all the while as if she had come here to steal the silver. Glimpsing herself in a mirror on the way out she had had an inkling why. She looked frayed, haggard, dishevelled and a little crazed.

So she had emerged into the afternoon heat of the city.

There was an hour before her train left, and she wandered slowly towards Charing Cross. A muffled sensation came into her. She felt dimmed somehow, and cut off from the buildings and people passing on either side of her. Confronted with the failure of her mission, she began to wonder why she had embarked on it in the first place. What had possessed her to waste a day in such a senseless fashion? If she couldn't replace the button, she could find three others that would look just as nice as the sunflowers. Really, she told herself, it had been altogether rather a shameful exercise. And futile.

But even as she admitted these things, something in her rose obstinately to her own defence. There *was* something worth clinging to in the idea of perfection. A thing once blemished was never the same, however much you forgave it. At any rate she herself was so constituted as to be sensitive to the small things that made the difference. If that was a fault in her then so be it. She was not responsible for the aspirations of her own soul.

She marched on, squinting into a glare that seemed

to radiate equally from the street, the sky, and her own exhaustion. Turning a corner she came to a crossroads where the flow of people and cars was held up by what appeared to be the demolition of an underground public convenience. Giant excavating machines were grouped around a crater in which were exposed – among clay, rubble, creeper-like armatures of plumbing, and some patches of broken mosaic – several doorless toilet cubicles with the white porcelain bowls still nakedly in place. Verdigris-streaked pipes led up from them like stalks from enormous onion bulbs. A horrible odour hung in the heat. She tried to hurry by but the cordoned walkway past the site had narrowed pedestrian traffic to single file. For several unpleasant seconds she was caught in a slow-moving human crush. By the end of it a sweat had broken out on her lip, and she was feeling dizzy. Just as she emerged, a pigeon flew down slantwise right across her face, so close she felt a buffeting of hot air on her eyelids. She gave a soft cry and put her hand to her heart, which had at once begun knocking in her chest. The pigeon landed in one of those arid patches of earth left unpaved at the base of city trees. It scrabbled there with its wormy toes; a filthy bird, looking as if some passing god of the metropolis had seen fit to breathe life into a broken lump of pavement with a smear of oil on it. Muriel caught its bulbous eye as she paused for breath. Cigarette butts, sweet wrappers and bleached excrement lay around it on the sandy earth. It hopped between two gnarled claws of root, jabbed at the ground, and then took off with a wheezy flapping.

And there between the roots, pristine and gleaming,

as if the pigeon had just that moment laid it, was the sunflower button.

A sensation of hot triumph had come into Muriel as she stooped for it. She felt both elated and defiant, as if in retrieving the button she had confounded some opposing law of existence.

It was warm from the summer heat, and mysteriously communicative as only an inanimate object can be.

She had been even more sparing in her use of the coat after that, restricting herself for the most part to admiring it in passing as she picked something less hazardous from her bedroom closet. She hung it on its padded hanger, with a net bag full of cedar chips to keep away the moths. It was hanging there, of course, the weekend her son Billy came to visit with Vanessa.

An only child, born late in a marriage already entramelled in mutual if seldom articulated grievances, Billy's personality had seemed from an early age pale and indefinite, as if stretched thin by the diverging motions of his parents. As a boy he had been timid; as a teenager, after his father's death, he had seemed to make a point of forming friendships exclusively with the shiftiest-looking, most unappetising specimens of local youth. What they got up to when they sloped off together on Friday and Saturday evenings, Muriel had preferred not to imagine, though from an instinctive appraisal of their collective character, she had suspected it was confined to the pettier forms of disorder, and she silently thanked her stars that her son had not been cast in a more vigorous mould. Later, after he had left school, he had seemed to settle down contentedly, or at least without conspicuous dissatisfaction, to a job at a nearby estate agent. Gratified by the apparent change, Muriel began to enjoy his company; even to allow herself to depend on it. And while it was true that occasionally when she spoke to him he would meet her look with an expression of rather childish bewilderment in his eyes, Muriel had not suspected him of seriously chafing at the outward circumstances of his life. It had come as quite a surprise then, when he had arrived home from his job one day, a few months after the Falklands War, and announced that he was going to join the Royal Navy.

He had met the girl, Vanessa, on his first weekend of shoreleave after a long tour of duty in the Arctic. It was unlike him to bring home a girl, particularly one he had known for no more than a few weeks. Sensing something momentous, Muriel had gone out of her way to extend a welcome. But her overtures towards Vanessa – a pallid girl with a loose, large mouth, and long fingers varnished pink at the nails – were received with what appeared to be a mixture of suspicion and amusement, and it had soon become apparent that the weekend was going to be a trial.

By Saturday night the young lady had distinguished herself by lounging around the house with next to nothing on, feeding Muffy chocolates till the poor thing was sick, sitting on Billy's lap at mealtimes, spoonfeeding him, cooing babytalk at him, signalling at him while Muriel attempted to make conversation with him about his tour of duty, until with a sheepish grin he had sidled off after the girl and followed her upstairs. Muriel had not been born yesterday, but there are certain sounds that she considered a mother's ears

better off not hearing, and she had had to go outside
and prune the roses in the twilight rather than endure
them, though even there she had heard her son's name
called out in a startlingly piercing cry: *Billy, Billy* . . .
My God.

It was as she had suspected. On Sunday morning
Billy took her aside to ask what she thought of
Vanessa. She had begun to make a reply, choosing her
words carefully, with an equal view to truth and tact,
when Billy burst out that he had proposed to the girl
and that they were going to get married on his next
leave.

So that Muriel had felt it her uncomfortable duty to
take them to the Sandbourne Hotel at lunchtime, for
a celebratory glass of champagne . . . The girl's idea of
dressing up had been to exchange her négligé for a
lederhosen outfit with a loose, sleeveless top that
seemed designed to draw every male eye deep into the
ripe shadows of its shoulder halters. It had certainly
caused a stir in the lounge of the Sandbourne, and the
girl had clearly revelled in the attention, letting her eye
stray about the room, babbling her silly nonsense in a
loud voice that got louder the more she drank.

Under the circumstances it was difficult not to con-
template the crude perils awaiting Billy in his long
absences at sea. But with luck perhaps the young lady
would find herself unable to manage even the few
months of solitude that lay ahead of her, and Billy
might learn his lesson without the added humiliation
of being actually married to his teacher.

Shortly before they left the hotel, something behind
Muriel caught the girl's attention. Her eyes kept
moving slyly to a point just over Muriel's shoulder,

then sliding back to Billy's with a look of suppressed mirth. A few times Billy looked covertly over at the bar, then met Vanessa's glance with expressions that changed gradually from perplexity to the same reined-in hilarity as if he were slowly cottoning on to some private game. Muriel did her best to ignore it, but at last turned round to see what they were looking at. There was an elderly man in a brass-buttoned blazer sitting at the bar: red-faced, white-haired, and with long, stiff, white moustaches twirled and waxed at the ends and sticking out absolutely horizontally above his lip. He was drinking gin and tonic and sitting with a very straight back. He looked with a stony or perhaps merely blank expression at Muriel's party.

Muriel turned reproachfully back to Billy, but before she could speak, Vanessa broke out with a peal of giggles, and after a feeble attempt at self-restraint, gave in to a fit of wild and rather terrifying laughter which seemed to Muriel, however mysterious its precise cause, to be formed unmistakably of an inseparable cruelty and dirty-mindedness, and which twisted and crumpled the girl until, with tears streaming down her face, she had run off to the Ladies' Room.

That afternoon Muriel had decided it would be in everyone's interest if she absented herself from the house for a few hours. Apart from anything else it might earn her a little of Billy's attention in the evening.

On the pretext of errands to run she drove off with Muffy to the nearby reservoir where a footpath led around the shore.

People were out sailing in dinghies – snub-nosed

Mirrors, and the flotilla of pretty, leaf-shaped Larks owned by the Sailing Club. It had been warm for days, and dry for most of the summer. The water level had sunk quite low, leaving a wide band of dried froth and ribbon weed on the pebbly shore.

Muriel clipped the lead to Muffy's collar and set off along the dusty footpath, bordered by the reservoir on one side, and on the other by a flat wilderness of broom, gorse and bilberry bushes. There was a smell of warm creosote from the Water Authority huts dotted along the shore, and an occasional dank algal breath from the lapping water carried upward on the breeze.

The place had always had a calming effect on Muriel, and it was not long before she began to feel a little less agitated.

She thought about Billy and Vanessa, and reflected that a father might have been useful to Billy at this moment in his life; even his own father, who had maintained high standards in his judgements of others, if not of himself. It was a pity, too, that Donald and Billy didn't get on – not that anything had been said, but it would be hard to imagine Donald offering to take the boy aside for a chat, let alone Billy submitting to such an offer.

Anyway, much as she loved her son, she knew that he was in some respects a fool, and that even if he were saved from this particular folly he would sooner or later find another one to commit in its place.

And then too, she thought with sudden gentleness, there was always the chance that Vanessa herself would improve. She was very young after all. The shrillness and flimsiness of her outward manner might disappear over time, and reveal a decent sort of soul. Her faults might not be deep; at any rate might not be irredeemable. You never knew what might happen to a person; it was a mistake to trust only in the worst.

A couple with a labrador approached along the footpath. Muffy stood still to be sniffed, then sniffed the labrador in return. She trotted towards the owners with her tail wagging, and Muriel let her stay a moment to be patted, though she kept the leash tight and watched her closely: Donald had said Muffy had probably been beaten as a puppy, and would never be a hundred per cent dependable.

She had appeared at Muriel's door one winter morning, her skin covered with bald patches and sores, and her skeleton visible beneath it. One ear had been badly chewed up, and one hind leg was in the air, apparently too tender to put on the ground.

Muriel had thrown her some bacon rinds, which the dog came warily forward to snatch up, limping off with them through the wet grass into the woods at the end of Muriel's back lawn. That evening she had returned, soaked and shivering. Muriel had thrown her some more scraps. The dog gobbled them, this time staying where she was, and staring up at Muriel with her head cocked to one side when she had finished. Muriel had been touched by the sight, and had called her inside, giving her more food and putting down a blanket for her on the floor of the cloakroom.

An acquaintance had recently suggested she get a dog for the companionship now that Billy was gone. She had taken no notice of the idea, never having considered herself a dog lover, but she found it difficult to turn the animal out of the house the next morning, and she soon realised she was becoming attached to the creature.

It had sharp, almost dainty features, like a very small Alsatian. Its cindery ochre coat had a reddish tinge on top that suggested red setter. After a few days Muriel had decided to adopt her, and enquired about a vet to have her examined. It was in this way that she had met Donald.

Under his care, the dog recovered from her sores and grew back the fur on her bald patches. After a few weeks in a splint, the fractured bone in her hind leg mended perfectly. She lost her slightly unpleasant derelict odour, and began to smell of ginger biscuits, if rather stale ones. She grew healthy and sleek and alert; turning in fact into a very pretty animal, with bright girlish eyes, and a way of tilting her head to form a certain pathetic expression that never failed to arouse a pang of protective affection in Muriel.

Her nervousness had been slower to cure. She barked furiously at anyone who came to the house, and had once chased the child of a neighbour out onto the road, after which Muriel kept her tied up whenever she was outside. But in time the sedate rhythms of Muriel's life seemed to soothe the animal, and she had grown less noisy and excitable, becoming even a little bit slothful in recent months.

Muriel passed the Sailing Club, which marked the half-way point of her circuit. The sun was low in the sky, and a lance of light was probing across the reservoir. From the far shore ripples shot across the water like footprints of a swift, invisible herald. A breeze blew up. Sails filled out and surged forward, tilting over as they were hauled in for speed.

Muriel remembered bringing Billy to the Sailing Club once when he was a small boy, and watching anxiously as the little Lark he was put in with an instructor raced off across the water at what had seemed a dangerously unstable angle. He hadn't enjoyed the experience any more than she had, and never showed any desire to repeat it; a fact she had not failed to remind him of when he had told her of his intention to join the navy.

The breeze died, then came back, stiffer than before. By the time Muriel completed her circuit, the reservoir had blossomed with brightly striped spinnaker sails billowing out in front of their craft and towing them along so fast that even the smallest cut a wake of orange light on the water. For a moment she stood and watched. They were lovely to look at, and she felt gladdened and lightened by the sight.

She drove home in good spirits, exercised and refreshed, sanguine about the chances of a civilised final evening with her son.

There was a note on the kitchen table when she got in:

GONE TO THE PUB. SEE YOU LATER.

Assuming this meant they would be back in time for supper, Muriel put the casserole she had prepared into the oven and set the table. For a while she sat in the living-room reading the papers. But she was unable to concentrate, and fearing that her good mood might not survive if she sat there with just her thoughts, she went back outside to finish pruning the roses.

It was almost dark by the time she finished. Billy and Vanessa had not returned. She raked up the pruned stalks and carried them in bundles to the steel basket incinerator at the bottom of the back lawn. Putting in as many as she could, she poured petrol over them and set them alight. Flames shot up into the dusk. A few pearl-sized drops of water glinted in the firelight, falling to earth. She hadn't realised it had started raining.

Back inside, she ate her supper and cleared it away. Thinking it would be a triumph of sorts if she were to wait up for Billy and Vanessa and receive them without a trace of reproach, she went back into the living-room, and had another go at the papers.

But the silence of the room, so familiar to her, and usually not oppressive, made her suddenly desolate. It really was a little inconsiderate of them to disappear like this, she couldn't help thinking, though she immediately chided herself; probably Billy had wanted to celebrate with some of his old friends from the village. Well, that was understandable. She resisted the temptation to feel hurt by him; there was no limit to how far you could slide in that direction once you started.

She stood up and went upstairs, thinking her best bet would be to go to sleep.

To her surprise she could smell Vanessa's scent as she went into her bedroom. She turned on the light. The slide door to the closet was open. She went over to inspect it. A pair of high heels on the floor had been tipped over. A tweed jacket had been taken out and put back with its collar twisted. There was a padded hanger with a net bag of cedar chips at a gap where the row of clothes had been divided. The yellow coat was gone.

Muriel sat back on the foot of her bed, a little stunned. For a while she neither moved nor formed a thought, but merely sat, coiled into herself like a person who has just been hit. Then gradually she began to make an assessment of the situation.

Obviously the girl had not taken the coat in order to spite her. She knew nothing of its preciousness to Muriel. She had taken it because the evening had turned out to be cool and she needed something to wear. No doubt she had asked Billy's permission, and Billy had told her to help herself.

It was unfortunate that the weather had broken, but Vanessa could hardly be blamed for that. Anyway, Donald's warning that rain would ruin the velvet might well have been alarmist – he did tend to be a little over-cautious. But even if he was right, so what? It was only a coat after all, and one shouldn't make a fetish of such things. She had perhaps set too much store by it in the first place; certainly her day in London in search of the button filled her with a half-shameful feeling whenever she remembered it.

These last reflections were formed more in a spirit of wishfulness than conviction, but they helped Muriel stave off the feelings of annoyance that had begun to rise in her.

She felt it necessary to do this; in recent months she had noticed herself becoming prone to fits of irritation, often for quite trivial reasons. Something would vex her, and before she knew it she would have passed into a dream-like state of silent fury, where the most violent punishments would be meted out in an atmosphere of obscure malediction. She would emerge from these states feeling shaken and vaguely guilty, as if after an over-indulgence. She had no wish to end her days in a permanent twilight of bitterness and anger. Why such a fate should threaten her, she had no idea; these things were apparently not in one's hands. But it was becoming a matter of conscious vigilance to maintain a pleasant disposition, and keep the more disagreeable tendencies of her imagination in check.

She no longer had any desire to go to sleep, and went back downstairs.

Passing the open door of the cloakroom she saw a short red suede coat on a hook and remembered that Vanessa had brought this with her. Because of the fine weather, she had not worn it all weekend, and Muriel had forgotten about it. Seeing it now was like being struck again. For this argued, did it not, an indifference verging on contempt?

A feeling that had in it both dismay and bewilderment came into Muriel. She pictured the girl putting on her own coat then discarding it and running upstairs to Muriel's bedroom and riffling through her closet, trying on one thing after another, posing in the mirror, calling out to Billy for approval. The idea was peculiarly distressing; it unfolded in Muriel like an extremely unpleasant physical sensation.

So that it was again necessary to get a grip on herself.

She went into the living-room and sat in an armchair without turning on the light. She thought of ringing Donald – it might have helped to talk to someone – but dismissed the thought. Idle telephone chats were not a part of their arrangement. Donald would assume a calamity had occurred and start flapping, then wonder why she had rung. Worse, he might attempt to rise to the occasion and encourage her for once to pour out her heart, and she dreaded to think what that might bring forth. Either way, she was certain to regret disturbing him.

And at this she found herself struggling against a sudden impulse to denigrate, even to revile, her friendship with Donald. What sort of friendship was it after all? What did it mean? An infinitely deferred promise of love; an offer of intimacy that would never survive being taken up . . . She thought of him with his sombre, considerate manner that seemed to invite confidences, yet somehow always contrived to deflect them; his elaborate attempts to procure a frail feeling of enchantment that was really nothing but a kind of sweetened anaesthesia . . . Was that all she could hope for any longer? A feeling of disgust rose in her: for his tepid notion of happiness, for her own collaboration in it, for his fussy habits, his clean hands, his cabinets with their carefully labelled curios, his cautious driving, his conscientious gifts and notes . . . God, he was like the ghost that didn't know it was a ghost. He was like the void of a person not there . . . And if their time together was an improvement on their respective solitude, it was only as an exchange of the despair that knows it is in despair for the despair that imagines it is not, and is therefore even further from hope . . .

She felt as if the darkness of the room were seeping into her soul. Morbid and bitter thoughts began to take hold of her. She saw herself quarrelling with Billy and Donald – even heard herself spit out the withering remarks that would bring about these quarrels – then

sitting alone here in the living-room like someone in a
ship drifting towards some vast and empty darkness.

She stood up and went outside.

Cool, light rain was falling steadily now, pattering
on the grass, swishing through the woods at the end
of the garden.

She walked to the garden gate and stood looking
along the lane that led to the village. In her mind's eye
she saw Vanessa putting on the coat as she and Billy
left the pub, and going out into the rain. She followed
the girl's carefree steps, imagining the first drops of
rain falling onto the material of the coat. A sharp spasm
of anger went through her, but it was followed by a
feeling of helplessness.

Smells of wet soil and wet vegetation filled the air,
sweet and fresh under the acrid driftings from the incinerator. In a few days the first brown marks would be
appearing on the roses. Trees that had fallen in the big
spring winds would start succumbing to mosses,
fungus, lichen; the wood growing soft, pulpy, then
powdery, eaten up by insects and mould, blackening,
disintegrating, disappearing into the soil . . . She had
heard woods described as being like an hourglass: the
life sifting from the trees into the earth, then the hourglass turned around and the life sifting back into the
trees. The new grew off the old, the living off the
dying. But it was never the same thing that grew back.
Life poured into you, then the hourglass was turned
and it began to pour out of you.

The moon was high in the sky above her, muffled
in cloud, its light falling in showers through the upper
air, glittering in dimness on the wet hydrangeas and
feathery yew shrubs of the house opposite, pooled in

the giant leaves of the gunnera plants in the border along the fence, dripping from branches, pouring in plaited trickles from the gutter on the garden shed.

After a while she heard the girl's voice from far off. The two figures appeared, Vanessa hanging on Billy's arm, both of them walking a little unsteadily. The girl's hair was plastered to her skull, giving her face a rudimentary look: a knot of sense organs. The coat looked more silver than yellow in its sheen of rain and moonlight.

Spiders and Manatees

A familiar name appeared on the screen, above a little American flag. The figure in goggles and ski hat, crouching at the top of the jump slope, could of course be anybody. Still, Victoria peered forward, wondering whether she might glimpse some recognisable feature among the phosphorescent colours framed in her old television.

The figure launched himself onto the steep slope, elbows tight against his hips. His name still hung above him as he plunged towards the lip of the jump, and Victoria had a distinct memory of seeing it in a similar square-angled computer print at the top of a series of papers on Greek literature. Was this the same Carl Pepperall? His face was too masked, his body too crouched, for her to tell. She turned the volume knob, but the commentator must have fallen silent for the build-up to the jump. The figure gathered speed through the rush of static. A different camera showed him in profile slicing across the screen, and for the first time Victoria felt less than amused by the blotting-paper definition of her set. Could it be him? He hurtled down towards the lip, and with a final convulsion of his doubled-up body, took off into the lurid blue sky. But instead of turning into a sleek missile of compacted limbs and skis, he seemed to trip over some invisible rift in the air, and open out into an ungainly assemblage of flailing, wheeling spindles that tumbled through the sky like an enormous daddy-long-legs.

Victoria watched askance as the man crashed to the ground and lay there in a heap, abruptly motionless, the unnatural colours of his ski clothes bleeding into the snow around him.

The commentator started to speak again, but Victoria lunged forward and turned off the television, wishing she had done so before the sports coverage had begun, though glad at least to have been quick enough to protect herself from a knowledge she did not wish to possess.

She took up her work again, and edged herself back into the mood of delicate scorn with which she had been reviewing her old professor's latest offering on Epicharmus (how invigoratingly difficult it was to have a reputation for an unflinching critical eye!). The words flowed easily until, like a sudden *whump!* of oxygen into a smouldering fire, a glimpse of something vast, shadowy, and unnameable opened up in her.

The year before, Victoria had taken a teaching job at the small college of Branderhaven, in Eastern Connecticut. From her classroom she could see across the campus to a buttressed gothic fantasy that had been built to house what the prospectus described as a gym of unrivalled sophisication. It would already be full of students when she arrived to teach her morning class, and however late she left at night, there would still be

dozens of young men and women exercising on the
mysterious contraptions gleaming in the golden interior
light.

   Occasionally they make a sortie, she had written to
her colleagues back in London, *for a lecture or seminar,
but reluctantly, and you feel a little cruel dragging them
away, even though it looks like a Bosch hell in there.
Mens Sana indeed. The faculty are the same. Not for
them the salt of bracing interdisciplinary debate as
seasoning to their (epicurean!) lunches; no, any remarks
that don't bear directly on the subject of fishing are
considered practically scandalous. My contributions are
lavish, as you can imagine. Do you remember Bill Plat-
kin, the 'corn-fed Oklahoman'? The men are all like
him, though the head of Humanities – a Hadley or
Bradley – does show minute signs of life. He has offered
to escort me around New York. No flowers please.*

A hard blue light was at work on the city; chiselling
and bevelling angles, glazing planes. The cold sky
looked packed with cut crystal. The place produced its
customary effect on this latest initiate:

   'It's like being inside a diamond,' Victoria
announced. They passed a luminous violet tanning par-
lour, a shop selling the flowering parts of tropical
plants. 'No, I'll tell you exactly what it's like, it's like
a mixture of London, Rome, Madrid and Venus.'

   The brilliance of the morning and the affability of
her companion had released a surge of effusive spirits
in her, and she talked as she had not done since leaving
London. Her phrases grew steadily pithier and more
daring.

   'There's a saurian strain to everything, even the

people,' she informed the head of Humanities, Bradley Crane, who had obligingly agreed to show her Manhattan. 'They seem alert to different disturbances, do you know what I mean? As if they get their energies from different food sources. Any second now we're going to see a coiled tongue dart out to catch a fly.'

'Why, what are they eating in London these days?' Brad said, hoisting his amiably gloomy, hound-like jowls into a smile.

Victoria felt herself fuelled by his apparent pleasure. 'That car – it's like a hybrid of a Mercedes and an anaconda. What on earth is it?'

'Just a stretch limo.'

'A stretch limo! Even better!'

They were lunching in the West Village when Victoria, in full cry, experienced a distant pang of a kind she associated vaguely with the first suspicions of material loss – a lost wallet or set of keys. For a while the feeling hung in abeyance, unconnected with any discernible source. But its strength gathered until it made her falter mid-speech. The interruption seemed to startle Brad, and although he had shown no visible signs of inattention, he now smiled guiltily at Victoria, as if he had been caught drifting off. She resumed her flow, but in the fractional pause, her sense that she had been captivating this comfortable, weatherbeaten armchair of a man, had already begun to cloud. When had she lost him? Had her appreciation of his city been too pert for his liking? A few days ago he had seemed like one of those miracles that arrive in your life so matter-of-factly you hardly remember the anguish, the aridity, that preceded them. The smell of his big, damp sheepskin coat had intimated such vastnesses of friend-

ship and repose. Surely she can't have been mistaken.
She could feel a shrillness in her voice. She suspected
she ought to be quiet, stopped talking for a moment,
but Brad said nothing, and the silence pushed them
apart like a spreading pool. An ill-looking man went
by the window leading a poodle with a bondage stud
collar.

'Enter the age of sex by proxy,' Victoria said with
a little laugh.

Brad smiled, but seemed unamused. Or was she
imagining things? She tried again, but all her words
came out off-colour, or faintly condescending, and she
wished she could shut up. But the more she felt herself
grating on Brad, the more she felt it imperative to
regain his attention. As they left the restaurant, she
gave a rendering of her dinner with the dean on her
first night in Branderhaven, roguishly quoting the
catchphrases that had been bandied about, the *hidden
agendas*, *significant others*, 'Oh, and yes, Brad, *serendi-
pitous moments*, I counted three *serendipiti* . . .' But
he wasn't to be tempted into the cosiness of a secret
conspiracy, and his non-committal, barely audible
response made her feel shallow and treacherous; 'you
mustn't think I'm being disloyal, now,' but that only
made it worse . . .

All the while, however, she retained a provisional
quality in these feelings. She was quite possibly imagining things; one was seldom anywhere near as awful as
one feared.

In a tunnel of the 14th Street IRT subway, they
turned a corner and came face to face with a man
defecating. The man stared at them brazenly, furiously,
from the ghetto of his hood. As they passed by,

Victoria began to say something – not, as it happened, anything to do with the man – but Brad silenced her unceremoniously with an abrupt, upward gesture of the back of his hand.

'I mean,' he said, at once conciliatory, 'I guess that doesn't require any comment.'

Victoria was too crushed to explain that she had actually been about to ask him if he had ever taken a Mediterranean Antiquities Cruise.

There were tulips on her desk the next morning, white ones with feathery waves bred into the curl. She recognised them vaguely, but couldn't remember where from. There was no note. Brad? It seemed unlikely after the silent, humiliating train journey home last night. But there they were – white, fresh, cleansing the air about them. Perhaps Bradley was one of those men who have to insult you as a way of testing their own feelings. She smiled. She was not averse to the idea of a little combative wooing.

Her performance in class that morning was freer and lighter than usual, leavened by her secret excitement. At one point, several students spontaneously began taking notes – a sight that was always astonishing and gratifying. Even the curly-haired, tracksuited Carl Pepperall, who sat at the back in a permanent foment of suppressed callisthenics, was unusually attentive. He was gazing at her with a look of shy wonder. Had his ears been opened at last to the riches of Greek verse? She asked his opinion of a Sapphic conceit. A panicky look came over him. She smiled, and asked another student. A breath of the tulip fragrance sent a flutter of delicate apprehension through her.

After the class she made straight for the faculty
building. Ita, Brad's Maltese secretary, eating a Danish
pastry from a box in which glistened several more, gave
her a grin and asked how she'd enjoyed New York.
Victoria thought she detected a trace of archness in the
woman's voice, though it was hard to tell with the
chomping and swallowing going on.

'It was very pleasant, thank you.'

'Bradley sure enjoyed himself.'

'Did he?'

'Sure!' *Shewer*; Ita bellowed it with a shower of
crumbs and a rolling of eyes, as if her word had been
doubted. She put a finger to her chin, tilted her head,
and stared.

Victoria had attempted to make a motherly confid-
ante of this woman, but there was something not quite
satisfactorily maternal about her, despite her bun of
silver hair and the voluminous softness of her figure.
She was oddly dilatory over the small administrative
matters Victoria had asked her to settle, and she was
prone to quirky sulks.

She pointed at the door to Brad's office and said
with a little twinkle, 'He's in there now,' as if Victoria's
single ·thought had been emblazoned on her forehead.

In fact, the woman's peculiar clairvoyance disarmed
Victoria to the extent that she found herself opening
Brad's door in a state of dreamy suggestibility, without
even stopping to think of an excuse. Brad was lounging
back with his feet on the desk, and fiddling with a
quiver of small, brightly coloured feathers. He glanced
up.

'Hi Victoria. What can I do for you?'

Victoria faltered. Brad began to wind thread about

the feathers while she tried to think of something. His hands were absolutely steady. He did not have the air of a man who had just sent an anonymous gift of fancy tulips.

'I wanted to thank you for a lovely time yesterday,' Victoria improvised.

Brad gave her an empty look.

'Oh, sure.'

She stood helplessly. She felt mortified, but she couldn't bring herself to leave. She watched herself in horror as she stepped forward and touched the little posy of feathers in Brad's hand.

'It's pretty, what is it?' she said.

Then she felt something prick her, and simultaneously heard Brad roar 'fly', or seem to, making the word sound so much more like a command than an answer that she jumped back and fled from the room, smarting.

Ita avoided her eye, busying herself with a sticky finger; a look of sly, sullen amusement on her face.

For a few days Victoria made efforts to find out who her anonymous admirer was. Men who were courteous enough to sit next to her at lunch, or say hello to her in the faculty building, found themselves at the receiving ends of alarmingly piercing looks, that in no time had them retreating into the iciest of professional formalities.

A whisper of quiet panic began to greet her wherever she went. She was too shrewd not to notice the rout – the contortions of evasive behaviour; eyes beseeching rescue, mid-sentence flights for forgotten books, the quick getaways made under cover of a dazzling smile . . .

She realised she had better get a grip on herself. *Anyone would think I came here to get a husband*, she wrote to her old colleagues, and she resolved to cut a figure of dignified aloofness in the remaining months of her appointment. She dropped her investigation, and in a mood of combined pique and defiance, withdrew from Branderhaven's small social arena. *If they choose to see me as an academic* gastarbeiter *imported from a nation fallen on hard times, then far be it from me to embarrass them with social obligations. I shall henceforth conduct myself with the meekness of a governess in a nineteenth-century novel* . . .

She applied herself to her classes with added diligence, spending long hours preparing intricate summaries and appraisals, going through the students' papers with an attention vastly out of proportion to anything that had gone into their making. She ate lunch at a table on her own unless she was specifically invited to join the others, which happened rarely, then not at all. And at night she retired early, proudly, with a Sanskrit primer.

The magnolia flowered hard and bright all over the campus. A week later it fell and the ground was covered with drifts of rotting blossom. An early summer brought the class out in silks and pastels. Music came on the breeze from the steps to the gym where the students gathered in the warm, lengthening evenings. Victoria watched them as she worked at her desk. They strolled out of the big glass doors in loose tunics and togas, a little more glowing flesh on show every night.

It's the baths of Caracalla over there, Victoria wrote, *soon we'll be down to thongs and loincloths . . .*

Bradley receded into the background. There remained something silently contemptuous about his presence whenever it encroached on her horizon, but he was not difficult to avoid. She seldom thought of the white tulips now, remembering them merely as an irritatingly mysterious interruption of her life's natural medium, like a blizzard in a desert. Stoicism and work were to form her natural continuity. She pledged herself to them with a fierceness that was intended to purge every other inclination from her heart.

One evening she was making notes for a class on Greek metrics, when her concentration – usually excellent – began to stray, and would not be brought to heel. She had long ago discovered the flagellant's secret of control, which is to make things harder when they are hard, rather than easier. She turned from the notes to the more arduous task of memorising another passage of Homer (she had resolved to learn the *Odyssey* by heart before her thirty-fifth birthday). When that didn't work, she pulled a newspaper from her bag, picked a column at random, and began translating it into Greek, an exercise she relished for its sublime purity of purpose.

She had worked herself into a cold blaze of effort searching the ancient language for epithets that would do justice to a modern fashion article (in what terms would Pericles's Athenians have conceived of day-glo and mohair, of spandex, chenille and distressed leather?) when the door opened and the bare-footed figure of Carl Pepperall appeared inside the classroom.

He looked at her silently for a moment. He seemed

very far away, obscured in a tissue of soft sounds and
night scents that had trailed in with him, and then
further removed by an afterswirl of dictionary print
milling before her eyes like a gnat cloud. She heard
him speak – 'Oh, excuse me, ma'am' – and had the
odd impression of seeing his lips move out of time
with his words. 'I think I left my sneakers in here.'
He rummaged for them under the table, stood up, and
grinned at her. She hoped he would go now. She was
aware of him peering at her, and of herself sitting
there without speaking or moving. She must have been
straining her eyes. The room looked very dark, and
everything in it seemed to pulse. Light dissolved from
the boy as if he were a body of light steeped in dark
water.

'Are you alright?' she heard him say. The words
seemed spoken in a foreign tongue. He was approaching, a look of concern on his face. She had an urge to
hide the work she was doing, but her limbs felt too
heavy to move. He stood by her, looking down at the
desk. Her forehead tingled coldly, as if at the onset of
fear.

'You're translating the *Times* into Greek,' he said;
'what are you doing that for?'

She could hardly look at him, let alone answer his
question. Her head was bowed in shame. After a
moment's silence he gave an unexpectedly assured
chuckle. 'Why don't you take a break?' he asked.
'Come over to the gym.'

She was on a walkway above an echoing, cathedral-
like space lit so brilliantly she was at first only aware
of a multiplying gleam of chrome and glass and

polished wood. She had been led there in what amounted to a state of suspended volition. Protests and practicalities had crumbled in the face of Carl's polite, confident insistence. (Where had he got that sudden flow
of confidence from – her own ebb? Some power source
unknown to her?) Her glimpses through the windows
of the gym had not prepared her for the size of the
interior. She remembered her arrival in New York.
Here was the same dazzle, the same power of pure
scale: a broad central aisle given over to game after
game of basketball and tennis; glass-partitioned votive
chapels full of weightlifters, masked fencers, squash
players hurling themselves at walls like flies in a jar; a
huge blue swimming pool scribbled over with glyphs
of gold light (the ringing air above it somehow darker
and more solemn than elsewhere). The locker room,
where she changed into a borrowed tracksuit, had a
primary, carnal reek. How odd it felt to be back where
the body was the measure and arbiter of reality. She
had seldom ventured into this empire since childhood.

She met Carl by the aerobics machines.

'We'll start with some stretching,' he said. 'If you
just copy me.'

She allowed her gaze to settle squarely on his body
for the first time. There was an unsightly scar – a livid
rose – at the back of his thigh, but otherwise she had to
concede that he looked as a human male was probably
intended to look. The few others she had eyed with the
same licence were spiders or manatees in comparison. A
smooth plait of muscle was visible under his string
vest, which flowed like chain-mail over the burl of his
shoulders as he plunged forward on alternate knees.

Victoria sounded herself for a reaction. Was she

impressed? Amused? (What would her old colleagues think if they could see her with him like this?) Ignited? None of these exactly, though when he turned to smile silently after the receding figure of a girl in a walkman and tight, metallic green leotard who had flipped him with her towel as she went by, Victoria felt the lapse of attention like the chill of a sudden draught.

'What did you do to your leg?' she asked.

He turned his attention back to her.

'Propellor got me. I fell out of a boat in a power race off Virginia Beach.' He grinned. 'I have a lot of them. They're my souvenirs. Here, harpoon dart from the Caribbean, St Croix.' He showed her a sheeny white gouge in his shoulder, then touched his hip. 'Got a steel pin in there from a hang-gliding fall. The wind decided to drop just as I did. That was in Northern Spain, Asturias Mountains. My mom swears she dies every time the phone rings when I'm off on a trip . . . '

There was something touching about the unembarrassed, intimate disclosures. He seemed to take a guileless pleasure in fixing her attention on his body. Without noticing the point of transition in her own thoughts, she found herself trying to picture him stealing through the icy fog of a March dawn with a bunch of white tulips in his hand. She looked at him afresh. The image shimmered in and out of plausibility. There seemed all at once an irresistible hint of affinity between the flowers and the boy's fair curls and limbs gleaming in the neon light. If he had been a god visiting a mortal in a dream, Victoria reflected, he might have left such flowers as his tokens of remembrance. She smiled, and tried to shrug off the idea; the boy must be more than ten years younger than herself.

'Now we'll try the machines,' he said.

He sat her on a bicycle and explained the principles of aerobics. He was standing beside her, just outside her field of vision, so that he was both looming and abstract. His voice was impassively polite, like an airline steward's. It was difficult to get any purchase on him, or on her relation to him, now that they were outside the simple geometries of the classroom, and now that the spectre of the tulips had risen again in her mind. She didn't know whether to feel flattered or obscurely insulted by the way he was ordering her around. Then too, she thought, there was the matter of his papers – those punctual, immaculately presented reports on classical literature that arrived on her desk like lambs to the slaughter, so virginally innocent were they of anything approaching originality or even cogency. The students were graded at the end of the semester, and in all conscience it was going to be difficult to award Carl anything more than a bare minimum 'pass'. It would be a pity if he should think he had done anything to make her vindictive. Awkward too. It crossed her mind that she might have been incautious coming here with one of her students. A delicate suggestion of impropriety flittered through the air. She didn't know what to do. She didn't even know what she wanted to do. The situation seemed globed in a complex burnish, like that of a vase under several layers of glaze, with a dozen different shades and hues. And at the point where her own feelings might have been expected to guide her, the shades merely deepened to a pitch of absolute mysteriousness.

Without warning, Carl touched her throat. As it turned out, he was only taking her pulse, but it felt like a detonation, and in the few silent seconds in which he let his fingertips rest near her jugular, her blood seemed to perform a drumroll right beneath them, and in her agitation she pedalled furiously, as if trying to reach a speed that would persuade the fixed machine to move.

'You probably should exercise more,' Carl said, and prescribed ten minutes each of cycling and rowing.

She sat on a ledge in the women's steam-bath, stupefied by pain and exhaustion. *See you later*, Carl had said. Did that mean goodbye or later on this evening?

At first, on the bicycle, the extreme physical effort had been an adventure, and she had reported on it to Carl in her customary style. 'I feel like a maternity ward for newborn muscles screaming into life,' she had informed him, and 'the more pain you're in, the longer each second on the stopwatch seems to last. There must be a point of convergence between absolute agony and eternity. I suppose that's where hell is.'

But at a certain level of exhaustion, her body had begun to reel her mind in like a kite, until it was wrapped so closely about her limbs it seemed merely a dim radiance from them, barely distinguishable from the sweat and heat. No more thoughts occurred in it; only the notation of strain and lung-burn, and the wish to stop.

'I can't do any more,' she gasped after the first ten minutes.

'Quick,' Carl said, 'it's important to keep your pulse up.' He led her to the rowing machine, and was strapping her feet to the boards, heedless of her protests.

'Now pull.' It seemed she must.

The seat slid back on the horizontal spine as she dragged at the weighted chain, her feet braced against the boards. The chain drove a geared bicycle wheel with flaps fixed all around it, which fanned her as she sweated. Carl stood over her, again a little behind, issuing curt instructions – *a little faster, pull harder now, keep that speed up* . . .

A pattern had emerged: she would reach a peak of agony, slacken, be admonished, protest she had had enough, then feel a downsurge of shadow as Carl leaned forward, an indistinct mass of male form, to touch her throat. And once she had discovered the degree of protest that would bring him, she had half-consciously summoned him, as one does summon again and again the thing that most perplexes. She still wasn't sure what it was his touch induced. It felt like a panicky lurch, as over a forgotten step, or perhaps more like the lurch from a step that isn't there. It was always this way in matters of physical experience; one was more than ever the proverbial Greek in Rome: a creature of refinement thronged by the unpredictable barbarians of appetite. One never quite knew what was going on. A limitless, treacherous obscurity would open up, accompanied by a feeling of helplessness that kept her to the task. She was only capable of doing what she was told. She recognised the feeling from three or four other occasions in her adult life – the same unaccountable surrender, the same excruciating pain, the same blind obligation to go through with it.

'Okay,' he said at last. 'You can stop now.'

She lay prone, awaiting further instructions. But he was already leaving.

'See you later,' he said with a smile, and was gone.

Now what? A drama of folly seemed to be unfolding in some shadowy zone between the real and the imaginary. How would it proceed, she wondered: towards a moonlit confession under the magnolias? A silent entanglement in the locked classroom? She felt quite numb towards the eventualities, as if she too were suspended in that indeterminate zone. The steam appeared to have dissolved her skin. It swirled and bloomed inside her. Blurred pink figures moved softly around the room.

And then a paler one came in and sat down opposite. It was the girl in the walkman and tight green leotard she had seen earlier on; the girl who had flipped Carl with her towel. Her skin was almost as white as the steam-room's porcelain tiles, which boosted the bits of colour on her. She swept back a damp mass of reddish ringlets, yawned, wrinkled her nose, and gazed into the steam with a look of self-satisfaction.

But before that, her eyes had flickered briefly over Victoria's, and in the instant the older woman had felt the ripple of banished illusion. One flickering look and it was gone! She wondered at her capacity for missing the obvious. How could she have imagined Carl would be remotely interested in herself when a creature like this was at his disposal? It wasn't as if she had even desired the things she had imagined, unless a weakness for the flattery of being desired be itself considered a desire. If she felt anything now, it was more like relief for what she had been spared.

How familiar this turn of events felt. Fantasy, disillusion, relief: the cycle seemed peculiarly her own. Even when the fantasy happened by chance to land her in a grapple with one of those spiders or manatees, there would always be a moment when something rock-like reared up with an unarguable veto to any pleasure she might have had from it, and in retrospect this moment would always seem one of deliverance. It had even been so, she realised, with Bradley, after that day in New York. She had been too preoccupied with her humiliation to notice it at the time, but after it was all over, something in her had breathed an unmistakable sigh of relief.

Meanwhile, as she looked at the girl, she could feel the knotted burden of Carl, and the tulips, and the strain of overwork, unravelling, and it was like a physical sensation of loosening in her body.

Gradually, a mood of benign calm settled on her. She smiled ruefully to herself, thinking of Carl and the girl together – an affinity of toned flesh. She felt an almost protective magnanimity, as if she were an old priestess presiding over their nuptials. Steam made the blood tingle in her capillaries. She had never known anything quite so luxurious as this steam-room; one felt almost afloat in the assuaging cloud. She stared at the girl, glazed in good feeling. It wasn't often that she was able to forget herself in this way. She wondered whether the supposedly warmer, more candid palette of American emotion was at last beginning to colour her own feelings. Waves of tenderness seemed to be pulsing out of her.

The girl caught her eye – a green glint – then looked away. Pink blotches had appeared on her skin. The corners of her dark red lips were drawn up further, and to a finer point than most, as if they had been detailed by an unusually expert hand. How nice she would look if she smiled. Victoria found herself feeling extraordinarily well-disposed towards the girl, towards everything! It seemed to her inexpressibly wonderful that Carl and the girl should be lovers. She smiled, picturing them together. The steam plumed obligingly into boas, bulged into pillows and glistening cherub clusters. Again the girl caught her eye, and it was like a splash of sea-green against the portholes of a sinking ship. How delightful to sink like this; into a whirlpool of soft contours, mild brush-strokes of bluish shadow, steam-darkened braids and knots of copper . . . Victoria had always considered any form of body fascination to be infantile. She refused to read certain novels: *boredom not prudishness*, she would tell people; *it's like having a travel book that does nothing but tell you about the workings of the car.* And even now she had a suspicion that she ought not to indulge these feelings. But where was the harm? His hand would descend through the meadow of freckles sloping from each sunburned shoulder to an areola ringed, she noticed, with dainty marks that might have been cast from the pawprints of a thimble-sized lion. She imagined the contact of hand and breast. Another green wave crashed as something exulted in her blood.

'Jesus!' the girl exploded, and jumped up, covering herself with her hands. She spat out another word as she left the room. Victoria coiled as it tore into her, bulleting through what seemed like a series of opaque veils through which she was able to glimpse briefly the source of her imagined exultation . . . The glimpse faded as the rips healed, though she was not altogether spared the knowledge, because in the flurry of violation something brilliant and silken had rippled out of her memory, and to her astonishment she was seeing a vase of those white, feathery tulips in the faculty room at the very beginning of the semester, an overheard voice saying *yes, they're pretty, my neighbour gives them to me, he's a commercial breeder*; the voice female, accented, muffled by sounds of chewing and salivation.

It took a few days for the glare of revelation to fade. Something in the mixture of cruelty and craving in Ita's gesture gave it a certain lingering fascination. But eventually Victoria was able to consign the image and all it insinuated back to the darkness from which it had arisen. A sense of having in an obscure way been made a fool of, was all that remained of the episode.

Was this what her Greeks thought of as *Ananke*: Necessity; the force that draws all things forward to their designated place, do what they might to resist it, so that even one's defiance of its decrees is taken into account?

A day of blinding sunshine . . . the shadow-etched campus emptied for some annual, end-of-semester joust between seniors and alumni . . . cries drifting over from the sports field behind the gym . . . Victoria was clearing out her desk in the classroom when a woman knocked on the open door and strolled in. She took off a pair of sunglasses. She was handsome, clear-skinned, her blonde hair grained with grey; blue eyes that appeared lit from the back with mauve. She smiled at Victoria, extending a hand.

'Hi. I'm Sophie Pepperall. I think you know my son.'

What followed had a dream-like, faintly incredible quality, even at the time. The woman had stood before her, pleading for her son, though pleading was not quite the word, as she seemed sure of getting what she wanted, as if she were going through the motions of an elaborate ritual, purely out of some vague nostalgia for more courtly times. She was relaxed, almost playful, sunglasses dangling from one hand, the other trespassing lightly and confidently on Victoria's arm.

Her gist was that Carl's place at the business school his father had attended was contingent on a grade average that he might have scraped if he hadn't done so badly in Victoria's class.

'It's not a particularly high average they're looking for,' Mrs Pepperall explained, 'but on the other hand they don't appear to have too much flexibility.' She paused for a moment, smiling at Victoria. 'Bradley Crane told me it was unusual for a student to get a grade that low, especially in this kind of a subject . . . ' She looked at Victoria candidly, leaving the pleasant spill of colour from her eyes to express the thing that even her idea of propriety stopped her from saying. Carl's face stared out from hers, boyish and vulnerable beneath her confident smile.

Victoria remembered the acute discomfort she had felt as she answered the woman – the astonishment at what was being asked of her, the desire not to betray the angry thudding of her heart, to sound measured, reasonable, in perfect command of herself . . . It had taken several very painful minutes to convince the woman that her decision was a solid, objective fact, and not open to negotiation.

She was still recovering from the effort a few minutes later, when Brad strode in without knocking. He was carrying the computer print-out of the student grades, and he looked more dour than Victoria had ever seen him.

'I'd like you to reconsider this now,' he said, holding the print-out towards Victoria.

She tried to keep her voice steady. 'I've just been asked to reconsider it by his mother.'

'Yes, and now I'd like to ask you again.' It seemed he had thrust a pen into her hand, which was poised above the print-out. He stood waiting, his expression stiff and remote.

'I'm afraid it's out of the question,' she heard herself say.

It was more a matter of *can't* than *won't*; a sense of almost physiological impossibility, like a fish being asked to breathe air.

'You can change it yourself though, if you want to. I won't tell anyone.'

She flinched as if from an expected blow, as Brad leaned over the desk towards her and snatched the pen back from her hand.

He folded up the print-out.

'Very amusing,' he said, and walked out, leaving her with a sense of victory which even at the time felt curiously incomplete.

She sat in the wintry shadows of her flat, facing the darkened screen of the television where the figure had tripped and lurched and spun out of control. For a moment she felt an urge to switch the set on again, not that the programme was likely to be on the same subject any longer. But even suppose it was, she told herself, and suppose the figure was indeed her Carl Pepperall, and suppose, purely for the sake of hypothesis, that something unpleasant had happened to him; what did any of that have to do with her? She assured herself that she had done nothing to be ashamed of, that she had acted out of the same high, unflinching principle as she was now bringing to her old professor's book on Epicharmus. In the end one could only shrug, and dismiss the episode, if there even was an episode, as a grotesque coincidence, of the kind that life occasionally throws up in imitation of those engineered by the lesser tragedians. It would be a mistake to look for any meaning in it. She switched on a light, and returned to her review.

But she was in tumult. She saw the white tulips again, the treacherous steam, and the vibrant white blur of mountainside with the body sprawled on it. She saw the mother again, and the son's face buried in her features. A tremor went through her. She sensed briefly the cold touch of eternity that had used her intricate, coiled-up soul as its instrument, and felt how exquisitely it had fingered the keys.

The Volunteer

There was a new resident at the shelter. She was small and bony with dark, olive-coloured skin. Her face was a little puffy, which might have been from bruises, or prolonged sleeplessness, or dissipation of one kind or another. She wore a tracksuit of faded mauve cotton, with frayed drawstrings dangling from the hood, and elastic cuffs that looked as if they had been nibbled at by mice. Her eyes were narrow and pretty; scimitar-shaped slits with yellowish-brown pupils and unhealthily discoloured whites. The lashes were soft and curled, and she had emphasised them with make-up; a striking contrast to her otherwise drab appearance. Her name was Tina.

The shelter was in the crypt of St Ursula's, a Catholic church in the part of Manhattan called Alphabet City. It consisted of a long, raftered, stone-floored gallery, with bathrooms, a kitchen, and a TV room off to the side. There were statuary cornices under the rafters, and a few crayon Sunday-School pictures on the walls; but the windowless, overheated space was not especially pleasant, and it was up to the residents themselves to make the atmosphere congenial.

There was room for fourteen residents, male and female. They and the night's volunteer ate a communal meal at a refectory table in the kitchen, cooking and cleaning up by roster. Afterwards they would chat or watch television, drinking coffee, and turning the unventilated air blue with cigarette smoke. At a quarter past ten they wheeled out the folded, prison-built beds and set them up in the long gallery; men at one end, women at the other.

We, the volunteers, had a curtained-off annexe to ourselves, at the bottom of a ramp that led up from the crypt to the main body of the church itself. We slept on the same uncomfortable beds as the residents; short, with thin, slippery, plastic-covered mattresses that didn't hold the sheets.

I had been working as a volunteer at the shelter once a week for two months, and I was now considered trained, which meant that I didn't need another volunteer to work with me. Our job was to let in the residents at seven-thirty in the evening, open locked store cupboards if extra supplies were needed, turn out the lights at ten-thirty, and make sure everyone was gone by seven in the morning. If an argument broke out we were expected to settle it, or get help if we couldn't; if residents turned up showing signs of intoxication of any kind, we were supposed to send them away. In practice such occurrences were virtually unheard of: the residents were screened before being referred to the shelter, and quite apart from it being in their interest to keep the place in good order, they were aware of what expulsion meant. Several of them had spent time at the city's Public Shelters, and what they said confirmed all the worst rumours of squalor and violence in circulation at that time.

Our role was largely symbolic then: we represented the domiciled among the homeless, and this gave us our authority. Because of the kind of people we were, and because almost nothing untoward ever occurred, we carried this authority awkwardly, like a burden, and tended to compensate for it with an exaggerated humility, an over-eager solicitousness with the residents, which made relations with them intricate and sometimes anxious. I was no exception in this.

Nevertheless, in my two months there, I had become attached to the place. I got on well with most of the residents, and I had even become fond of the physical surroundings. The metal cupboards and calcium-bearded radiators, the soiled woollen curtains dividing off the volunteers' annexe (the wool itself like carded dust); the bits of carpet remnant in the TV room; the opaque lamp globes, each with a fuzz of city soot like a shaven head; the refectory table in its sticky sweat of wax: the whole dingy, grimed-over place with its almost human air of shrugging unillusion, had become familiar to me and unexpectedly comforting.

Almost as soon as we sat down to dinner I saw that Tina, the new resident, had not settled in.

The communal meal was the focal point of the evening; for many residents undoubtedly the highlight of their day. From my first visit, I had been struck by the warmth and liveliness of the occasion: these were people who had been exposed to prolonged and quite extraordinary hardship, but between what for many of them were the more or less blank hours of daytime

wandering, and the oblivion of sleep; against the bare
surroundings of the shelter itself, an atmosphere of
surprising cheerfulness and neighbourly goodwill
flourished for an hour or so each evening.

It was here that the more extrovert among the residents came into their own: Subalowsky with his
wheezy chest and paralysed hand; Pam, young, acne-
scarred, with her candid but strangely impersonal
descriptions of her counselling sessions and Antabuse
treatment; Selwyn from Arkansas, always stylishly
turned-out, flamboyant, with an elaborate courtesy in
all his gestures; Lucky with her boxer's black eyes,
cropped hair, white stubble on her chin, and raucous
laugh that retroactively turned anything that prompted
it into a dirty joke . . . The talkers talked, but the shyer,
more dazed or withdrawn were also included in the
general current of conviviality. They participated
quietly, with sympathetic smiles or other small gestures
of attentiveness, and even the most depressed among
them would seem briefly distracted from their problems.

Tina however, the newcomer, appeared to be making
little effort to enter into this spirit. If anything, she
seemed to be keeping herself deliberately aloof. She sat
a little back from the table, holding her plate in her
lap and concentrating on it with a severe, preoccupied
look. I saw that most of the people talking attempted
to include her in their audience, though even then, still
relatively soon after she had first come to the shelter,
there was a noticeable hesitancy in their gaze as it
settled on her, as if she had already accustomed them
to having their attentions rebuffed.

At one point she turned conspicuously in my direction. Selwyn was joking about his attempts to join the National Guard in Arkansas –

'I said I wanted to be the first negro married to a president of the United States. Apparently I had the wrong attitude . . . '

While he was talking Tina caught my eye with a distinctly contemptuous look in her own. It was as if some lofty and scornful pact existed between us. Other residents noticed this, and watched for my reaction. I had hardly spoken a word to Tina so far, and her gesture – unaccountable, oddly decisive in its execution, impossible to ignore – took me by surprise. Aware of the delicacy of my position, wishing neither to snub the newcomer nor offend Selwyn, I assumed a diplomatically abstracted look, and the small tension of the moment passed. However, it left me with the impression of a strong and not very likeable personality.

The following week Tina gave me a grin as she came through the entrance of the shelter.

'Hello Simon.'

She was carrying an empty-looking valise. I noticed a jerkiness in the way she walked; a faint, puppet-like tottering movement in each step.

While dinner was being prepared she stood near me as if she wanted to talk. I gave her my volunteer's smile, and she sat down next to me at the refectory table, where I was shredding lettuce on a chopping board. She pulled her chair close to mine, glancing around at the other people in the kitchen. When she spoke, it was in a low, whispery voice, so that I had to lean towards her in order to follow. As I did, I caught a musty smell of sandalwood.

'So, Simon, you having a good time?'

'Yes thank you. Are you?'

'You been working here long?'

'Two months. A little over.'

'How old you are?'

'I'm thirty.'

'You from Europe or someplace, right?'

'My mother's English. I used to live in England.'

'What's your other name?'

I told her my surname.

'What name is that?'

'It's Jewish, if that's what you mean.'

'How long you been in this country, Simon?'

'Two years, on and off.'

'You like it?'

'On the whole. What about you, do you like it?'

'You got family over here, right?'

'Hey Tina – ' this was Selwyn, laying the table with the kitchen's yellowing silverware and unbreakable plastic plates, ' – what is this, some kind of interrogation?'

Tina ignored him. I busied myself for a second, loading the shredded lettuce into a tupperware bowl. Another helper put two sagging loaves of sliced white bread beside it. A thick, sugary smell drifted from the stove, where store-donated cans of Franks and Beans had been emptied into a big saucepan.

'My father's in Vermont,' I told Tina. 'He has a sister here in the city.'

Selwyn turned away with a shrug.

Tina went on; 'Sister, huh? She have children?'

'She has two sons.'

'Your cousins.'

'That's right – '

'You been married?'

'No, I've never been married. What about you?'

'You a homo?'

'No, I'm not as a matter of fact.'

'Girlfriend, right?'

'Not at the moment. Shall we help them set the table?'

'She leave you for some other guy?'

'No – '

'You leave her?'

'I suppose so, yes.'

Tina grinned. 'Uh huh. Uh huh. I got a favour I might have to ask you Simon.'

'Please do. I'd be very glad to help.'

'You a lawyer right?'

'No, I'm afraid I'm not a lawyer.'

'Oh. But you a Jew?'

'Yes, why? What did you want to ask?'

Her eyes slid away, then settled again on mine. They were delicately curved at the outer corners; thin little oases in the otherwise harsh landscape of her face. She broke into a whispery laugh.

'I'm jiving you man. I'm jiving you.'

She put her hand on my wrist. The hand felt light and hard as a bird's foot. She went on with her questioning. After it ended a strained feeling lingered with me, as if I had been exposed to something more turbulent and oppressive than had appeared to be the case.

At dinner on my third week since Tina's appearance,

I saw that people no longer attempted to bring her
into the conversation. Subalowsky, demonstrating how
he had got the repetitive motion injury that had paralysed his hand (he had been a barman, and he mimed
a drink-pouring action with his stiffened, fin-like limb),
managed a curious rift or lacuna in the arc of his gaze,
that succeeded in excluding Tina entirely as he looked
around the table, drawing in his tribute of laughter.
She sat in her own dark sphere; small and isolated. I
thought I could see in her expression something of a
shunned child's defiant pride in proving to itself a kind
of negative mastery of circumstances. In a professional
way I felt concerned for her. But I had not taken to
her personally, and my sympathies were with the other
residents, whom I knew to be unusually tolerant of the
foibles and weaknesses of their fellow humans.

That night, as I came out of the volunteer's bathroom
at the top of the ramp that led up from the annexe to
the sacristy entrance of the church, I heard a sound to
the right of me, from inside the church. Looking
through, I saw Tina standing next to a pillar, lit by the
dim glow of the sconce lamps that hung over the main
entrance. She was wearing a bathrobe of brown towelling. Her feet and legs were bare.

'Hi,' she whispered.

'Hello, Tina.'

'How you doing?'

'I'm fine, thank you. How are you?'

'Alright.'

I waited, still standing by the bathroom door, several
paces from her. Except in emergencies, this part of the
building was strictly off-limits to residents, and by my
distance, as well as a deliberate sternness in my manner,

I was intending to convey the suggestion of a rebuke on behalf of the shelter, without going so far as to say anything direct.

'Was there something you wanted?'

She grinned, putting a finger over her lips. Then, beckoning at me to follow, she stepped away from the pillar, further back into the shadows of the church. Uneasy, but reluctant to assert myself any more forcefully at this moment, I followed her into one of the wooden pews. She slid along to the far end, patting the space beside her. I sat where she had motioned. We were in near-darkness here, the surroundings visible only as pale strokes of light over prominences or the uneven parts of polished surfaces – stone wings, the angled lip of the pulpit. Two parallel gleams like dim copper showed in Tina's lap where her thin thighs came out of the bathrobe. The same stale, dry scent of sandalwood that I had caught before was upon her. As a purely physical sensation I was aware of her flimsiness, her physical vulnerability and near-nakedness beside me. I felt the awkwardness of my position, and sensed that I should not have allowed myself to be led here. Possibly, it occurred to me, there was an element of gratuitous manipulation on Tina's part; a simple revelling in being able to make the volunteer do what she asked. Thinking back to our conversation the previous week, the mention of a favour, it crossed my mind also that she had come here to beg or perhaps beguile a sum of money from me. I looked up at the ceiling, bracing myself for a difficult conversation.

Beside me on the pew there was movement; an arm rising, a whisper of clothing. I became aware of Tina's

hand sliding under the lapel of her robe as if to with-
draw something.

'Look,' I heard.

Her hand was at the lapel, cupped tightly as if she
were half afraid to reveal its contents. It took me
several seconds to realise that what she was showing
me was in fact a thickly folded wad of dollar bills.

'Two hundred seventy dollars.' She held it out
towards me. 'You take it.' It seemed she was urging
the small bundle onto me. 'You hold it for me, okay?'
I said nothing, not fully comprehending. She spoke
again, in a hoarse whisper. 'You look after it for me,
right? I'm not legal in this country. I can't get a bank.
You be my banker.'

She found my hand in the darkness, and pressed the
money into it.

In my private embarrassment at my earlier conjec-
ture, my grateful surprise at having had it proved
wrong, I heard myself agreeing with alacrity to do
what she asked. I wasn't even able to bring myself to
count the money in her presence.

I counted it under the bedside lamp in the volunteers'
annexe and saw that it was as she had said: two hundred and seventy dollars. The bills were very soft and
frail, the print worn off in places from repeated fold-
ings. They were warm too, and gave off a fragrance of
sandalwood.

In the morning I handed Tina a receipt for the
money, with my telephone number on the back of the
piece of paper. In case she needed cash during the
week, I put the money – the bills themselves – into a
desk drawer at my apartment.

It grew there, a little larger every week. Tina didn't

offer to tell me where it came from, and in keeping with the tacit code of conduct for volunteers, I didn't ask. It would have been difficult to imagine a legitimate source.

The bright air of late autumn dissolved into blustery rain and sleet. The city, almost South American in summer, shed the last of its carnival colour, and turned into a chilly European metropolis; grey, wet and miserable. Darkness poured into the day at both ends. Under the projects the leafless pin-oaks and ailanthus trees caught their winter foliage of tattered plastic bags.

In fairness to myself I should say that I realised almost immediately that I had made a mistake in allowing myself to become involved in Tina's affairs. Quite apart from the fact that the shelter organisers would almost certainly not have approved of one of their members acting as private banker for a resident, it soon became apparent to me that the arrangement was having little or no stabilising effect on Tina's behaviour at the shelter. She continued to be unsociable, if not downright aggressive, and this made me nervous about my position.

By the time the pile of bills in my desk drawer had risen to almost five hundred dollars, I was beginning to think that I should disengage myself. One night I made an attempt to do so.

We were at the top of the ramp, by the sacristy entrance to the church, where Tina had come, as usual, to give me the week's instalment. I put it to her that she might feel safer keeping her money with the shelter organisers than with me. I said I was sure the coordinator would be willing to make a similar arrangement, and that there would be no danger of him reporting her to the Immigration authorities.

'What's the matter,' Tina said immediately, 'you don't want to help me no more?'

'No, I just had a feeling you might not be happy with the way things stood at the moment.'

An expression that was both wounded and suspicious came into her face.

'You don't want to help me no more.'

'Of course I want to help you Tina.'

'No, man, you don't want to help me.'

She stood in a stiff, angular poise, breathing deeply through her nostrils, as if absorbed in sombre and disturbing reflection. Her hand was still at the lapel of her bathrobe, where it had gone in anticipation of giving me the money.

'What can I say, Tina? I want to help you very much.'

'You saying you don't want to help me. That's what I'm hearing.'

Her voice was rising. I felt trapped and agitated, sensing a convergence of ancient, unknowable sorrows with a possible talent for histrionics. I wondered too whether I was perhaps after all being too scrupulously cautious. In my own conscience I already stood accused of lacking genuine sympathy for her, and it struck me now that I might be also guilty of setting my own peace of mind above hers, in a way that was both cowardly and unnecessary.

'I was only making a suggestion,' I heard myself say in a yielding voice.

She looked at me with her lips tightly closed. I felt unable to press the point any further.

'Why don't you give me the money and we'll forget I said anything?'

I held out my hand for the money. But with her instinct for the psychological advantage, she tightened the towelling robe at her neck instead of giving me the money, and stepped back. She stared at me, saying nothing. A bright moistness showed under the soft bluish lashes of her eyes. I looked back at her, unsure what to say or do.

'Why don't you give it to me?' I said gently.

Again she tugged at the lapel of the towelling robe, leaving her forearm across her breast with a protective air. The soles of her feet showed light and yellowish under her heels.

'You don't like me.'

'I do like you, Tina.'

'No, man, I don't think you like me.'

I put my hand appeasingly on her arm.

'Come on Tina, I like you very much.'

'Why you don't want to help me then?'

She stood stiffly, looking obstinately away from me. For a moment something quite acutely touching and poignant seemed expressed in the posture. I squeezed her arm lightly with my hand. She softened in my grip. Looking into my eyes, she took a step forward. As she did, I felt an unexpected stirring: almost as much in response, I think, to a sudden glimpse of her reality as a human being, unobscured by the veil of ideas and surmises which in my ignorance I had woven around her, as to the sense of her reality as a woman. I drew back, surprised at myself. Her eyes flickered over me. She looked pretty and knowing.

'Come on now,' I said, reverting to my brisker

manner, 'let me take the money and we'll go on with things the way they were.'

She drew the limp, dust-grey and green bundle from the inside pocket of her robe, and held it close to her.

I put my hand out to take it, but she continued to hold it back.

'Give it to me Tina. I'll look after it.'

Still she didn't offer the little bundle. An almost playful look of contrariness came into her face, as if on an inexplicable whim she had now decided to tease me with the money. Exasperated, both with her and with myself for handling the situation so badly, I spoke impatiently –

'Give me the money Tina!'

It came out more harshly than I had intended, but the effect was swift. She gave me a peculiar smile; at once submissive and satisfied.

'Okay Simon' – she spoke in a tone that I can only describe as coquettish – 'you the boss.'

She handed me the money and walked away with light, quick steps. I stood for a while, uncertain what had passed between us, sensing that I had in some way been appropriated into the fantastical afflictions of a soul more disturbed than I had yet realised, and that far from bringing our arrangement to an end, I had become more deeply implicated in it than before.

In December I spent a week at my father's farmhouse in Vermont. His wife's two daughters were there with their husbands and children. Four feet of snow lay on the ground outside. In the afternoons we went up into the sparkling woods on cross-country skis, watching the landscape unfold beneath us as we climbed; frozen ponds and diamond-bright meadows, church spires sharp as the icicles dangling from the eaves of the gold-windowed Capes and cabins. Leafless maples rolled through the dark evergreens. At night, after the children had been put to bed, we sat in the resplendent glow of the glass-doored stove in the living-room, talking and drinking, gazing out through the windows at the white birches standing luminously against the shadowy volumes of my father's barn; an enormous, bulging building, stocked like an ark with two or more of everything – two cars, two pick-up trucks, two deep freezes, two canoes, skis two by two in racks along the walls . . .

I arrived back in New York on the day I was due at the shelter, and went straight there from Penn Station.

There were lilies in the crypt, and a jug of yellow chrysanthemums on the refectory table.

I had never seen flowers at the shelter before, and the sight startled me.

Looking about, I noticed that the place had been given a thorough clean. The soot on the globe lamps had been wiped off, and the opaque glass sparkled overhead. All the surfaces were gleaming. A clean, pleasant smell of furniture polish filled the TV room.

In the volunteers' annexe I opened the cupboard where emergency numbers and occasional messages were left. There was a note inside. 'To those of you I haven't yet reached: Tina D'Oliveira arrived two nights running under obvious influence of narcotics, and we had to ask her to leave. This is very distressing for us all, but you'll appreciate we're obliged to enforce our few rules strictly. In Tina's place we have a newcomer, Geraldine Leal, who as you will see has already made her presence felt in the shelter. As ever, please do all you can to make her feel welcome at St Ursula's.' The note was signed by Abel McCormick, the coordinator of the programme.

I closed the cupboard door and went back into the kitchen to put on coffee for the residents. I remember standing at the shiny zinc counter, spooning coffee grounds into the big, frilled filter. The chrysanthemums on the table were a brighter yellow than the kitchen's low-wattage bulbs, giving their tangled heads an over-brimming, incandescent appearance that fused itself into the still not fully absorbed impact of what I had read, and seemed at that moment the vehicle of imminent catastrophe pressing through from the hypothetical into the real. I reminded myself that I had given Tina my telephone number, and this gave me a feeling of at least provisional calm.

At dinner I asked what had happened.

'They throwed her out,' the woman called Lucky said with a shrug.

Subalowsky described it: 'She showed up Sunday night barely able to stand on her two feet. The volunteer said he couldn't let her into the shelter in that condition. He told her to straighten out before she came back. Next night she comes back even worse. Jessica was the volunteer that night. She told Tina she couldn't come in, but she wouldn't leave. She pulled out a sheetrock knife and stood in the doorway yelling and screaming, threatening anyone who came near here . . . '

Selwyn broke in – 'She spit at me! She spit at me!'

'Jessica had to telephone Mr McCormick. He came over right away. Told Tina she was out of the pro-

gramme and to take her things and leave right away or
he'd call the cops.'

'And she left?'

'Yep. She left.'

There were no expressions of sympathy, and the
conversation soon turned to lighter matters. I had the
impression that the residents were satisfied, not just
with the removal of an unstable element from their
midst, but with the severity of the shelter's rules; that
they took a stern pleasure in seeing them enforced.

After dinner I went straight to the volunteers' annexe
and sat on the hard plastic chair. Contented murmurs
reached me from the crypt. The heating knocked in
the pipes and hissed with a long, bubbling suspiration.
I thought of the money in my desk drawer at home,
and told myself again that I had given Tina my telephone number; that even if she had lost it, she could
get hold of me through the shelter.

But with the image of the soft, sweet-smelling pile
of bills nestling among my papers, came a feeling of
oppressive disclosure, as if I were being presented with
a sudden privileged inward glimpse into my position
at the shelter. In what was still effectively the shock
of the moment, the circumstances seemed to me to
embody more than they could perhaps be said to contain on the basis of a rational analysis. As I write now
I think of Frantz Fanon's austere stipulation: 'it is
necessary at all times and in all places to make explicit,
to demystify, and to harry the insult to mankind that
exists in oneself.' Precisely that passive, unintended,
but nevertheless culpable relation was what seemed
exposed in me, and no doubt what this connection
lacked in logic, was more than made up for by my

abundant willingness to take a symbolic or even super-
stitious interpretation of anything pertaining to my
own uneasy status as volunteer. What was a volunteer;
someone who wanted to help or someone who wanted
to guard the door? Were our motives ones of simple
charity, or did we suffer from some morbid wish to
enact within our own psyches, to illuminate by our
own lives, the essential relations between one part of
society and another, just as the sin-eaters of another
century elected to absorb into themselves both the
wrongs and the due punishment of their sinning breth-
ren? It was like being shown an X-ray of some part
of your body, your chest for instance, the physician
pointing to a bright, calcined maculation behind the
ribs: a surprise, certainly, but one that nevertheless
seems to confirm something you had always known
without knowing that you knew it.

The next day I made enquiries with the police and at
other shelters in the city: nobody had heard of Tina.
At that point I told Abel McCormick what had
happened. He apparently thought it unnecessary to
reprimand me for allowing myself to get into such a
situation, and instead merely suggested that I hand over
Tina's money to the shelter, on the understanding that
it would be given back to her if she turned up to claim
it. I wrote out a cheque at once, and used the cash
she had given me for my own expenses. The smell of
sandalwood lingered in my desk, and long after I had
spent the last of the bills the sweet, dry fragrance would
rise up from the folds of my wallet whenever I opened
it to make a purchase.

Two or three weeks passed without a word from

Tina. Whether she ever turned up at the shelter after
that to claim her money I have no idea. In February
I began a new job, and I no longer had time to work
as a volunteer.

I did however see Tina on one more occasion.

I had turned into a quiet, dilapidated block just south
of Houston, on my way to have dinner with a friend
in the Lower East Side. Light, sharp sleet was falling,
briefly fluorescent where it slanted down through the
red and gold illuminations of a store on the corner.
Granular residue shone on broken stones where the
sidewalk had erupted under pressure of tree roots or
burst water pipes. Fire escapes clung to the fronts of
the tenements on my side of the street; saggy and
rusty, with a ponderous ornateness like the weavings
of a battalion of cast-iron spiders. Most of the opposite
side was empty lots – boarded-up or fenced-off with
padlocked chainlink and looped razor-wire.

On that side, near the far end of the block, a figure
had emerged from a gap between two sheets of corrug-
ated iron, and set off swiftly in my direction. As we
came closer to each other I saw that it was Tina. A
feeling of relief surged in me, though it became rapidly
tinged with apprehension as she approached.

She was walking at a fierce pace. Her hands were
working at her sides, and she seemed to be expostulat-
ing as she moved. She hadn't noticed me, or at least
hadn't seen that it was me. I looked at her as she came
nearer. The jerkiness in her walk was more pronounced
than I had seen it before – a suggestion of involuntary
movement flickering over each footstep. The
impression was of some hostile emotion metabolised
into the actual musculature; echoed strangely, like a

kind of livid afterglow, by the indecipherable but peculiarly expressive graffiti on the boards she passed, the word-forms midway along an apparent regression from alphabetic to hieroglyphic; some spattered out, some creamed out in a bendy, lubricious strut, others glowering in a hallucinatory rainbow smoulder; all of them suggestive of some dense extrusion of human fury and wonder. A rapid, unintelligible mutter became audible: imprecations, by the look on her face. Either side of her, her stiffened, spread-out fingers were jabbing at the air. She looked packed tight with violence, like a bristling mine ready to explode at the slightest touch. As we came level, I saw from a rolling whiteness in her eyes that she was probably not in a condition to recognise me.

'Tina!' I called out.

She plunged on past me. I crossed over, feeling a lightness in my limbs as I ran after her.

'Tina,' I said, catching up with her. She strode on, fast and oblivious, her muttered words no more distinct at this proximity than from across the street. I reached out with my hand.

'Tina, it's me, Simon,' I touched her on the shoulder.

She spun around. A look of terror shone in her narrow eyes, which seemed not to see me so much as to search for me through an enveloping veil of darkness; one of her hands appearing partly to grope, partly to pummel at the space between us. I reached into my coat, intending at the very least to make her take whatever I had in my wallet. As I pulled it out I felt what seemed like the whiplash of a white-hot wire across my knuckles; a sensation that left me stupefied for a moment, with nothing in my mind except Subalowsky's phrase *sheetrock knife* flashing there like a message on a console in an empty office. I stood there with my hand spread before me, a string of blood-beads swelling across the shallow cut, the smell of sandalwood hanging in the air – fragrance of a desolation beyond the reach of pity or even understanding; of a reproach too deep and bitter for forgiveness – while Tina sped off with the same peculiar stammering articulation, as if in the painful embrace of some invisible, ratcheting, mechanical apparatus; the big, glittering coils of razor-wire running along the wooden boards above her like a new and savage decorative order.

Three Evenings

1

Jonathan was twenty-two when he met Katie Vairish, and he was new to London. Katie was older than him by six years. A cousin of Jonathan's introduced them at a wedding reception in Surrey, where Jonathan had grown up and several of his relatives lived. The cousin described him as an aspiring journalist, and the ghost of a smile crossed Katie Vairish's face.

She wore high heels and a sleeveless crushed velvet dress with fingerprint-like smudges gleaming all over it in the electric light. Her brown hair was cut in a short bob, leaving the smooth curves of her neck and shoulders bare except for a thin necklace of coral and silver. Her name sounded familiar to Jonathan; vaguely, and for some reason also a little forbiddingly. She made him nervous, but whether out of capriciousness or because his diffident manner genuinely endeared him to her, she seemed to make up her mind to like him. Before they parted she wrote down his number and promised to commission something from him for the magazine where she worked as an editor.

He had finished university six months before, with a degree in history, and the offer of a place to do postgraduate work, which he had declined. To the extent that he believed a moment would arrive in his life when he would be the author of a number of written works, his cousin's description of him was not wholly inaccurate. What these works would be about he had no idea, but this didn't trouble him.

He was dark, and of slight build. His eyes were brown but the pigment was thinly concentrated in the vane of the irises, giving them a translucent look that was the most striking aspect of his appearance.

Otherwise there was an indistinctness about him: he was like something that had not quite set. He was aware of this but it didn't trouble him any more than the content of his unwritten books did. He believed what he had read in Kierkegaard about the self: that its task 'is to become itself'; and he felt that he had a long time to accomplish this task. At a certain point his nature would declare itself more forcefully and he would step forward to take his place in the world. How he occupied himself in the meantime was unimportant. It didn't matter to him that the walls of the room he rented in Acton were streaked yellow with damp, that the furniture was hideous, the curtains and carpets embedded with the dirt of his predecessors. Nor did it matter much to him what he did for money: he interrogated train passengers for a market-research company; he taught history 'O' and 'A' level at a crammer in Holborn. All of this was temporary and unimportant to him; he was just camping down in his life for the time being.

Over a period of two years Katie commissioned per-

haps a dozen pieces from him – trivial things mostly;
reviews of consumer exhibitions at Olympia, interviews
with up-and-coming actors or chefs. It amused him to
write them, though after a while he took the work less
because he needed it than for the excuse to visit Katie
in her office high over the Euston Road.

Unalike as they were – she with her trailing aura of
gossipy dinner parties, her six years' seniority; he with
his taciturn and slightly provincial air – a subdued but
nevertheless suspenseful interest in one another had
grown up between them. And although the intervals
between his visits were long, each one brought about
a perceptible deepening of this interest.

She was pretty in a languid, rather over-delicate way,
with big, long-lashed eyes, high cheekbones and bluish
skin. She was very thin, a heavy smoker, always well-
dressed in furling outfits of black or grey, with a rose-
bud or a brooch or a hand-pleated silk scarf for colour.

In the soft leather chairs of her office, with the blinds
half-closed against the evening sky and the rush-hour
traffic crawling like two metal-scaled serpents in the
dusk below, they would drink gin and tonics and talk
together with a warm and effortless intimacy. It was
perhaps this quality, this effortlessness, that Jonathan
valued most about their friendship. He felt relaxed with
Katie and under no pressure to disclose what wasn't
yet ready for disclosure. Other women tended to take
his quietness as a ploy to keep them at arm's length,
or else as the sign of a superior wisdom, which usually
resulted in disappointment; when in fact it was just
that he was still more or less a mystery to himself.
Katie on the other hand, with the simple egotism
of an attractive woman unused to probing her own

inclinations, merely adapted his quietness to her own needs: she made him the repository of her confidences, and this suited him. He was a good listener, and many of their conversations consisted of little more than Katie complaining about the men – the barristers, merchant bankers or television producers – that she got herself involved with, while Jonathan murmured sympathetically in response.

At the same time, with a characteristic disregard for apparent inconsistency that lent her life a curious plasticity, she flirted with Jonathan when the mood took her, and it was settled between them that they were attracted to each other; a fact that gave their discussions of her lovers an undercurrent of faint tragedy.

When they parted company for the night, Katie would say goodbye in a way that made it seem as if their separation was simply an inconvenience, a quirk of fate that had to be put up with for the time being, but would eventually be corrected. She would put her mouth to his, and on one occasion she opened her lips a little, without actually opening her mouth, but staying like that for a moment, looking up at him intently from under her long lashes, before pulling away. He happened to be involved at that time with a woman at the tutorial college where he taught; a fact which Katie knew perfectly well. He went home feeling exhilarated and bewildered, the after-impression of her lips lingering in a sweet taste of perfume and cigarette smoke.

Sometimes they would go out together for a drink or a meal. Once, about a year and a half into their acquaintance, when Katie had moved into a new flat, they went to an auction in Fulham. Jonathan hadn't been to an auction before.

'You've never been to an auction? Oh, they're the most exciting things. It's like going to the races only being the jockey as well as the person betting.'

The auction house was in a quiet street between an office building and a row of antique shops with their shutters down. It looked as if it had once been a warehouse: sombre Victorian brick on the outside, chilly and cavernous inside, with bare floorboards and dusty white globe lamps hanging on chains from iron beams.

There was a pulpit, a real pulpit, for the auctioneer. Rows of chairs stood in front of it, waiting for the prospective buyers to settle. Around these, and spreading back through several more rooms, pieces of furniture and cabinets of bric-à-brac were heaped densely together, stark-looking, and mysteriously drained of colour by the glare of the white lamps.

Dozens of people, most of them smartly dressed and in couples, milled about the cluttered rooms examining table-legs and sofa-backs, looking for hallmarks on cutlery, pressing the keys of upright pianos, checking tea-sets for cracks, and oriental rugs for stains. Amused, slightly sheepish expressions were visible on many faces, as if their owners were unsure of the dignity of the ceremony, or at least felt it necessary to build up a playfully ironic attitude toward the imminent public declarations of taste and acquisitive will. There was a slight tense gaiety in the air, as at the beginning of a social function. Against the orphaned clutter with its faint aura of misfortune, the human beings looked bright and predatory.

Katie and Jonathan wandered about, looking at the

estimates in the stapled catalogue they had picked up from the entrance, and marking off items that appealed to Katie – a mirror with a pear-wood frame; a sloping school desk with an inkwell; woollen fruits under a glass dome.

'This is fun, isn't it Jonathan?'

Jonathan smiled at her, catching the look of antici-pated pleasure in her eyes.

She was carrying her coat, and wearing a short dress with the flowery black lace tights that were fashionable that year. Her lithe figure drew glances from the men who passed her. Normally a little pallid, her face took on a delicate glow against the inanimate background. Against these things she had the pale, slightly improb-able incandescence of a winter flower against snow. Her scent rose, now and then, lightly over the dull must of wood and iron. Looking at her Jonathan felt a momentary, curious anguish, and a wish to deny to himself that he thought her beautiful. He wondered if people could tell that he and she were not a couple furnishing their home together. He thought that they probably could, and he tried to work out why this should be so. Without forming any very definite con-clusions, he found the thought converging unexpec-tedly with his sense of the effortlessness of their relations with each other, and the idea that these two things might be connected disturbed him so much that he immediately turned his attention to something else.

They came to a partitioned room that appeared to be devoted to lighting fixtures. There were upright lamps, table lamps, wall sconces, track lights, lamp-shades of every description. At the far end were chan-deliers, hanging from a bar, or sitting on the bare floor.

Most of these chandeliers were glass, with cobwebby riggings and thick coats of dust over their faceted lustres, but on the floor in the corner was a more resplendent-looking one, made entirely of gilded ironwork. A man in a camel-hair coat was bending over it, fingering the matt gold radial of looping bulb-holders. Clusters of oak leaves and acorns sprouted all over the armature, very delicately moulded in the same gilt iron; the leaves almost leaf-thin, wobbling a little in the light as the man examined them with a thick finger and thumb.

Katie paused to look at it from the doorway.

'God, isn't that lovely?'

She went over to the corner, moving in deft steps and turns like a graceful forest animal through a small grove of standard lamps, and leant down to touch the chandelier. Jonathan followed behind.

'Don't you think it's rather wonderful Jonathan?'

'Quite nice,' Jonathan said.

'I mean it's nothing special but it's cheerful, and I could do with a few cheerful things . . . '

The man who had been examining the chandelier stood up. Katie smiled at him vaguely. He looked away and moved on, marking his sheet.

'Yes, I think I might bid for that.' Katie said. 'Do you see what the estimate is?'

Jonathan looked through the catalogue.

'Sixty-five pounds.'

'Well, I should think it'll go for double that. They usually give a low estimate, to make you start thinking of it as your own. But that's alright, it's worth double, wouldn't you say?'

'If you can afford it.'

'I think so. I'm quite taken with it. I think I could go up to a hundred and thirty for it.' She turned to Jonathan; a lively look had come into her eyes.

He smiled at her.

'No higher though,' she said, 'you have to make up your mind in advance, otherwise you get carried away. Stop me at a hundred and thirty, would you?'

'Alright.'

'I mean it. Shut me up at a hundred and thirty if the bidding's still going.'

'If you say so.'

'I do say so.'

Soon after that a bell rang and people took their seats for the auction.

A young man with a bow tie and yellow silk handkerchief mounted the pulpit. Porters in green boiler-suits collected below him, and a bespectacled woman sat at a table with a ledger. A big reflector heater was switched on and the two thick bars glowed brightly in their wire cage, sending out a wave of raw heat into the chilly room.

After winking and mouthing hellos at various members of his congregation, the auctioneer banged his gavel, and went over the rules of the auction.

'Signal clearly, I can't read your thoughts. Those of you with epilepsy or St Vitus Dance kindly sit on your hands unless you wish to leave here with a large amount of unwanted possessions. All successful bids are final and binding. A porter will take your name between lots and I will personally have you gently poached in fish broth if you try telling Phyllis here that you've changed your minds . . . '

There was a little laughter. Katie leaned in close to Jonathan, smiling excitedly. The auction began.

It was fast and efficient. Movable lots were brought rapidly across the front by the porters. The heavier items were described by the auctioneer, always with a little self-important glimmer of facetiousness. There were more than two hundred lots, and after a while a mesmerising rhythm set in.

Four or five pieces that Katie had marked were sold off in bursts of bidding that she took part in briefly, with a short, excited flare like dry tinder being swept over by a grass fire, clutching Jonathan's arm with her free hand while she bid, and letting it go when her limit was passed.

She hadn't bought anything by the time the light fixtures took their turn in the procession of objects passing beneath the pulpit. Jonathan could sense a keener attention stirring in her as they appeared. He himself felt more alert and invigorated; following as always when he was with her the fluctuations of her mood.

Lamps went by in quick succession, seeming by the steadiness of movement more to metamorphose into one another than give way to each other. There was a stream of glass shades with frosting and floral ornamentation. Then the chandeliers began; slung on poles between porters like strange shot-down creatures of the upper air, their dusty glass plumage hanging limp. Katie sat forward on her seat, her back very straight, her lips pursed in concentration. In one hand she held the catalogue, rolled up like a baton. With the other, as her chandelier made its entrance from the wings, she grasped Jonathan's arm.

The bidding started at twenty pounds and rose rapidly, with bids from all over the room. After sixty-five pounds – the catalogue estimate – the pace slowed a little. The seven or eight people bidding dropped to four, and at eighty-five pounds there appeared to be only two other people apart from Katie. Looking around, Jonathan saw an elderly woman, who had already bought a number of things in a rather professional, detached manner, nod when ninety pounds was asked for. Katie raised her rolled-up catalogue at ninety-five, and a figure – the man in the camel-hair coat whom they had seen examining the chandelier earlier – turned round from two rows ahead of them, catching sight of Katie's signal before turning back and nodding at a hundred pounds.

'One hundred pounds. One hundred pounds,' the auctioneer said. 'I'm bid one hundred pounds. Who'll give me one hundred and five. Yes, madam. Yes, other madam, one hundred and ten . . . '

The chandelier hung in the reddish light from the electric heater, looking bright and festive with its delicate sprays of oak leaves and acorns.

'One hundred and ten pounds. Am I bid one hundred and fifteen?'

The auctioneer looked at the elderly woman, who gave a dry little shake of her head.

'One hundred and ten pounds then.'

Jonathan prepared himself now, like an actor with a small part girding himself up for his entrance. He sensed that Katie had given him this role as a way of making him feel he was wanted, and he appreciated the gesture; the more so because of the uncharacteristic thoughtfulness it conveyed.

The man in the camel-hair coat nodded.

'Yes. One hundred and fifteen.'

Katie raised her catalogue. Her other hand had tightened on Jonathan's arm, and he could feel her excitement in the grip.

'One hundred and twenty. One hundred and twenty-five. This is a superb piece, as you can see. Comes from a most distinguished home. Knew its father and mother myself . . . '

Light laughter escaped briefly from the hush of the room.

'One hundred and twenty-five pounds.'

Jonathan whispered to Katie, 'Remember this is your limit.' She raised her catalogue.

'Yes, one hundred and thirty pounds.'

The man immediately bid.

'One hundred and thirty-five pounds.'

Jonathan tapped the hand that was holding his arm. 'Stop now.'

Katie frowned briefly without turning to him, and raised her catalogue.

'Yes, madam, one hundred and forty pounds. I'm bid one hundred and forty pounds . . . '

Jonathan wasn't sure what to do. He had not anticipated resistance, and now he was unsure of the seriousness of Katie's request. The man in front nodded and Katie at once raised her catalogue. Her eyes were wide open, and there was a look of taut, gleeful determination on her face.

'Yes sir. One hundred and fifty-five pounds. Still a bargain at that *if* I may say so. A charming piece, one hundred and sixty pounds, yes. One hundred and sixty pounds.'

What should he do? The situation seemed to rebuke him for lacking force. He took hold of Katie's shoulder and shook it firmly. 'You're over your limit,' he whispered, trying to sound good-humoured.

The man in front nodded and glanced round. He was short, but very broad across the shoulders, with a fleshy, pugnacious face and thick ginger eyebrows. Jonathan squeezed Katie's shoulder again as she raised her catalogue.

'Katie,' he whispered sternly. 'Katie, stop now.'

'Oh be quiet.' She wriggled free of his grasp and gave him an angry look. He sat back feeling as if he had been slapped.

'Am I bid one hundred and seventy-five pounds? Magnificent piece of craftsmanship. Former ear-ring off a giantess, no. Yes. One hundred and seventy-five pounds. One hundred and eighty. One eighty-five. One ninety. One hundred and ninety pounds. I'm bid one hundred and ninety pounds.'

Jonathan looked at Katie. Her face was flushed, her eyes were bright with an intent, malevolent look of pleasure in them. She had never spoken to him in that way before, and he didn't know how he should react. He felt taunted and in a dim way responsible for it himself.

The man in the camel-hair coat bid a hundred and ninety-five pounds. Katie at once signalled two hundred.

'Two hundred pounds,' the auctioneer crowed, pursing his lips in a way that seemed to suggest he was sharing a joke with certain select members of the audience. 'I'm bid two hundred pounds. We rise now in increments of ten pounds. Am I bid two hundred and

ten pounds? Two hundred and ten?' He looked at the
man in the camel-hair coat, raising his eyebrows. There
was no signal.

'Two hundred pounds it is then. For two hundred
pounds this, ah, illuminating creation, going, going,
gone!' He banged his gavel and proceeded to the next
lot.

After the auction was over Katie paid the cashier, and
they made their way out of the building. Jonathan
carried the chandelier, which was heavy and awkward
to hold without bending the sprigs of oak leaves and
acorns. His feeling of injury had not disappeared; if
anything it seemed to be growing stronger.

'You didn't do a very good job of keeping me under
control, did you?' Katie said with a smile.

'What was I supposed to do? Tie you up and gag
you?'

Katie shrugged, declining to acknowledge the petu-
lant note in his voice.

As they left the building they caught up with the
man who had bid against Katie for the chandelier. He
had lit a small cigar, and the whole of his stocky,
corpulent frame seemed absorbed in smoking it. Night
had fallen and it was cold outside. Katie put on the
short suede coat that she had been carrying, and gave
a little shiver. She turned as she passed the man.

'I hope you didn't have your heart set on it – ' she
tilted her head at the chandelier in Jonathan's hands.
A grin with a distant look of insolence in it turned up
the corners of her lips. The man stopped and looked
at her, drawing on his cigar. Under his coat he wore
a grey suit and a pin-stripe shirt with a white collar

that seemed too tight for his thick neck. Starched cuffs with mother-of-pearl cufflinks showed at his wrists. There was a glowering and dissipated look about him; a heavy metropolitan ripeness of early middle age. Removing the cigar from his mouth, he gave a dry look.

'I'll survive,' he said.

Katie eyed him with an abstracted expression for a moment. Jonathan hung beside her, holding the heavy chandelier. People jostled past them along the lamplit street, many with satisfied looks, their arms full of plunder.

'I've just moved into a new flat,' Katie said. 'I hadn't thought of getting a chandelier. I think the glass ones are fairly vile. But when I saw this I thought it would go rather well.'

The man considered this, glancing briefly at Jonathan and turning back to Katie. In his consternation Jonathan shifted the weight of the chandelier, pointedly, but Katie did not appear to notice.

'Well, there you are,' the man said, and gave a little nod. 'It's yours now.'

'You don't feel deprived then?'

'I expect if I'd wanted it badly enough I'd have got it.' He made to go. Jonathan looked at the loose, heavy flesh of his face, willing him away.

'I bet it was a present for someone.' Katie called out.

The man turned. 'As a matter of fact,' he said, then gave a thin, superior smile of his own, 'as a matter of fact that's none of your business.'

Katie laughed. 'Well, don't worry, there's always something here. I come just about every week at the moment. I usually find something I like.'

A flush of dismay went through Jonathan. His arms ached from the heaviness of the chandelier, and the unpleasantness of the situation seemed to add to its weight.

The man nodded again, and marched off. Jonathan watched his squat figure disappear down the lamplit street. He turned to Katie, who gave him a distracted smile and looked about for a taxi.

At home he lay on his bed, going over the evening in his mind.

He thought again of how Katie had asked him to stop her from overbidding, and how he had failed to do so. Well, he could hardly blame himself for that. He had no authority over Katie, and there was nothing in their relationship that gave him any claim on her obedience, even as an instrument of her own will. The sensible reaction would be to shrug off the incident as a case of perversity on Katie's part, that perhaps didn't reflect well on her, but said nothing about himself.

But the incident had lodged itself in him with an oppressive weight, and he was unable to shrug it off. It seemed to accuse him of a weakness that went deeper and deeper, the more he considered it. He saw that either he should not have allowed himself to get into such a position in the first place or, having done so, he should have been effectual. On what basis, by what actions, he could have asserted the necessary authority, he did not know, but he sensed that it could have been done, and that another man might have managed it in his place.

He thought of the casually imperious way in which Katie had shut him up, and a feeling of bitterness welled in him. It struck him that he should have walked out there and then. Anyone with an ounce of pride would have done just that. He pictured himself doing so, and finding in the image a certain satisfaction, pictured it again, and then again. But at the time it hadn't even occurred to him! And not only had he stayed, but he had also meekly carried the chandelier out of the auction house like a lackey; or no, like a prisoner forced to parade in public carrying the instrument of his own torture . . . And as if that wasn't enough, having allowed himself to be insulted and used as a convenient pair of arms, he had then stood by uncomplainingly while Katie had obliquely but unmistakably made an assignation with another man!

He thought of his own lyrical, tender, patient desire for Katie; of how with the minimum effort she kept its ardent little flame alight, and of how he had contentedly accepted that this should be so. It came to him that he disliked her. At the same time he felt a harsh and narrow craving for her.

He got up and closed the heavy curtains. He undressed and went to the basin in the corner of the room. In the mirror over the basin he saw his face, and what he saw did not please him. The pale, translucent eyes that Katie herself had once told him were beautiful, seemed to him unbearably soft and beseeching. He poured a glass of water and lay back down on the bed.

Gradually his feeling of dissatisfaction spread from Katie into matters that had nothing to do with her. He saw that he was the same withheld, closed-up individual that he had been when he left university almost two years before. But whereas then he had been confi-

dent of the presence of all sorts of splendours preparing
themselves inside him, he now found himself wondering if there was anything of interest there at all.

He thought of his unworldliness, and for the first
time suspected it of being no more than a kind of
congealed immaturity. And his days coaching the 'O'-
and 'A'-level failures, or walking up and down the
corridors of trains; the nights in the bed between the
wardrobe with its cracked veneer and the gold rivulets
of damp coursing down the floral wallpaper; were these
situations perhaps slyly taking advantage of his dreamy
passivity to exchange their transitory status in his life
for one of permanence? A mortified feeling came into
him. He turned off the table lamp. The gas fire was
on and he left it to burn up the fifty pence he had put
in the meter. Under watery-blue flames the clay glowed
bright pink and orange, throwing crimson shadows into
the dark room.

2

Not long after this Jonathan decided that it would be a good thing for him if he went and lived abroad for a period.

His natural inertia, as well as an exaggerated idea of the difficulty of earning a living in a foreign country, kept him from acting on this decision for a few months, but over that period he confided it gradually to most of the people he knew, and in this way it took on the galvanising force of a fact with an existence independent of himself.

The offer of an introduction to the editor of an English paper in Rome gave a more precise focus to his thoughts. Addresses, further contacts, and helpful tips followed on, some of them from quite unexpected quarters: the woman he did his market research for had once lived in Rome herself, and gave Jonathan the address of a rental agency that specialised in flats in the old quarter, the Centro Storico; someone else knew of a language school in Parioli that paid a living wage . . .

A plan for living in Rome began to develop, unfolding with a surprising ease and rapidity, which gave it in Jonathan's mind a seal of rightness and predestination.

He enrolled in a short course for teaching English as a foreign language. As part of it he was filmed giving a class to his fellow students. Once again he saw himself as if from the outside, and once again he was dismayed at what he saw: there was something in his bearing that was so shy and innocent, so timidly self-effacing, that he became quite alarmed, and felt more than ever the urgent necessity of putting himself through an experience that would toughen and anneal him.

There had been a slight cooling in his relations with Katie after their evening at the auction house, but in the weeks before Jonathan's departure, they began to see each other regularly again. Soon they were meeting more frequently than ever.

Katie would ring him late in the afternoon and ask if he wanted to have a drink or see a film, and even if he had made some other arrangement, he would usually get out of it. The truth was he still cared more for Katie's company than anyone else's. He found her casual acceptance of all the less reputable instincts of her own psyche strangely soothing and relaxing. Careless, egotistical, amoral, and transparently manipulative as she may have been, he would always feel a definite freeing of certain internal constrictions when he was with her, as if at other times he was permanently anxious and on his guard. He knew that he would prefer to spend an evening with her than with anyone else, even if that meant the risk of being hurt.

Under the pressure of his imminent departure, their friendship took on a new, valedictory, sweetness. The latent attraction between them which had never been quite extinguished, flared up as the days went by.

Jonathan was offered the lease on a flat near the Ponte Sant' Angelo, starting from the beginning of October. Late one afternoon in September he went to meet Katie in her office for a drink.

She greeted him warmly, wearing a girlish frock he hadn't seen before, ruched at the front like a pinafore, with bright cotton embroidery.

Jonathan sat in one of the low leather chairs while she went to the drinks cabinet. When she came over with the drinks she knelt on the floor beside him.

'So, Jonathan, you really are abandoning us.'

She spoke in a quiet voice, looking at the ground.

'Well . . . ' He hadn't seen it in quite those terms, but he felt flattered by the idea, even if he knew Katie well enough to sense also the intention to flatter. 'I'll be back from time to time.'

'Yes, but it won't be the same. You'll just be passing through. You'll find us all unimportant.'

'No, I won't, Katie.'

'Yes you will. Then after a while you'll just forget about us.' This was stated as a simple fact.

'I think it's more likely you'll forget about me.'

'Very funny.' Katie looked up, and to Jonathan's surprise she seemed hurt by his remark.

'Katie, I'm sorry – ' He touched her shoulder and smiled at her.

They went to a pub and sat at a table out in the garden. It was a warm evening. The tops of buses were visible over the trellised palings of the garden. When the breeze blew, an occasional prematurely brown leaf would fall from the plane trees outside and lie on the ground like a dropped glove.

They drank and talked steadily.

'What are you going to *do* in Rome Jonathan?'

'Teach, write articles I hope.'

'No, but what will you do with yourself? You'll get a lovely Italian girlfriend won't you? A student with a bicycle and long black hair, and every night you'll go to the Tre Scalini and eat tartuffi with whipped cream.'

'I don't even know what a tartuffo is.'

'You'll find out.'

She put her hand over his. 'Jonathan, I can't bear to think of you going.'

He turned his hand over to hold hers, which was cool, with long, straight, well-manicured fingers.

'I'll certainly miss you,' he said.

'I'll miss you too.'

They slid their fingers together, looking at each other.

After closing time they walked towards Baker Street. They didn't speak. The air was warm, and the quiet streets still smelled of summer foliage. Streetlamps were couched deep in the branches of trees along the pavements, their light crevicing the dark domes into planes of shoaled leaves, silhouetting them, turning their thin fringes amber. At Baker Street Katie hailed a taxi. They stood by the open door and started to say goodbye. Katie brought her lips to his. The smell of her perfume went sharply through him. She put her hands on his shoulders, turning her head slowly beneath his, and he felt the soft body of her tongue against his own. The taxi waited by them on the kerb with its engine running and its meter turning. A feeling of melting sweetness came into Jonathan. The moment seemed both inevitable and utterly surprising. 'You could come with me,' Katie said. They climbed into the taxi together, and the city's lights slid across the tinted windows.

Katie lived in a basement flat near the Old Brompton Road, with an entrance down a sunken stairwell. Jonathan hadn't been here before. There was a little parquet-floored hall that smelled of polish. One side of it was taken up by a portrait of a scarlet-jacketed cavalry officer on a rearing horse.

They went into the living-room and lay on a sofa in near darkness. They kissed seriously and intently; Katie entering into this role with her characteristic ease of transition. A concentrated attentiveness took possession of Jonathan. The situation seemed to be surging just ahead of him, drawing him along in its wake. He slid the straps of Katie's frock over her shoulders and even at this moment was a little surprised at the action of his own hands.

They made love quietly, almost stealthily, with suppressed cries, as if a part of the pleasure lay in a certain pretence of furtive concealment. Afterwards they bathed together in a deep, old-fashioned bath on four claws, with a curved lip and tall taps that made Jonathan think of two butlers. Water gushed from them and the pipes knocked. Katie lay on her back in his arms, humming to herself while he ran soap over her shoulders and breasts. In a way he felt more intimate with her bathing than making love; more that had been withheld seemed now laid bare.

For several minutes they lay in silence. Vague sensations floated through Jonathan's mind. The sight of Katie's green toothbrush, standing in a glass by the steam-shrouded mirror over the basin, drifted into him on a ripple of inexplicable tenderness. He felt numbed, and richly content.

'What if you didn't go?' he heard Katie say lazily. 'What if you didn't go to Rome?'

He smiled and kissed her wet earlobe. Her nails played lightly across his thighs.

The water cooled. They got out and rubbed them-

selves dry. Katie put on Jonathan's shirt and went to
the kitchen, showing Jonathan to the bedroom and
saying to wait there for her.

This was an untidy room, un-aired, with a smell of
sleep and stale scent. Clothes and magazines were
strewn about. There was a marble bust hung with necklaces and an old green cabin trunk marked Mombasa,
with scarves and sleeves dangling from under the lid
like tentacles from a sunken sea-chest.

Up above the bed hung the chandelier, its candle-
bulbs blazing, and the sharp little knots of gilded ironwork shining brightly. For a moment it was like seeing
an old enemy, and a reflexive annoyance flared in Jonathan briefly. But on consideration, its bracketing of the
elapsed time since he had last seen it gave a sense of
progress that was actually quite satisfying. Here he
was, after all. The thought filled him with an almost
proprietorial pleasure. He stretched out on the candle-
wick bedcover, fully naked, warm and languid from
the bath.

The palms of his hand were softened and still acutely
sensitised; tingling with the memory of the flesh they
had held and caressed. In them and in the tips of his
fingers his sense of Katie, and of what had occurred,
seemed stronger than in his mind. They seemed to hold
the impress of the whole evening like that of a physical
object. He remembered carrying the heavy chandelier
from the auction house. The thought came to him that
he lived almost entirely by physical sensations. Even
his emotions were really no more than codified clusters
of physical sensations. Warmth and cold; hunger and
repleteness; pain and pleasure. He wondered if this was
true of people in general, or if he was in some way

more rudimentary and animal-like in his consciousness than others. He did seem animal-like to himself. He was like a private and solitary animal: something dark and velvet, nocturnal perhaps, neither hostile nor friendly; a little fastidious . . .

Katie reappeared with French bread and a pan full of scrambled eggs. She lay by him and they tore off bits of bread to scoop up the eggs, which were hot and buttery, with chopped chives and freshly ground pepper mixed in with them. They tasted good, and Jonathan ate eagerly.

'We're starving,' Katie said.

Lying there beside her, Jonathan formed the impression that their being together like this – himself naked, Katie wearing his shirt – had a denser reality than most of the scenes he had lived out so far in his life. Whereas those had all been more or less improvised out of the chance furnishings of the moment, this had come, it seemed to him in his slightly exalted condition, as the result of ancient preparations and stately, inflexible natural laws, like a solar eclipse or the appearance of a comet.

As far as he had analysed things before, he had thought that his attraction to Katie was more or less confined to the erotic sphere, with both the force and the limitation that that implied. Now he wondered if there was something more to it. Not love – the blossom said by someone to break miraculously from the sturdy timber of mutual regard – there was none of that upward-aspiring freshness or candour. But he felt something over and above the physical revelry of gratified desire. Thinking about it now, he saw that it was like a fascination, but a fascination that travelled inward rather than outward, that promised to lead back into himself; an inverted narcissism perhaps, with a sweet blemished taste in it like the fruits that can only be eaten in a state of decay, or like an ember's fascination with air. It answered a need that he suspected now had been present in him long before he had met Katie, though he had not been aware of it until then.

She put the pan on the floor and turned to him. One hand supported her chin while the other started stroking his hair.

'Don't go to Rome,' she said.

He smiled as he had before, looking upward at the ceiling.

'Don't go Jonathan. Stay here in London.'

She spoke in a quiet voice, turning a lock of his hair about her finger.

'Stay here in London Jonathan, why don't you?'

He turned to her and saw that although she was smiling she was not joking.

'Katie,' he said. He took her head in his hands and looked at her.

'You don't have to go away Jonathan.'

He was touched and surprised. He didn't know what to say. He put his arms around her and they kissed again, more slowly than before, as if they had found something new to kiss about. She drew away, gripping his arms.

'Don't go.'

'Katie, what do you mean? Are you being serious?'

'There's no need for you to go, you could just stay here.'

She looked at him with an expression of doting

fondness. He kissed her throat. She lay back, sinking into the pillow. He undid the buttons of the shirt and saw her naked again as if for the first time. He was struck by how lovely she was; how simple and at the same time extraordinary it was to be seeing her breasts rising from two ridges in her ribcage, the nipples dark and oval like whorled knots in pine. He took them in his mouth; one and then the other.

'Ah, God.' She clutched him, her fingernails sharp in the small of his back.

'Say you won't go Jonathan.'

Her eyes were closed; screwed tight as if she were willing his acquiescence with all her strength. A part of him remained quite cold and detached and disbelieving. Into another part, however, that stood in relation to this first like an alembic beginning to seethe mysteriously under the eye of a sceptical but intent observer, came the first stirrings of a strange confusion. What he felt now began to commandeer the excitement and adventurousness he had been experiencing for his imminent departure for Rome, while that departure in turn seemed to be taking on the sadness and staleness he had once felt for the idea of staying in London.

'Say it Jonathan. Say you'll stay.'

She moved from under him, kissing his chest and stomach. She took him into her mouth. Everything around him, all the clutter of the room – magazines and clothes, the marble bust and green cabin trunk, the gold chandelier glittering like a knived chariot wheel – seemed vibrant and aflame. She drew back again, panting, her cheeks flushed, her eyes dark and blazing.

'Jonathan, I don't like anyone except you.'

He looked at her and felt the softness of his nature

yielding beneath hers. Is this what I am? he thought. He wondered what had happened to him and when it had happened.

'Say it Jonathan, say it. Say you'll stay.'

He opened his mouth to speak, not knowing what he was going to say until he heard himself saying it.

Two days later he phoned and arranged to meet her for lunch in a wine bar. She turned up late, wearing high heels and a business suit. Glancing at her watch, she remarked how she envied him setting off for a new life in a new country.

He looked at her, not quite believing he had heard correctly. She met his eye with an expression of calm indifference. After she had drunk half a glass of wine, she excused herself, saying that she had to interview someone in St Albans.

At home he took the shirt that still smelled of her from under his pillow, and threw it in the laundry basket. He looked in the mirror and told himself that what he saw was the face of a fool who had been given an undeserved reprieve for his folly. Half believing it, he sat at his desk and drew up a final list of things that needed doing before he left for Rome.

3

The expatriate life suited Jonathan. After a few months of settling in, he began to feel as if he was emerging from a long hibernation. He was calm and happy. For the first time in years he felt free of a pervasive melancholy that had coloured even his more contented moments in the past.

He got a job at the language school in Parioli. The work was uninteresting but it paid his expenses, and the impersonal atmosphere of the place was made up for by the camaraderie of the offices of the English weekly newspaper off the Corso Vittorio Emanuele. Here, after he had written some short pieces that the editor had liked, he was given part of the 'Visitors' section to produce, and then a section of his own.

At the Food and Agricultural Organisation, where his editor had sent him for a series on International Agencies based in Rome, he met Lydia, a Canadian agronomist. She was younger than Jonathan, fair-haired, with mild blue eyes and a high, smooth forehead. She owned several white dresses and wore a straw hat in the Roman sunshine.

A lofty tone was set during their courtship. Lydia's assumption about love was that it was above all a matter of growth and mutual improvement. Earnest discussion, and vigorous, forthright debate were her preferred means. A good argument about aid policy or the military/industrial complex brought more pleasure into her cheeks than wine or flowers. 'Say something contentious,' she would sometimes command Jonathan, who seldom initiated such discussions. She gave him a list of her favourite books, and asked him for a list of

his, ordering them at once from the Lion bookshop on
the Via del Babuino bookshop, and reading them as
they arrived.

'I love you darling,' she would say as they lay in
each other's arms between the clean sheets of her bed.
Jonathan would pass his fingers over her clear forehead
and through her long, brushed hair.

'I love you too,' he would say.

But even at their most intimate there remained something formal about the way they behaved with each
other. At times she seemed to him glazed in a radiance
of virtue and wholesomeness that was simply impen-
etrable, and it would feel oddly futile to make love to
her. A little like taking part in some kind of civic
ceremony, he thought.

Sensing this perhaps, she made a surprising suggestion one afternoon.

'Darling, why don't we go to bed and get drunk.
Wouldn't that be fun?'

With a determined look she emptied several glasses
of Scotch into her stomach. She became rapidly drunk,
and this unleashed, briefly, an uncharacteristic lasciv-
iousness in her.

Afterwards she was badly sick, and for several days
she could hardly bring herself to speak to Jonathan, as
though the experiment had been his idea and not hers.
He didn't protest; under the apparent unfairness of her
tacit accusations, he sensed a true and just apportioning
of blame.

Some time after this, in a bar in Trastevere, he saw
a girl with a pretty, freckled face, and bare arms with
thin silver bracelets on the wrists. She was by herself,
and from time to time she glanced in his direction. He

went over to her table and asked if he could join her. He had never done such a thing in his life. The girl made a pleasant, rustling gesture of acceptance. She was wearing a strong perfume, and he sat down by her with a sense of subsiding into a sweet, fragrant cloud. She was Dutch; a student on holiday. As they talked, Jonathan felt as if he was converging into some hitherto purely hypothetical version of himself, and flooding it with reality.

He didn't contact Katie on his visits to London. They had almost no mutual friends, and he heard little news of her. For a couple of years an occasional scrap of gossip reached him via the cousin who had first introduced them. But the cousin gradually lost touch with Katie, and then Jonathan lost touch with his cousin.

Four years passed. When he thought of their night together or their evening at the auction house in Fulham, Jonathan no longer felt any resentment at Katie's behaviour or chagrin at his own. He would go over his memory of the events quite dispassionately, with a scientific curiosity. It would seem to him that certain facts about his nature at that time had been brought to light, and regardless of how unflattering those facts might be, it was satisfying to know them.

Owing to a crisis in the Italian timber industry, the government was offering tax subsidies to publishers provided they bought Italian wood pulp. The proprietor of the English paper took advantage of this to launch a colour magazine. For the first issue the editor decided to run a piece on Italian and English Palladian houses, along with the people who lived in them. Jonathan put himself forward for the English part of the assignment, as it would pay for a visit to his parents, whom he had not seen for almost a year. The editor gave him the job.

He arranged his interviews and flew to London. For several days he drove around England in a rented car. It was October, mild with a drizzling mist that followed him south from Derbyshire.

· The owners he visited received him warmly, pressing him to stay for meals, and sometimes for the night. They were eager to show him their painstaking repairs to cracked cupolas and pilasters worn down by acid rain. He was guided through libraries smelling of beeswax, and drawing-rooms furnished assiduously in period style even when that had meant a sacrifice of comfort. Palladian window entablatures were pointed out to him; he was given tours of grounds with porphyry fountains, ornamental lakes, and sheep huddling in drenched grass under cedars and limes. One elderly couple spent the whole afternoon of his visit talking very slowly about their grandchildren, and then, when it was pitch dark outside, insisted on showing him their garden by the light of a tiny electric torch. He took his own pictures, except when he wanted landscape shots, when he would return with a professional photographer.

The journey led him mostly along minor roads that wound through open countryside and small towns. It was pleasant and strange. He was struck by the thought that he no longer lived in this country. The damp air with its pervasive smell of burning leaves brought the sombre fields and hedgerows sharply into his senses. Now and then a sight would fill him with a nostalgia that was sometimes mixed with an unaccountable anxiety: a yellow and brown copse with a black pond glinting between the tree-trunks; a soft-drinks bottling plant in a cropped field full of Chinese geese . . .

He wondered what the undetectable something was that makes a place a place . . . You come to a group of dwellings; hardly a village – silent, a pale rain-shine on the brick walls. There is a stock car with a joke shark's fin on the roof. A Crystal Refrigeration truck dwarfs its owner's bungalow. The place is quiet, deserted, but undeniably a *place*, with a little atmosphere and language of its own, that is spoken by the stock car and the refrigeration truck, and then, in another voice, by glistening green dollops of pruned yew trees that seem to contain, swelling through their feathery branches, some liquid light essence of rain and greenness. And then as you turn a corner, the place with its miniature but self-sufficient economy of shapes and surfaces has vanished, leaving you with a feeling of pleasure, or loss, or even dread, as if something in it corresponded to something in yourself . . .

On a Sunday afternoon, towards the end of his journey, he drove through the Chilterns into Berkshire and came to the gates of a house called Felstead, a few miles outside Wantage.

A drive wound through ploughed fields and past a farm with two grain silos gleaming like pewter in the whitish afternoon light. The drive climbed through a belt of beech trees; smooth-limbed with black, squid-like eyes where lower branches had fallen or been lopped. Rolling parkland followed, leading to the house itself, which was built of sandstone, and gave off a soft

yellow glow through the mist. It was smaller than the
size of the estate had led Jonathan to expect, though
it was in better shape than some he had seen. The tall,
panelled windows in the symmetrical wings gleamed
with clean glass and fresh white paint. Rawer-looking
blocks among the masonry of the semi-circular front
portico suggested recent renovation.

Jonathan parked his car and went up the three steps
to the domed entrance. A man came to the door, smiling and extending a hand.

'Mr Bennett?'

Jonathan nodded and said yes.

'Francis Trenillin. How do you do?'

The owner of the house shook Jonathan's hand
firmly. He was a tall man, quite portly in the middle,
tapering to dainty feet at one end, and at the other a
narrow, long head with sparse hair that might have
once been red. A moss-coloured tweed jacket hung, a
little shabbily, from his slightly stooped shoulders, and
at first Jonathan took him for a much older man than
on closer inspection he turned out to be.

'I thought perhaps we'd see the park first, then go
over the house when we come back for tea. You'll stay
for some tea, I trust?'

'That would be nice.'

They set off along an avenue of chestnut trees. The
grass was covered with fallen chestnuts, and Mr Trenillin collected several of these, discarding the prickly
pods and putting the glossy nuts into the pockets of
his jacket.

'I thought perhaps we'd have them roasted for
tea . . .'

The avenue led to a lake with a small island connec-

ted by a balustraded bridge. Some orange-billed moor-
hens swam for the rushes on the far banks as the two
men approached. On the island was a weeping willow
– all spokes now – with a wrought-iron seat beneath
it. Mr Trenillin came to a halt and stared out across
the water. Red and yellow leaves floated on the lacquer-
black surface. Splintery reeds and brown bullrushes
with their match-like tops beginning to disintegrate,
grew thickly along the shore. Mr Trenillin stood in
silence, looking across the lake. Jonathan waited beside
him. The silence continued for several seconds. Jonathan waited respectfully. From a certain solemnity in
the man's presence, he sensed a good-natured and possibly gloomy personality.

'Do you know these plants?' Mr Trenillin said after
a while, pointing to the ground. 'They grow in sections
which you can pull apart as if they were assembled
rather than grew like that. Look . . . ' He stooped and
showed Jonathan how the thin, fringed tubes of the
strange-looking plant slotted together.

'I believe they're called Mare's Tails.'

They walked around to the other side of the lake
and up a steep hill that gradually opened a view onto
the whole property. As they climbed, Jonathan ques-
tioned his host about the house and land, and his life
there.

Mr Trenillin's grandfather had bought it after returning from East Africa with money from copper and
manganese mining. His son, Mr Trenillin's father, had
sold the mining business and put the money into property in London, most of which now belonged to Mr
Trenillin himself. There was an office in Wigmore
Street to which Mr Trenillin commuted three or four

days a week. A frown crossed his face as he spoke of
it, and it was apparent that he didn't enjoy his duties
as a landlord.

'My wife likes London and we keep a *pied-à-terre*
there, but personally I much prefer it here. This is
where I was born, and I have to say I'm rather child-
ishly attached to it.' He cast a sidelong look at Jonathan, who realised he was being appealed to for reassur-
ance.

'That seems perfectly natural to me.'

'I've been researching into the history of the place.
It's quite interesting – '

A happier look came over Mr Trenillin as he talked
about his researches and his plan for restoring the park
and building to their original glory.

'Grandpa was a complete vandal. If he didn't like a
room the way it was, he simply bashed a wall down
or punched in a new window. We don't have the draw-
ings so we're having to consult historians and ferret
out original descriptions by visitors in the eighteenth
and nineteenth centuries. I'm not a scholar but I have
to say I'm enjoying myself tremendously. My sister
helps me. She's been staying here with us – and she's
better on the house than I am. My speciality is the
park, and the question here is which original do you
restore it to: Repton? Bridgeman? Capability Brown?
They all worked here, or at least their followers did,
each of them digging up and pulling down their prede-
cessor's work – '

He became quite animated now, as he pointed out
plantings of trees characteristic of this or that period,
showed where a wall had been replaced by a ha-ha
to open the view from the house to the surrounding

countryside, speculated on whether a rise here might be the remains of a mediaeval saltory, whether the chestnut avenue might once have formed part of a *patte d'oie* of avenues fanning out from the house . . .

They reached the top of the hill. A strong breeze blew, whipping drops of rain into their faces. Mr Trenillin was out of breath, and stood panting, his cheeks glowing brightly.

'Up here there was a folly once. Look, you can see where the foundations must have been – ' there was a circular dip in the earth ' – somebody must have pulled it down. I can't think why. I should think it was a little Greek temple. Possibly something more pagoda-like, but with a folly I think it's permissible to go with your own preferences and I prefer the idea of a temple. Anyway we've decided – ' here a look of excitement came into the large man's eyes, as if he were letting Jonathan in on a secret – 'to commission a miniature replica of Bramante's Tempietto. That ought to interest them in Rome.'

Jonathan made a polite murmur. Between the man's bulky stature, which seemed to suggest quite a jovial soul, and the rather finicky connoisseurship to which he appeared to have dedicated himself, there was an incongruousness that suggested to Jonathan an element of strain.

Lights had come on in the panelled windows of the house. The greens and browns of the surrounding countryside were easing into a grey sleep. Rain had begun to fall steadily.

In the distance, beyond the lake, a pair of headlights appeared from around a hill. Their brightness in the bluish dusk obscured the car itself, which travelled about a quarter of a mile towards the house, before veering off in another direction. Mr Trenillin, who had been following the car's progress, turned away without a word and led Jonathan back down to the house.

They went through the portico into a chequered marble hallway. A woman appeared from a corridor.

'Ah, there you are,' she said in a mild voice.

She turned with a smile to Jonathan and Mr Trenillin introduced her as his sister, Cressida. She looked older than him, with short grey hair and the same oval build. A pair of glasses hung on a beaded chain from her neck.

'I wasn't sure whether to put the kettle on. Shall I put it on now?'

'Yes, why don't you? I'll show Mr Bennett around the house.'

As Cressida went off towards the kitchen, her brother called after her –

'Any telephone calls?'

She turned around, putting on her glasses as if she needed them in order to think.

'No, not while you were out,' she said, then took off her glasses and went towards the kitchen.

Upstairs, in a small room that had been turned into a study with a desk, a sofa, and bookshelves around all the walls, Jonathan saw Katie Vairish's chandelier.

Either it was hers or it was another one identical to hers. There were the sharp sprigs of oak leaf and acorns that had dug into him while he had carried it out of the auction house, and there were the little candle bulbs that had burned above Katie's bed, the night they had lain there together four years ago.

A tingling went down his spine. He felt the rush of a half-forgotten complex of sensations: the animal sweetness; the feeling of being concentrated or compacted into a narrower part of himself; the peculiar tension. He opened his mouth to ask where the chandelier came from, but stopped himself.

'This is a pleasant room,' was all he said.

'My wife's study.'

Jonathan looked at the chandelier again. There was no mistaking it. An odd feeling went through him, as if the years since he had last seen it were an interval of distance rather than time, and he was looking at it from a vertiginous height.

'She works here then, your wife?'

'Occasionally. You might meet her later on. She's sometimes home in time for tea.'

They went out of the room, and continued the tour of the other upstairs rooms. It was difficult for Jonathan to pay attention. The sight of the chandelier had had the momentarily eclipsing effect of a too-bright light.

They went back again; down the fanning marble staircase with its round-edged steps like thick ripples of cream, into a drawing-room with stucco wreaths of camellias and mignonettes. Straight-backed sofas and chairs stood on an oriental rug. In the corner was a spinet inlaid with brown and white marquetry. A fire had been lit and the flames gleamed on the dustless surfaces of porcelain vases and walnut cabinets. Looking at these things, thinking of the grounds with the lake and avenue, the rolling acres of grass, the sense of a sublime and fantastical misappropriation arose in Jonathan. He wondered if it was really as he imagined.

He tried to picture Mr Trenillin as Katie Vairish's suitor, her husband. Sensing the imbalance, or an equilibrium precariously maintained by money, a feeling of sympathy, even solidarity came into him. At the same time the impression of some jubilantly contemptuous appetite glimmering behind every detail of the property, filled him with a harsh joy.

'This is lovely,' he heard himself say dutifully.

Cressida brought in a tea-tray and poured tea into translucent china cups. She handed one by its saucer to Jonathan, and another to Mr Trenillin. The three of them sat around the fire, balancing the cups and saucers on their knees. Outside it was dark. A glass clock on the mantelpiece struck the hour with a soft, whirring ring, and Mr Trenillin checked it against his watch. The pockets of his jacket bulged with chestnuts, but he appeared to have forgotten about them, and Jonathan didn't think it would be polite to remind him.

They talked about the house. Cressida carried most of the burden of the conversation. She herself lived in Oxford, she explained, where she had a fellowship in history at St Hilda's. This year she had taken a sabbatical, and was staying at Felstead to help Francis with the restoration.

'We had the mouldings repaired with real egg stucco. I've never seen so many broken eggs in my life...'

Mr Trenillin seemed distracted. Cressida looked at him with an expression that wasn't tender, was even a little cold, but nevertheless conveyed a certain sisterly concern. Every now and then the swishing sound of a car on the wet road beyond the lake could be heard, and the three of them would fall silent for a few seconds until the sound faded away.

Jonathan accepted another cup of tea and tried to interest Mr Trenillin in the other houses he had visited for his article. The man nodded his narrow head and smiled vaguely, showing his crooked yellow teeth. He sighed.

'Sunday evenings . . . ' he said. 'There's something terrible about them even at the best of times. I wonder why that is?'

'No doubt our punishment for not observing the day of rest,' Cressida answered pertly, with a smile.

Francis Trenillin continued: 'I can be sitting here having spent days and days in absolute contentment, and suddenly find the most awful feeling of dreariness creeping into me like a sort of freezing liquid, and when I ask myself what on earth's the matter, I realise. Of course! It's Sunday evening.'

He sat back in his armchair and looked into the fire, his long legs sprawling from his broad waist and hips, the tiny tea-cup forcing a curious mincing appearance into his thick, fleshy hand.

There was a silence.

'I should probably start making my way,' Jonathan said. The talk was growing strained, and he had no further pretext for staying at the house. Little effort was made to detain him, but for a while he didn't stir. He sipped the sour dregs of his tea, and debated asking Mr Trenillin if his wife was Katie Vairish, but again thought better of it. It seemed to him some awkwardness would be involved in his declaring he knew her. Then too, there was something that appealed to him about not declaring it: her own sport of gratuitous stealth, but also the obscurely satisfying thought that she might discover from her husband who had visited that afternoon, and then wonder if he had known whose house he was in . . .

'It's been a very pleasant afternoon,' he said, setting his tea-cup on the floor.

Cressida put on her glasses.

'We shall look forward to reading about ourselves. You'll send us the article, won't you?'

They all stood up.

'I'll fetch your coat,' Mr Trenillin said.

As he was walking towards the door, the hum of a car engine came through the rain, which was now falling heavily outside.

The three of them stood still, following the sound with their ears. It rose, and a swishing was heard on the road beyond the lake. It travelled in a wide arc about the house, ebbing and rising, each time slightly fuller on the return, so that it seemed to be approaching in waves. Lights broke through the beech wood separating the park from the farm, and the swishing turned to a sizzling as the car came up to the house. By then Mr Trenillin had forgotten about Jonathan's coat, and was on the bottom step of the lit portico, holding an umbrella. Cressida waited in the portico, while Jonathan hung back behind her, in the drawing-room doorway. Through the hall window he saw the slim, familiar figure climb out of the car into the shelter of the waiting umbrella. He saw her kiss her husband on the lips and slip her arm through his as they walked briskly up the steps to the house. Mr Trenillin was smiling eagerly.

'Oh, you poor thing. You poor thing,' he was saying as Katie gave an amused, voluble account of traffic jams and motorway diversions.

They entered the portico where Mr Trenillin paused to shake out the umbrella. Katie lightly relinquished his arm, and took in its place her sister-in-law's.

'Cress, hello. How are you?'

'I'll put the kettle on for you,' Cressida said, patting Katie's hand and disengaging herself.

'Oh, and I got chestnuts for you,' Mr Trenillin cried, catching up with Katie, who took off her jacket and hung it on the coat rack.

'You sweet thing.'

Passing into the hallway, Katie came to a halt. She stood still, looking across the hall in silence.

'Ah yes,' her husband said, 'you're just in time to meet Mr Bennett. He's the journalist . . . You remember . . . Mr Bennett, my wife Katie.'

Jonathan stood in the doorway while Katie came towards him. He saw that she had changed a little. The years that had passed seemed to have brought into final balance and definition all the delicate features of her face. Her cheekbones were more prominent than before, and the line of her jaw was a little harder, giving her face a gem-like, ghostly beauty.

He was about to feign the surprised recognition that the moment seemed to call for, when Katie said, 'How do you do Mr Bennett,' holding out her hand with a steady gaze in which the mirth was only visible as a faint suppressed movement about her lips.

'How do you do,' Jonathan heard himself say. He shook her cold hand and followed her, or was somehow swept, back into the drawing-room. He felt as if he was in a dream where something at once dangerous and immensely gratifying was taking place. Mr Trenillin was at the fire, kneeling on the floor and rooting

at the embers with a copper shovel. Katie sighed and
breathed in the warmth of the room. Her eyes shone,
full of the dark night that she had been driving
through; lit at the back with a subdued but teeming
glimmer that Jonathan remembered well, and that
seemed to beckon onto some bright perpetual revelry
within. She ran a finger along the keys of the spinet,
then touched an arrangement of helleborus roses in a
vase and turned to Jonathan.

'So my husband has been showing you the place?'
He nodded.

'And you're writing it up for a paper in Rome?'

'That's right. An English paper.'

'I see. That explains why you're English. I was
expecting an Italian.'

He didn't know what he should say or do. Apart
from her evident amusement at pretending he was a
stranger, it was hard to tell what she was feeling. Perhaps nothing more than that amusement. The watchful
dependency on her whims and moods that had consumed him when they were together in the past, rose
in him on a strong, sweet current of memory. He
saw that her self-possession had reached a point of
apotheosis where it was indistinguishable from cruelty.

'Won't you stay for supper?' she asked.

'Well – I was just on my way . . . '

Jonathan looked to Mr Trenillin, and Katie too
turned to her husband, her hand resting on one of the
cabinets in a lazily proprietorial way.

'You didn't invite the man to stay for supper, darling?'

'Well, I – '

'Shame on you! Sending a fellow out on a night like this without a morsel to eat.'

Her husband had turned his head while his body remained kneeling towards the fire, his large behind facing out into the room. He looked sheepish.

'Dear,' he said, 'I'm sorry. I didn't think . . . '

He took a handful of chestnuts from his jacket pocket and tumbled them onto the tarnished copper shovel.

'Well then. And I've told you before, darling, not to stuff things into your jacket pockets. It ruins them and makes you look ridiculous. Like a schoolboy.'

Mr Trenillin frowned and turned back to the fire. Katie sighed and looked at Jonathan.

'I hope you'll join us then?'

She held his glance. A brilliant, unashamed hilarity showed in her eyes. Again he felt as if he were in a dream, or else the faint delirium of a sickness, the symptoms of which were distributed as much beyond him as within; taking in the bright room with Mr Trenillin kneeling on all fours at the centre, Katie poised with her hand on the swirling-grained surface of the cabinet, Cressida approaching with the tea-tray, and pausing at the sight of the two apparent strangers staring into each other's eyes, the chandelier upstairs with its gilt sprigs of leaf and acorn, and the cold, rainy night outside; and as he accepted her invitation, looking half at her, and half at her sister-in-law who was standing alert and motionless at the edge of the oriental carpet, he felt that if it was a sickness in him that these things denoted, then the sickness was entering a new and more definitive phase. And among other things this filled him with a curious, sombre satisfaction.

— uses ...
— very precise with words ; page 33